Aromaticus Kauai

A Renae Lapin Mystery

D1707801

ISBN: 9798395157935

Cover and author photos: Ronald J. Caddy
Cover and book design: Naomi C. Rose

Printed in the United States of America

*Dedicated to my husband Ron
who continues to be my best
friend and navigator.*

—RL

5 Star Reviews on Amazon
for *Quitclaim Sedona*

Superb first mystery from the author, with an intriguing cast of characters whose multiple layers of interaction enrich and deepen the reader's interest. But the real protagonist is Sedona itself, whose character and role in the unfolding narrative are never far from the surface. An excellent, well-written first effort in what promises to be a string of subsequent thrillers. —DL

The book was extremely enjoyable and hard to put down. Lapin combines mystery, great characters and wonderful descriptions of the beauty of Sedona. —RA

I LOVED this book! The characters are so well developed, you feel you know them or at least want to! As the story unfolds you find yourself rooting for them as individuals and as a collective. The author puts you right there in Sedona, sharing its beauty and community customs...I am so happy to hear this is just the first book of a series!! —SN

This Renae Lapin Mystery is a wonderful book! The author's love of Sedona is evident throughout. The book engages the reader from beginning to end as the very well developed characters interact in a fascinating mystery. The good news is that it is the first in a series! —HM

Captivated my attention all the way through! Well written and thought provoking. Must be read. —MK

Loved the imagery, ease of read and intrigue into character connection. Imagery vivid and Storyline flowed - loved reading it while in Sedona! —MJ

This is a wonderful mystery with excellent character development. The reader gets a great sense of each of the characters in the story as well as the Sedona backdrop. Glad this is the first of a series and looking forward to the future books! —HS

The author lured me in, I felt like I was right there in Sedona on this adventure. I couldn't wait to read to the end to find out how the mystery was solved. I highly recommend reading this book. —TC

This was a very fun and enjoyable mystery to read. I kept needing to go to the next chapter to see if I could figure out all the relationships. It gets to the heart of life after tragic loss and how resilient humans can be. But it also winds the reader through a maze and you will keep reading to find out what is behind the next turn...It was refreshing to read about the beauty of Sedona Arizona...I can't wait for future books by this very talented new author! —JR

This is a unique and intricate mystery set in the magnificent nature of Sedona, AZ. You will feel like you have experienced Sedona's people, culture and hidden treasures. The story of long lasting friendships is at the heart of the book. You will find yourself rooting for the good guys, while helping them uncover the very curious mysteries they struggle to solve. Your heart will break, but you will be renewed through this engaging story. —DS

Contents

Contents

Contents

Prologue

Dani couldn't shake the feeling of being watched. As she scanned each room of Star's home, her discomfort grew deeper. The house felt ominous. Something was off. The Aromaticus bottles had been drained. Who would do that? Why? Nothing else appeared out of order. It couldn't be Star. They said she died in her sleep. But had she?

Finally, Dani entered Star's bedroom and a chill ran up her spine. Dani had to get out. Now! She grabbed the shawl and jewelry box. No time to get anything more. Then she sped out of the house as fast as her eighty-three-year-old legs could carry her.

Chapter 1
Sapphire

Sapphire woke up in a puddle of sweat with the same recurring dream. Third time this week. What does it mean? Whose voice does she keeps hearing? The distinctly whispered words echoed in her brain. *Keep the formula safe for when the world is ready.*

She heard the doorbell ring and recognized the sound of the UPS truck as it rambled down the street away from her home. Another delivery, probably the fabric samples ordered for her current client. Sapphire Designs, her architectural and design business had provided her with financial success ever since she launched her firm 35 years ago.

Sapphire took her time getting started for her day, a luxury she reveled in each morning. Being single had its advantages. The package could wait.

Hydrated, showered, dressed, and caffeinated, Sapphire finally opened her front door and reached down to pick up the package. It was lightweight, just as she expected, but the return address in Asheville, North Carolina was unfamiliar. The bold letters read *CONFIDENTIAL*. The box stared at her, and Sapphire stared right back, challenging it to reveal its contents. Finally, Sapphire gazed up at the cloudless sky and took a deep breath. Gratitude for living in Sedona filled her heart as she absorbed the Red Rock views ablaze in the morning sun. Sapphire recognized that each day of living was a precious gift.

She brought the package inside and set it on her simple juniper-carved desk. As she reached for the scissors, Sapphire heard a faint whisper. *Keep the formula safe.* No one was in her home. The voice must have come from inside her head, from the dream. Sapphire tried to remember more details of the dream, but the images slipped away each time she almost grasped them.

Returning to the task at hand, Sapphire carefully sliced the reinforced tape and slowly opened the box flaps. The first thing she noticed was the envelope on top, which ever so faintly exuded a familiar fragrance. It reminded Sapphire of Aunt Star. They shared the same first name until hers was changed to Sapphire when she was fifteen. Her parents had whisked her away to boarding school in Sedona for her safety, as their secret research brought increased danger to their only child. Changing her name further secured her anonymity. Now, at age sixty-one, forty-six years ago was a lifetime away. Aunt Star's fragrance wafted through the air and brought Sapphire comfort.

She reached toward her heart for the precious star-sapphire hanging on a gold chain. It was a gift from her parents. Sapphire clutched the treasured stone close to her heart. This instinctive habit of palming her neck jewel, brought Sapphire close to her parents. She was only fifteen at the time of their death. They were killed in a political coup in South America. Shortly before sending Sapphire to Sedona, her mother clasped the heirloom pendant around Sapphire's neck as she lovingly assured her, "You are named in honor of the star-sapphire. Its unique asterism reflects light and will always connect you to me. Your heritage is a long lineage of strong women. The strength exponentially multiplies, getting stronger and stronger with each generation." Her anxiety and fear swiftly transformed into resilience and confidence as she palmed the star-sapphire close to her heart.

Sapphire now continued to unwrap the contents of the package in front of her. With a calm sense of purpose, Sapphire carefully opened the envelope and removed the single-page letter. She somehow knew what the contents would reveal before reading the words.

Keep the formula safe. This time the whisper seemed to come from inside the box.

Chapter 2
Pandora's Box

The scent was certainly Aunt Star's, but the mysterious writing in the letter was not. **SAPPHIRE DOVER**, in hard block letters on the outside envelope almost looked like a business inscription. It starkly contrasted with the calligraphy in the letter. Her brain couldn't connect the writing with the soft fragrant scent.

Sapphire focused her eyes on the calligraphed words while she allowed the nostalgic scent to fill her nostrils. The last time she saw her aunt was two years ago. Now, when she touched her star-sapphire necklace, Sapphire ached with memories of her loving aunt. She missed her so much.

The fabric edge of her aunt's shawl peeked out of the tissue paper wrapping beneath the envelope. Sapphire froze. Her aunt always wore that shawl, taking it off only to lovingly drape it around Sapphire during her visits as a child.

Someday this will be yours and you will treasure it just as I have, her aunt would coo. Sapphire's heart beat faster. If Aunt Sapphire was no longer wrapped in her treasured shawl, then that meant she was no longer alive in this world.

Sapphire clutched the edge of the shawl as she read the letter.

> *Dearest Sapphire,*
> *My name is Dani Lake, and I*
> *am your Aunt Star's executor.*

Aunt Star's executor? Who is this person? She continued reading.

> *Star Ceres passed away*
> *peacefully in her sleep at home*
> *on June 18, 2020.*

Sapphire sighed at the word peacefully. She was hoping for that one assurance. But Aunt Star hadn't been ill. How could she die so suddenly?

> *Enclosed, please find special*
> *gifts willed to you from your*
> *dear aunt.*

A tear formed in Sapphire's eye, and it slid down her cheek. The pale pink paper stock was elegantly designed with roses, giving the stationary a Victorian look. It could have just as well be an invitation to high tea. She was feeling oddly peaceful reading the news of her aunt's death in beautifully scripted words. The last sentence read:

> *Please contact me when you receive this.*

It was signed:

> *Dani Lake, Aunt Star's executor.*

Below Dani Lake's signature was a telephone number. Sapphire looked up the area code. It was for Asheville, North Carolina.

Keep the formula safe whispered throughout the air. This time, it seemed to be coming from within Sapphire's heart.

What does that mean?

Before removing the sacred shawl from its tissue wrapping, Sapphire gently lifted it up to see the other contents in the box. A tiny silver jewel case appeared to wink at her. It gleamed from the lighting streaming down from above. Sapphire looked up at the golden sunlight that shone through her octagon-shaped skylight. She initially created that special feature for her own home and it became her signature for all the homes she designed. Sapphire felt inspired each time she viewed the dancing sunlight.

As Sapphire lifted the jewelry box, it almost slipped through her fingers. She felt light-headed. In her eagerness to look through the box, Sapphire forgot to eat breakfast. Low blood sugar was a struggle. It was Sapphire's only medical condition. She found it to be an inconvenience at times, but it was easily managed by eating small frequent meals. Sapphire got a drink of water, infused with the mint she grew on her windowsill.

As she sipped the water, she struggled to process the reality of Aunt Star's death. Eighty-one years old is an impressive age to reach, Sapphire considered. She grasped tightly onto her gratitude for Aunt Star. If one word were used to describe Aunt Star, the word would be gracious. Sapphire hoped she emulated her aunt's grace.

She took a breath. She would proudly wear Aunt Star's ring, a simple star-sapphire set in white gold. Sapphire knew that's what the jewelry box contained. Her aunt only took the ring off when going to the beach or swimming. It was those special moments that remained etched in Sapphire's memory. As a young child, she was allowed to try on the ring before it was ceremoniously returned to its special box. During those tender moments, Sapphire looked forward to the time that it would fit her finger.

My star-sapphire ring will be yours after I leave this earth, and you will treasure wearing it just like I do, her aunt would always say.

Sapphire knew she needed to eat breakfast before continuing with the contents of the box. Or she would get too dizzy. A protein-rich egg, fresh from her neighbor's hen would sustain her for several hours. In short order, Sapphire placed the perfectly poached egg on toasted sourdough bread from the Sedona Farmer's Market. She topped it with mashed avocado, chopped arugula, and roasted red bell peppers. Farm fresh sliced tomatoes and organic blueberries rounded off Sapphire's breakfast. Blueberries were sometimes joined with strawberries, raspberries, and blackberries. Sapphire ate blueberries daily, convinced about their numerous health benefits.

Sapphire enjoyed breakfast on her front patio as she watched the hummingbirds drink sweet nectar from three carefully positioned feeders. The delicate creatures tentatively sipped tiny amounts, barely a drop at a time. Sapphire was mesmerized. As a child, Aunt Star introduced Sapphire to bird watching. Only the hummingbirds interested her. It was the graceful way they hung in the air while flapping their wings in place. The variety of colors amused Sapphire and filled her heart with joy. The hummingbirds were her only pets, although they did not belong to her. But since they visited her daily, Sapphire felt she was entitled to consider them hers. She wondered if they noticed her sadness.

After washing her breakfast dishes, Sapphire made fresh hummingbird nectar with four parts filtered water and one part sugar, heated, dissolved and cooled to room temperature. The nectar needed to be refilled every three days during the summer months to keep the tiny birds from getting dehydrated in the scorching heat. Sapphire frequently hydrated herself as well and kept a gallon pitcher of room temperature mint water on her kitchen counter as a reminder.

Nourished in body and soul, Sapphire returned to the box, wondering what else it contained. First, she opened the jewelry box and tenderly placed the ring on the ring finger of her right hand, as if she had done so every day. Aunt Star wore it daily on her right ring finger and now

Sapphire would do the same. The star-sapphire twinkled at Sapphire as if to say, *I'm yours now.*

There was nothing further in the large box. Sapphire unwrapped each crumpled piece of tissue paper and smoothed them out flat to be absolutely sure. That was it. A four-sentence letter written in perfect calligraphy, a woven shawl, and a ring. Not much to an untrained observer, but it was the entire world to Sapphire. She wrapped the shawl around her trembling shoulders, took a close look at the ring on her finger, and finally broke down sobbing.

Chapter 3
Judith Soothes

Sapphire's sobbing slowed. She took several deep beaths and finally one long sigh. Her body was on automatic pilot while her brain was trying to catch up. She felt out of sync, like a badly dubbed film. She had cried a lot over the years. She cried for Fisher, her best friend since high school who died just a year ago. Further complicating her grief, Fisher Bond had been murdered. She had cried for her mother and father. They suffered a violent death as well, killed in Columbia. That was several months after they sent her to boarding school in Sedona at Wildhorse Academy. Now she had the loss of Aunt Star to grieve too.

Sapphire felt comforted knowing that Aunt Star died peacefully. The word *peacefully* reverberated in her brain and rattled around her bones. A new energy flowed through her. She sprung up, suddenly needing to move. Sapphire stretched her muscles, and her six-foot athletic frame felt like it grew an inch taller.

She directed herself to the back room of her home, marching with long strides. Sapphire gracefully positioned herself on her reformer, a piece of equipment designed for the practice of Pilates. She closed her eyes, methodically placed the balls of her feet on the foot bar and began a series of stretching exercises her muscles had memorized. On to her arches, then toes, with slow deep breaths through her nose and out through her mouth.

Falling from her horse when he was spooked led to three grueling months of recovery during her senior year of high school. After completing physical therapy, Sapphire adopted the practice of Pilates to maintain her strength, balance, and agility. Practicing Pilates three times or more a week, became a gift from her injury experience.

Sapphire purchased her own reformer when classes during the COVID pandemic had abruptly ceased. On Mondays, her instructor would come to her home to train her. Sapphire did her routine on her own on Wednesdays and Fridays. Today was a Thursday, but she needed the calming breathwork right now.

Sapphire allowed her mind to wander as each exercise filled her body with oxygen. Who could she phone for comfort? Her other best friend, Farrell, was not the comforting type. It was Sapphire who comforted him most times, like a big sister, taking him under her wing. Ever since high school, Sapphire, Fisher, and Farrell had been best friends, known as the three musketeers. Now that the third point of their triangle had died, her friendship with Farrell was off kilter. All year, they stumbled and struggled to lean on each other. Their special three-person bond did not easily convert into a two-dimensional form.

The thought to phone Judith entered her heart like a warm cup of tea. Judith lived in Miami, across the country from Sedona. They talked so often, it felt like she lived next door. Sapphire admired the way Judith burst onto the scene after Fisher died to help solve his murder. They became fast friends. She never met a feistier eighty-one-year-old woman. Yes, she would call Judith. Sapphire's cellphone found Judith's number in her favorites seemingly all on its own.

Before Sapphire could complete her thought, Judith's number had been dialed. Judith answered on the first ring.

"What's wrong, my dear?" Judith inquired. Sapphire always phoned her in the evening, and it was morning in Sedona. Sapphire burst into tears for the second time this morning while Judith patiently waited for her to speak.

"My aunt died," Sapphire finally spilled out the words. "She was so strong, so healthy, it doesn't make sense."

"Oh, my dear Sapphire, I'll be there as soon as I can," Judith said without a moment of hesitation. "I might even be able to get a flight out today. Tomorrow, the latest."

"Judith, you don't need to drop your life to come to see me. I just wanted to hear your voice."

"Well, my dear, you will hear my voice in person tonight or tomorrow. I'm checking flights as we speak."

Sapphire absolutely wanted a great big hug from Judith. But she didn't want to impose. She took a slow deep breath and sighed out loud. Once Judith made up her mind, there was no changing it.

As if she was reading Sapphire's mind, Judith said, "Don't even try to change my mind. You need me and I'll be there."

And with that, Sapphire realized she did need Judith. She wanted to tell Judith about the letter, the shawl, and the ring, but she would wait until she could tell her in person. Judith would know how to interpret the dream and voices too. She could almost feel herself melt into Judith's arms.

Chapter 4
Sapphire
Reminisces

After she hung up from her call to Judith, Sapphire collapsed into her chair and stared into space. She should make herself a cup of tea, but her body wouldn't. She sat in limbo for an hour. Her mind travelled back to the last time she visited Aunt Star. It was two years ago, right before COVID hijacked the travel plans for almost everyone. The humidity on Sanibel Island had felt heavier than usual. Each year, it seemed to get muggier and muggier. Sapphire had bites by no-see-ums over her entire body. Aunt Star had laughed and said that she was an exotic sweet treat for the insects. She gave her an ointment to soothe the itchiness and homemade herbal tea to drink. According to Aunt Star, the carefully researched combination of herbs would exude a scent from her pores that insects found unpleasant. It worked, surprising Sapphire.

Aunt Star was always combining various herbs for medicinal purposes. She had a concoction for chasing away headaches and another blend for insomnia. Sapphire wondered if the recipes for any of her aunt's special herb formulas and teas were preserved. She had a lot of questions for Dani Lake, the executor who sent her the box. Why hadn't Aunt Star ever mentioned this person's name? What other secrets did Aunt Star keep?

Sapphire had often tried to engage Aunt Star in conversation about her parents but learned very little over the years. She suspected there was more to their lives and deaths than Aunt Star would share. At first, Sapphire chose to wait until Aunt Star was ready to talk about it. But eventually she concluded it was unlikely that Aunt Star would ever reveal the secrets she held.

Although it was a struggle, Sapphire learned to accept her mysterious aunt on her own terms. In a way, Sapphire was like Aunt Star in that she too learned to be secretive. A heavy weight of invisible secrets followed Sapphire throughout her life, creating a veil of confusion and always tilting her a bit off balance. She kept secrets about her past from her best friends, Fisher, and Farrell. The one time Fisher accompanied her on a visit to Aunt Star, she and her aunt had an unspoken agreement to avoid talking about Sapphire's parents and her past.

The view from her window of flitting hummingbirds brought Sapphire back to the present. She scrounged up a pad and pen to begin a list of questions for Dani Lake, Aunt Star's executor. Question number one: "Were you a friend of my aunt?" Sapphire hoped Dani was. She felt a need to talk to people who knew Aunt Star, but she didn't have anyone to reach out to. Fisher was her only friend who met her, and now his memory died along with him. How many new complicated ripples of grief would Sapphire uncover?

Sapphire had always enjoyed the simple banter with Aunt Star. Her curiosity about the herbal insect repellant elicited amusement. *Will it repel people I don't want near me too?* Sapphire had teased.

You love everyone, my sweet Star. Aunt Star teased back. *I've never seen you find people offensive.* Aunt Star was the only living soul who still called Sapphire by her given name of Star. It always warmed her heart.

You haven't met some of the strange men who've tried to date me! Sapphire had replied. She immediately regretted opening the topic.

And how is that lovely fellow, Fisher? Aunt Star had needled her. Sapphire knew what was coming next. *I don't understand why the two of you never married.*

Sapphire long ago gave up her desire to marry Fisher, although they remained best friends until he was murdered last year. When she heard the news, Aunt Star had offered to come stay with her for an extended visit. But traveling during COVID was risky. Plus, Sapphire wanted to grieve alone without being observed, fussed over, and worried about.

Aunt Star was never a fan of the phone calls, texting, or emailing, which kept them farther apart over the past two years. Aunt Star wrote beautiful letters instead, although they had become fewer and farther between lately. Sapphire had been too wrapped up in grieving for Fisher to notice.

Sapphire had always loved her visits to Sanibel Island, the small island on the west coast of Florida that Aunt Star had made her home. Swimming in the salty Atlantic Ocean was a treat. On her last visit, a phenomenon called Red Tide, kept them out of the water. Toxic Red Tide algae from up the coast drifted down through the currents and left dead fish scattered along the shoreline. Tourists were repelled by the stench, and island workers struggled to clean the beaches every morning. Aunt Star took it all in stride, *Maybe we'll be able to swim next year,* she had said. Sapphire never swam in the ocean with her aunt again.

Now Sapphire wondered if she would ever go back to Sanibel Island. Without Aunt Star, the island had lost its allure. Sapphire suddenly understood why her aunt arranged for someone else to settle her affairs. Aunt Star knew that her niece could not face the task. If Aunt Star trusted Dani Lake, then Sapphire would trust her as well.

Aunt Star's colorful shawl caught Sapphire's eye. She wrapped herself in it like a cocoon. It smelled like Aunt Star, and Sapphire took slow deep breaths, inhaling the nostalgic fragrance. With each breath she took, Sapphire felt Aunt Star's presence, and it calmed her. She was ready. She picked up the phone and entered Dani's phone number. The crisp British accent on the voicemail startled her.

You have reached the confidential voicemail of Dani Lake, President of Aromaticus. Please leave your name and telephone number. A member of our team will return your call. Please remain on the line to speak with my personal assistant if your matter is urgent. Thank you.

Aromaticus? That was the name on the labels of Aunt Star's essential oils. The delicate calligraphy script of each label was etched in her mind since childhood. Sapphire's heart skipped a beat as she reached for the letter from Dani Lake. Same delicate script. Her eyes widened as she drew a sharp gasp. Dani Lake, the President of Aromaticus, must have known Aunt Star for many years. Why didn't her aunt ever mention her?

Chapter 5
Farrell Listens

Are you okay? showed up on Sapphire's text feed. It was from Farrell, an unlikely person to know instinctively that something was wrong. Farrell had been one of Sapphire's best friends since high school. On the other hand, Farrell had become more intuitive since their other best friend Fisher died last year. They remained close since high school, but Farrell struggled with being close to anyone. Most of his relationships were with business associates, and all his wealth management clients loved him. Farrell rarely dated and when he did, the relationship ended before it had an opportunity to become serious. He never married, had no children, and was considered a sixty-one-year-old eligible bachelor in Sedona. Women fell all over him trying to entice him with their charms. None succeeded. He remained devoted to his business and his best friend Sapphire.

Sapphire wondered why he was texting her now and how he knew that something was wrong. Was Farrell finally embracing his intuition? Just then, it hit her. They were supposed to meet this morning at eight to hike the Adobe Jack trail. Farrell rarely agreed to go hiking, but Sapphire replaced Fisher's role as the person who encouraged Farrell to hike. To refuse her cajoling, felt like he was doing a disservice to the memory of Fisher.

On your way? showed up on Sapphire's text feed before she had an opportunity to respond. Everything seemed to be in slow motion since she learned of Aunt Star's death. After telling Judith, Sapphire had no energy to tell anyone else. She knew tears would come bursting out each time she proclaimed the announcement. Somehow, the act of verbalizing the truth challenged her to accept it before she was ready.

Grief had a tricky timeline. Everything was still confusing. She continued the struggle to absorb simple thoughts and soon Sapphire became very sleepy.

Just as her eyelids closed and her chin dropped, the familiar *Money, Money, Money* ringtone blared from her cellphone and shook her awake. Farrell had established that song for his ringtone on her phone one evening when the three best friends drank too many bottles of fine wine. Sapphire and Fisher worried about Farrell's drinking from that night on.

Sapphire braced herself for his call and promised herself that she wouldn't cry. She pressed the answer button. "Aunt Star died," she eked out in a squeaky voice.

Farrell quickly responded with sincere concern. "Oh Sapphire, so sorry to hear this. Want me to come over?"

"Yes." Sapphire was surprised at her answer. She realized that being alone was not what she needed right now. Farrell would not press her to talk, and it would feel good to have a friend at her side.

When Farrell arrived fifteen minutes later, she fell into his arms and allowed him to comfort her. If quiet could be loud, Farrell had the loudest quiet listening ability of anyone she knew. Other people would make soothing sounds or try comforting comments. Farrell did neither. He simply sat there and remained silent.

Sapphire showed Farrell the letter from Dani Lake, her aunt's shawl, and the ring. He raised his eyebrows as he read the letter and smiled sadly as he admired the ring. "Whose initials are these?" Farrell asked as he pointed to the etched *JJM* inside the ring.

"I don't know," said Sapphire. "It's odd. Maybe it's a relative of my mother's. But none of them I knew had those initials."

Next, he tenderly touched the shawl, clearly recognizing how precious it was to Sapphire. It was the most intimate moment she and Farrell ever shared. Grief had softened him, even if he did not have the words to express it. Sapphire wondered if she would ever learn the secrets of Farrell's past. And would she ever share her past secrets with her remaining best friend? So much existed between them without a word being spoken. Their relationship was strong and silent, just like Farrell. Sapphire was able to calm down in his loving presence.

They suffered enough loss to know that grief would permeate life in ways they could never have imagined. As teenagers, both Farrell and Sapphire, like Fisher, had been abruptly removed from their home and family and sent to boarding school in Sedona. Their high school bond saved them, making Fisher's murder even more traumatic. Sapphire and Farrell continued to cling to their precious friendship. Yet, they both had deep secrets from their past that they still kept hidden. Would they ever reveal their secrets to each other?

Chapter 6
Sofia Assists

Sofia knew immediately, before she opened her eyes in the morning, that today would be significant. It had been a full year since she arrived in Sedona after inheriting Fisher Bond's home. As a therapist, Sofia often experienced a strong connection with her clients, but this was different. It was more than a premonition. Someone in her personal life was in trouble. She felt it in every fiber of her being.

She often wondered if she inherited more than a house from Fisher. His home, his community, his friends, and his artistic talent all came wrapped up in one package. It felt like Sedona was always supposed to be her home. And what a home it was! Designed by Sapphire Designs and carefully decorated by Fisher. Every inch contained works by local artisans. The home was infused by generations of loving artistic talent. Yet, it exuded a welcoming and comfy quality, unlike the staged homes in glossy magazines.

Fisher's best friends, Sapphire, and Farrell welcomed her with open arms. The home accepted her too, and she quickly became part of it. After a fulfilling career of forty-six years as a family therapist, Sofia finally retired. The opportunity to live in Sedona and pursue her creative expression was truly a dream come true. How thrilling to have a second chapter in her life at age seventy-one.

Stained glass art classes led to hours each day of getting lost in her newly fashioned studio. Sometimes, Sofia would walk into her studio just to stare at a beautiful piece of glass, unique in color and texture, daring her to create the perfect design. So far, she had created six pieces, all her own designs and each different than the others. The ideas swarmed her brain day and night, demanding to be expressed in the way only artists experience.

At first, Sofa wondered if she would feel comfortable working in the same space where Fisher was murdered. Would it feel spooky or ghoulish? But it was surprisingly comforting. Fisher's metal studio held more positive energy than pain. The invitation to open the studio and begin to create beautiful art felt like it came from within the abandoned room. "I belong here," Sofia told Lena, her best friend from college.

The studio was a separate structure connected to the main house by a simple set of red rock steppingstones. Entering the light-filled studio transported her to the land of creativity. Sun streamed through the floor-to-ceiling windows with a panoramic view of the majestic red rock mountains. It smelled like fresh rain and creek flowers.

Sapphire agreed that the original plan to demolish the studio didn't feel right. The idea to raze the studio in response to Fisher's murder was an initial gut reaction born from the agony of grief. Fisher wouldn't have wanted them to destroy the beautiful space Sapphire had created for him. Sapphire was the designer and architect, so Sofia accepted her blessing wholeheartedly. Fisher's metal working tools were artfully displayed on several shelves, to view and admire by all who entered the studio. Sofia paid homage to Fisher in silent appreciation every time she laid eyes on his tools.

Sofia also accepted Sapphire's sincere friendship and invitation to experience all the beauty Sedona had to offer. "My entire new life here feels like a *Twilight Zone* episode," Sofia told Lena, during their last phone call. Sofia told Lena everything, ever since their college days. Lena still lived in Ft. Lauderdale, but Sofia hoped to entice her to move to Sedona someday.

"I'm so happy for you to be living there, but Sedona is not for everyone," Lena said. Sofia knew that it was true.

Sofia was honored to be accepted and enveloped into the folds of community life. Introductions from Sapphire and Farrell smoothed her entry, sometimes making her feel like a debutante in a coming-out cotillion.

Now Sofia returned to her awareness that today would be significant. The sensation strengthened even before her morning coffee. As usual, Sofia decided to wait for the day to unfold to inform her of the source of her strong feeling. The answer arrived less than two hours later in the form of a telephone call from Farrell.

"Would you be able to go to Phoenix this afternoon to pick up Judith at the airport?" Before Sofia had a chance to respond, Farrell continued. "Sapphire's aunt died, and Judith is flying in to be with her."

"You know I'd do anything for Sapphire and Judith," Sofia responded. "How is she doing?"

"I stayed with her last night. It reminds her of losing Fisher and I don't want to leave her alone today."

Sofia felt grateful she didn't need to cancel anything today. Of course, she would have canceled her Pilates, hair appointment, or stained-glass lessons if they conflicted. She wondered if Sapphire would still be interested in dinner out for their usual Tuesday night routine. Probably not, of course.

Maybe she would bring dinner in from one of their favorite restaurants. The four of them would need to eat. She decided to talk with Judith about it on the two-hour drive back to Sedona from the Phoenix airport. Despite the dreaded truck traffic on I-17, Sofia was looking forward to seeing Judith. No one had a greater zest for life than the eighty-one-year-old diminutive Judith Saltan.

Sofia met Judith a year ago when she came to Sedona to help unravel the mysterious death of Fisher Bond. The background information she shared and keen observance to detail proved crucial in solving his murder. Judith had been the secretary and assistant to an agent in the Witness Protection Program when Fisher was relocated to Sedona as a teen. His father, a private pilot, had been murdered after the mob learned he was an informant for the FBI. As a teen, Fisher's father brought him along when flying the so-called businessmen around South America and the Caribbean.

He never told anyone about the relocation throughout his entire life. Farrell and Sapphire hadn't had a clue. They had only known that Fisher was secretive. They had secrets as well. *Don't ask, don't tell* was their unspoken agreement about their past. An enduring friendship between Fisher, Farrell, and Sapphire was sustained over the years by focusing on their present and future. Judith's surprise about Fisher being relocated by the Witness Protection Program stunned Sapphire and Farrell, and they were still processing the revelation.

Fisher led a fulfilled life in Sedona, embracing his cherished friends and career as a beloved forest ranger, before his untimely death at age sixty. Sofia met Fisher when she was his therapist in Florida, before his relocation. He gifted Sofia his enchanting Sedona home. It was his way of honoring her for sharing her passion for the red rocks, directing him to Sedona.

Judith, Sophia, Farrell, and Sapphire became entwined forever after teaming up with the FBI and local authorities to solve Fisher Bond's murder. Farrell and Sapphire represented Fisher's present life and past since high school. Sofia represented his life before being relocated and Judith represented his relocation transition. They all loved him differently in their own way. Despite no longer being part of this world, Fisher's presence continued to reverberate, absorbed forever in the bonds of their friendship.

Now, they would be coming together again, as a team to help Sapphire grieve the loss of Aunt Star. Not one of them had a clue as to the family mystery Aunt Star left behind.

Chapter 7
Judith Arrives

Judith's cell beeped as soon as she turned it on, after landing at the Phoenix Airport. She read the text from Sofia. *I'm waiting for you by the baggage carousel.*

Judith sighed with relief. She was dreading catching the tram to the car rental center, waiting in a long line, and driving through heavy Phoenix traffic. When the plane came to a stop, she stood up slowly and stretched her limbs. Everything ached. She eyed the other passengers with envy as they sprung up from their seats and effortlessly reached for their overhead baggage. Those days were now behind her. She even had to check her suitcase since it was too heavy for her to manage it on the plane. Packing a larger suitcase, instead of a carry-on helped cement the plan, leaving her no choice but to check her luggage.

Judith struggled to accept the reality of her diminished physical capacity. She ignored the fatigue that finally visited her aging bones. For many years, Judith was able to ward off typical signs of aging that others experienced. Exercise, clean eating, and strong genetics all mixed to form a capable body. It complimented her feisty personality. Up until now, Judith was almost unstoppable. Nothing lasts forever, she had told herself, knowing that she would have to slow down. Yeah, right! Judith answered her achy bones.

She deplaned and stopped at the restroom to freshen up. Looking in the mirror, Judith encouraged herself, *YOU GO, GIRL! YOU'VE GOT THIS!!* Watching herself in the mirror, she straightened up and assumed the fierce and feisty demeanor she was known for.

"Thank you for picking me up. I normally take carry-on but didn't know how long I'd be staying," Judith told Sofia as soon as they found and greeted each other. "So, I packed a large suitcase." Judith and Sofia waited by the luggage carousel with the other arriving passengers, watching it go round and round. Finally, Judith's suitcase appeared on the conveyer belt. She pointed it out, and Sofia lifted it up and placed it on its wheels. Judith grabbed hold of the handle and began rolling it as they walked toward the parking lot.

"We all need to support Sapphire. It's the least I can do," Sofia responded. "It's my pleasure, really." Sofia noticed something was different with

Judith. She wasn't sure what it was, but Judith's movements appeared to require deliberate effort and the cadence of her speech was off. Maybe the plane ride was turbulent.

"How was the flight?" Sofia inquired. "It's a long plane ride across the country. Sapphire will be so glad to see you." Judith ignored the veiled reference to her declining stamina.

"Have you spoken to her?" Judith asked.

"No, but Farrell has filled me in," Sofia said. "It sounds like she is still in shock. Normal grief reaction." Sofia had seen that often. "Farrell said that Sapphire learned of Aunt Star's death when she received a letter from someone out of state. Someone she didn't know. Apparently, her aunt's executor. But Sapphire never heard of her. It's gotten her rattled."

"I'm glad Farrell stayed with her. It's good for both of them." Judith said. She gratefully accepted the cold bottle of water from Sofia, noticing the dehydrating effect of air travel. Her throat was parched. She took small sips of water, then resorted to large gulps. It was taking longer than usual for her body to acclimate. The change in altitude made her sleepy. She rubbed her eyes which had already become dry from the lack of humidity. Judith ignored her lightheadedness and clogged ears. The lavender oil she applied to her pulse points helped calm her.

Sofia noticed Judith's subtle signs of aging since she last saw Judith only six months ago. The brisk stride in her steps was no longer there. She walked slower now, but she hadn't adopted the lumbering shuffle and drag of most women her age. Sofia decided to not say a word about it. She slowed down her own pace to accommodate Judith. Sofia had honed the professional skill of maintaining a watchful eye while appearing nonchalant. She also knew how to adapt her pace to match another's. Some professional habits served well in Sofia's personal life.

"Why don't you wait here while I get the car," Sofia offered.

"Nonsense Sofia! You think I can't walk to the parking lot?" Judith barked back.

"Well at least let me carry one of your bags," Sofia said. She reached out to take the rolling suitcase. Before she could grab it, Judith foisted her large tote toward Sofia. *MZ Wallace* was embossed in gold letters on the quilted expensive-looking carry-on.

Sofia's eyes opened wide. "When did you start buying designer bags?" she asked. "You always said you didn't want to be a free billboard advertisement for designer brands." The bag was heavy on Sofia's shoulder as she watched Judith wheel the larger suitcase with effort.

"A gift I thought I should use," Judith responded sheepishly. "It belonged to Jared Silver's wife Bonnie. He wanted the bag to be well traveled since Bonnie died before having a chance to use it." Jared Silver was the lead FBI agent who helped solve Fisher's murder. He worked through his grief and retirement issues in the process.

"How is Agent Silver? You keep in touch?" Sofia was curious. She had hoped her friend Lena and Agent Silver would get together. Maybe there was still a chance for that.

"Traveling the world with his great-nephew, Taylor. They just got back from New Zealand. It turned out that Taylor was the perfect traveling companion for Jared. He's an expert at internet research and has become quite the travel advisor. Started a blog, whatever that is. Jared said Taylor has thousands of followers. Do you know what a blog is?"

"Kinda sorta," Sofia said. "It's like an online diary that others can read for inspiration and advice. Maybe it'll lead to a career choice for Taylor. Doesn't he graduate high school next year?"

"You can make a career and earn money writing a blog?" Judith asked. "I must say, I'm having trouble keeping up with today's kids and their creative use of technology. Taylor is just starting tenth grade and he plans to graduate early.

"Yes," said Sofia. "Companies pay money to have their brand mentioned. The more followers, the more the ad placement pays."

When they finally arrived at the car, Sofia loaded the luggage. Then she cranked up the air conditioning. "Wait until the car cools down before getting inside," she told Judith. It was 110 degrees in Phoenix, another typical June weather day. Fortunately, it would be twenty degrees cooler in Sedona.

The drive up to Sedona went quickly as Judith and Sofia caught up on their lives the way old friends do. They were comfortable enough with each other to share their joys and hardships without censoring their honest feelings.

"So...you might have noticed I'm slowing down a bit," Judith confessed. She surprised herself to say it out loud. Judith let out a giant sigh that she didn't know was stuck in her throat. The tightness in her heart loosened. "You're the first person I've acknowledged that to, including myself," she continued. "It doesn't work to ignore it so I might as well embrace it. Oh, I hate that term. Honestly, IT SUCKS!" Judith burst out laughing, and Sofia laughed with her. The laughter brought relief to Judith, and she took more deep sighs.

"And I thought you were an alien with superhuman powers," Sofia said. "We all marveled at how you had more energy than the rest of us. What a relief to know you're human after all."

Judith smiled inside. "I liked being Wonder Woman. Now what will I be instead?"

"Simply amazing, as always," Sofia assured her friend. She clasped Judith's hand to emphasize her admiration. "I remain in complete awe of you. I hope to be as energetic and sharp as you are at eighty-one."

"Enough about me, tell me about you, my dear Sofia." And just like that, Judith accepted her natural aging with the same grace she embraced other aspects of her life. She was ready to move on, noticing that she had more energy as soon as her worry lifted. Sofia noticed Judith's private breakthrough and nodded with acceptance.

"This year's been full of surprises for me. I was happy with my life in Florida a year ago and had no idea that I'd be moving to Sedona," Sofia began. "Fisher was a client in my first year of practice as a therapist so many years ago. He ushered me into the profession. What synchronicity that he would be the person, even in death, to usher me into my retirement."

"So, you've given up your private practice entirely?" Judith expressed surprise. "No more clients at all?"

"Well, they can always contact me, but I'll warmly refer them to one of my colleagues. I've got a network of other therapists I trust and feel secure referring clients to." Sofia struggled with her plan to refer clients out but promised herself that she would. In the past, some would track her down and contact her many years later. She even treated the children of some of the teens who grew up and reached out to her after two decades.

The red rocks could be seen in the distance as Sofia and Judith approached Sedona. "Now on to more important matters. We're thirty minutes from Sedona. What do you think we should bring for dinner?" Sofia's stomach rumbled reminding her that she hadn't eaten since breakfast. She shook her head inwardly, chastising herself. Sofia recalled the countless times she had told others to remember to keep up the needed nutrition. She took a long sip of water from her glass thermos. At least she remembered to hydrate.

Judith also noticed being hungry. "Is that Italian restaurant, Gerardo's, still in business? Sapphire loves their vegetarian pizza."

"Perfect," Sofia quickly responded. "I'll call in the order. How about a Mediterranean salad and those pistachio cannoli too?"

"I still have their number saved to my favorites," said Judith. "Taylor showed me how to do that. I'll call in the order while you concentrate on driving. I'll give them my credit card number. My treat."

Sofia knew from experience not to argue with Judith when she had her mind made up. "Okay, but order double please so there will be enough for the four of us. The order should be ready by the time we get there."

Thirty-five minutes later, the enticing aroma of pizza wafted in front of Sapphire's front door as Judith and Sofia waited to enter. It would be the first meal the four of them shared in a year. Most of the clues in solving Fisher's murder were analyzed during scrumptious meals. Judith, Sofia, Farrell, and Sapphire were about to embark on a mystery journey again. Bon Appetit!

Chapter 8
Reunited

Farrell opened Sapphire's door before Judith and Sofia had a chance to ring the bell. He had been watching Sapphire's security cameras anxiously awaiting their arrival. The grief he had absorbed from Sapphire over the past two days had taken its toll. He felt heavy and sad. Now the cavalry had finally arrived. Judith was more suited for the job of comforter, Farrell thought. He was completely unaware of the immeasurable role he played in supporting Sapphire. The entire time he sat by her silently, Farrell struggled to find the right words to say. Little did he know that his silence was golden.

Farrell's two days being close with Sapphire haunted him. Every time he became emotionally close with a woman, Farrell suffered. He would find himself ruminating about one horrible night in his past. After forty-six years, the guilt and confusion lingered on. He wished he could remember what happened that night. Farrell later learned that an alcoholic blackout stole his memory. He had been only fifteen the night it happened, but it still felt as if it were yesterday. Lately, his heart was getting heavier. He would have to talk to someone eventually but didn't know how.

Now Farrell ushered Sofia and Judith inside, luggage, pizza, and all. Farrell couldn't figure out whether to take their food and bags or hug Judith first. He managed an awkward combination of both, nearly dropping the pizzas.

"Whoa, hold on there and let me put this food in the kitchen first and then get a proper hug," Judith said. She knew her way around Sapphire's home, having been a guest there several times in the last year. She placed the food on the counter and wheeled her luggage into the guest room she always stayed in. Judith's familiar scent of lavender lingered.

"Now come here Farrell and give me that proper hug," Judith commanded. Farrell always did what Judith said. Everyone did. Judith was there and was now in charge. She held on to Farrell just a bit longer and tighter than usual as if she were taking in the grief he had absorbed. He wanted to cry, but his hardened shell refused tears. Still, the hug helped, and Farrell felt a bit lighter. It was always been surprising that he was able to allow himself to be comforted by Judith. Would he be able to share the shame of his past with her some day?

Sofia's professional experience recognized that Farrell's body forecasted his inner trauma. Lines were etched on his face. The shoulders of his six-foot-tall frame slumped. Judith noticed too, wondering if Farrell's sadness was more than sympathy for Sapphire. She made a silent promise to inquire more. Not now, though. Her mission for this visit was to devote her entire attention to Sapphire. Farrell's secret burdens would still be there later. Although Farrell was a grown man, Judith sensed his emotional growth was more of a teen than an adult. When the time came, she would have to tread lightly or risk him shutting down and shutting her out completely.

Sapphire emerged from her bedroom, red-eyed and bedraggled looking. Judith had never seen Sapphire with rumpled clothes and uncombed hair. She appeared dazed as she stared at Judith, almost as if she was surprised to see her. Judith and Sofia exchanged a quick knowing look. Both ran to her at once, encircling her into a warm embrace. She collapsed into their arms.

Farrell observed the feminine bonding of the three women he was closest to. He felt a galaxy away, as if he belonged on another planet. It was more than an amusing *Men are from Mars / Women are from Venus* experience. This had no humor. Farrell longed to be part of their connected circle. He longed for a stiff drink even more. In desperation, he began setting the table for dinner. Farrell knew he could avoid having a drink by busying himself with a task until the overwhelming compulsion became manageable. He set out plates for the pizza, bowls for the salad, napkins, silverware, and glasses. Needing more busy work, Farrell filled a pitcher with Sapphire's mint-infused water. He opened various kitchen drawers to look for a pizza cutter and salad tongs. What else, he thought? Farrell found small plates for the cannoli. For a final touch, he placed a vase of fresh flowers on the table as a centerpiece.

Gentle soothing sounds drifted to the kitchen from the trio in the living room. Then a bit of laughter. What was so funny?

At the table, Judith teased Farrell. "When did you become so domesticated? You set a beautiful table."

Sofia smiled as she admired his work. "Very nice, thank you, Farrell," she said with sincerity. "I'm starving, let's dig in!"

Sapphire giggled which made it all worth the effort. Farrell couldn't help but smile as well. He hadn't seen Sapphire crack a smile for two days, and her giggling was music to his ears. Sapphire walked over to him with a straighter spine and gave him a long hug. "Thank you for being here to help me through the worst part. You're my best friend and I'll always remember how you are here for me."

"I'll be here for you whenever you need me, Sapphire, just as you've always been there for me." Farrell couldn't keep a few tears from sliding down his cheek. He had done a good job in supporting his friend. What a relief.

"Let's eat! before one of us faints," Judith declared. And since they all always listen to what Judith says, they obediently filled their plates with pizza and salad. The only sounds that could be heard were munching and the all too familiar *mmm* from all four. Not a morsel remained as the famished foursome devoured their feast. The quantity of food consumed was as if they were preparing for a marathon. Somehow, the four friends knew that something important was ahead of them.

Chapter 9
Dani Lake

Dani Lake squinted at the caller ID on her office phone. She quickly reached for her reading glasses hung on a chain around her neck. The caller had the area code of 928. This was the call from Sedona she had been waiting for. However, she wasn't ready to talk to Sapphire quite yet since she hadn't figured out how to tell her the entire story. Maybe she was just too nervous. The phone rang five times. She let it go to voicemail, but no message was left. The click of a hang-up jarred her. It triggered memories and pulled her back to the past when Sapphire's parents would call.

Back then, leaving no message was the message. Sapphire's parents would call the lab every day around noontime while Dani waited with high anxiety. They had worked out the number of rings as a code. One ring had meant *all was well*. Two rings meant *we're making progress*. Three rings signaled *wait for instructions on where to meet us*. Four rings meant *destroy all research and shut down the lab*. Five rings indicated that it was *safe to pick up the phone.* Dani had kept the habit of waiting for the phone to ring five times before picking up any calls that arrived around noontime.

Dani had been Sapphire's parents' research assistant since all three had worked at Aromaticus. Sapphire's parents, Jane Ceres and Andre Dover, met Dani Lake at the University of New Mexico in Albuquerque. All three were science majors and shared their passion for inventions. They spent many late nights experimenting with unique combinations of essential oils to investigate the medicinal qualities. They longed to discover a combination of essential oils that would benefit humanity.

Jane and Andre had become a couple early on, yet Dani had never felt like a third wheel. They'd been a team from the start and a force to be reckoned with. Their combined skill sets complemented each other, making their scientific projects fun.

When Dani came out as gay, Jane told her that she had already known. It had been the way Dani looked at other women. The same way Jane looked at Andre.

Dani had several long-term girlfriends over the years. One moved in with her. But keeping secrets from a live-in partner hadn't worked out well for building a trusting relationship. Dani had been sworn to secrecy regarding Aromaticus. When the girlfriend moved out, Dani closed the door on her heart to further romance. It hadn't been worth the risk. The stakes were too high and the closer they got to developing the secret formula, the more dangerous it had become for all of them. If their formula was a success, the major medical breakthrough would impact the population worldwide. The implications were mind boggling.

Jane and Andre were only thirty-seven when they died, having left behind their fifteen-year-old daughter Sapphire. Fortunately, they had sent her to boarding school for her safety. Three months later, they'd lost their lives. The newspapers had falsely reported that political activists were killed in a failed coup. They were farmers, not political activists. Dani hoped interest in Jane and Andre and their secret formula would finally die down.

Jane and Andre had taken their research science skills directly into a small town in Columbia. As farmers, they seamlessly embedded themselves into the same society they had lived in while researching plants and herbs. If powerful interest groups learned of their research, the formula could fall into the wrong hands. They had to be discreet and needed a plausible cover for being in the farmlands, near the Amazon Rainforest.

Their cover was more than plausible. They ran a lucrative farm, and no one questioned their business. The Dovers' also championed the movement to improve the living conditions of migrant workers, having sung Joan Baez ballads along the way. It was the seventies and many ex-pats had joined forces with activists in foreign countries to overthrow corrupt governments and promote democracy. Marches and demonstrations led to violence. Yet, Dani doubted that Jane and Andre had become involved with marches and demonstrations. She didn't believe that their deaths were a result of their politics.

Dani remembered being in the lab when the dreaded four rings signal had come in. One ring, two rings, three rings, and finally four. Then nothing. The ringing had stopped. Had she counted wrong? But then it happened again exactly five minutes later. Four rings, then silence. And finally, one last time, ten minutes after that. Jane and Andre had known that Dani would've needed to be sure.

Dani later learned that the Dovers had instructed one of their trusted friends to place the calls in the event of their deaths. The same friend destroyed all records in the Dovers' make-shift lab on their farm, as they had requested. The friend never suspected that the top-secret documents held a miracle lifesaving formula. Instead, he thought he was destroying their farm business records to prevent the documents from falling into the hands of corrupt government inspectors.

Dani had immediately shut down her small lab at the Aromaticus factory in Asheville, as they had agreed. She slyly informed the product safety department that the plants and herbs in the lab became contaminated with mold. Dani also deceptively warned Aromaticus that the contamination from her lab could lead to a highly contagious bacteria that would damage the products being manufactured in the entire factory. The company president thanked her for her professionalism, had the lab fumigated, and wrote off the loss.

Over the ensuing years, Dani worked hard. She rose through the ranks and had finally become the company president. She later purchased Aromaticus when the owners retired. Dani had been married to her job for the past sixty years. At age eighty-three, she was still going strong and was genuinely respected by her company employees.

In present times, Aromaticus manufactured organic, medical quality herbal products. They produced over thirty different items ranging from tinctures, ointments, and essential oils. The essential oils had become highly sought after, and Aromaticus increased production to meet the demands. Mail order shipments in companies worldwide overtook in-store divisions, increasing profits tenfold. Dani Lake followed the online trend, bringing her company into the twenty-first century. The competition could not keep up with Aromaticus.

Before their death, the Dovers had entrusted the written details of the formula to Jane's sister Star. She was two years younger than Jane, and people had thought they were twins. Since it had been unsafe to record it in writing, the formula was creatively hidden in secret code. It was ingenious and only four people had known about it. Now that Star had died, Dani was the only person left who knew where Star hid the formula. She had to tell Sapphire and had to tell her soon.

Over the years, Dani denied the existence of the formula to various governmental agencies, research associations, and private contractors. There had been suspicions. After Star's death, Dani suspected that Star's home on Sanibel Island had been searched thoroughly before Dani had a chance to arrive. Small items had been left out of place. Had secret video cameras been installed to watch her sift through Star's belongings? These tenacious operatives were sinister and had been desperate for the formula. Money, power, greed, and influence were strong motivators. Now, she worried. Was her life in danger?

Dani knew the world wasn't ready for the formula. It wouldn't be used to save lives and reduce suffering for the masses. Instead, corporations would profit, and a small number of CEOs would get wealthier. Maybe, hopefully, sometime in the future the world would be ready. Dani suspected that it wouldn't be in her lifetime. Maybe not in Sapphire's lifetime either. It would be up to Sapphire to keep the formula safe and pass it on to the next generation until the time was right. Since Sapphire didn't have children of her own, selecting the right heir would be a daunting task. It was an extraordinary responsibility, and Dani hoped that Sapphire possessed the strength for this mission. Otherwise, the formula would be gone and forever forgotten.

Dani decided on a plan of action. She would arrange to meet Sapphire in person. A neutral location would be selected, one that would appear innocuous. It had to be far away. Sanibel Island wouldn't be safe. Star's home was likely still being watched. Dani Lake knew the perfect place.

She hoped Sapphire would agree to meet her. She also hoped that Sapphire wouldn't find the story preposterous. Dani planned to tell her the entire story from the beginning. That her Aunt Star didn't tell her the truth to honor her parents' wishes. Would she understand why Aunt Star had left instructions with Dani to tell Sapphire everything upon her death? Dani hoped Sapphire would accept the truth and understand the important role being passed on to her. The world needed the formula for the sake of future generations.

Chapter 10
Good Night

After dinner was enjoyed by all, Sapphire, Sofia, Farrell, and Judith sat comfortably at the dining room table, absorbed in their thoughts. The sunset bathed the home in golden hues. Everyone remained still in their reverence, sharing an unspoken appreciation for the beauty of nature.

Throughout Sedona and the surrounding Verde Valley, watching the sunset was a nightly ritual. Even the wildlife welcomed nightfall with their secret sounds, signaling that it was now their time to roam. Coyotes howled while dogs barked in alarm. Javelina sniffed out the roots of newly planted garden greens for their dinner. Mule deer snuck a drink in the homemade fountains. Hummingbirds fluttered around the colorful feeders, taking turns sipping the nectar through their slim beaks. It was the time of day when humans had no choice but to acknowledge who truly owned the land.

When the last ray of sunshine dropped below the red rocks, a reverse sunset treated the landscape with an encore. Wild orange and violet smudges whispered to the moon, enticing her to shine her light. Those who experienced it reacted with reverence and gratitude. Sedona was known for her mystical vortexes, but the breathtaking sunsets were truly unforgettable.

Cognizant of controlling his urge to drink, Farrell appreciated the special time with friends. The others were subdued resting in a carbohydrate haze. "Ladies," Farrell announced, "tonight I'm a full-service server. I'll clear the table, rinse the dishes, run the dishwasher, take out the garbage, and sweep the floors. You can thank me tonight and take over tomorrow."

"Who are you and where did my Farrell go?" Sapphire asked incredulously. She was glad for the help since she wasn't in emotional shape to assume her usual role of hostess.

Sofia and Judith shared a glance with a smirk. Men are celebrated when doing the daily chores that women do all the time, unrecognized. But tonight wasn't the night to speak about that. Instead, they both thanked Farrell for helping so much.

To his credit, Farrell sensed the unspoken words. "I know, I should do it more often. I just don't remember to. I wasn't brought up that way." Memories of growing up in an alcoholic family seeped into his heart, uninvited and unwelcomed. He wanted a drink. Farrell felt like a Pavlovian experiment with the same old stimulus and response cycle. Feeling sad led to an urge to drink. Feeling angry led to an urge to drink. Feeling anything led to an urge to drink. Not feeling anything led to an urge to drink. Drinking numbed him and it worked every time since his teen years. Same old pathetic depressing cycle.

One month was the longest Farrell had gone without a drink. He convinced himself that he could drink in moderation, and therefore couldn't accept Alcoholics Anonymous' first step of admitting that he was powerless over alcohol. Farrell knew people who found sobriety through AA, yet he continued to resist the support. He was sure that no one knew how much he struggled. Maybe one day, he would let them know. Farrell didn't want their pity, judgment, advice, or even their support. This was his private battle.

He finished the clean-up and sighed. His urge to drink had subsided. He had won the battle, at least for now. Farrell saw himself at that moment as an enduring warrior racking up more wins than losses. *Keep it up*, he told himself. *One moment at a time.* He looked forward to getting into his own bed in his own home and welcoming earned sleep.

Sofia left at the same time as Farrell, asking him to escort her to her car. Years of living in big cities taught her to be safety conscious. Even in the small town of Sedona, with little crime, she kept up her habit of having an escort walk her to her car in the dark. Sometimes she asked a friend to watch her get into her car as she left their home, if it was nighttime. Sofia got through her embarrassment by reminding herself that she was one of the very few women she knew who had not experienced an assault.

Sapphire slept soundly knowing that Judith was in the next room. Judith had visited Sapphire three times over the past year, each time staying in Sapphire's guest room with the beach decor. They had become even closer, after forming an instant bond right from the start. Although they had known each other for only a year, it felt like a lifetime for Sapphire. Judith had been like an aunt to Fisher when he was in the Witness Protection Program as a teen. Aunt Star functioned as a surrogate parent for Sapphire after losing her parents as a teen. How fortuitous that Judith entered her life as a surrogate aunt a year before Aunt Star died. Maybe she would call Dani Lake again tomorrow, with Judith by her side.

Something Sapphire said rattled around in Judith's brain. Aunt Star was strong and healthy. How could she have suddenly died? Judith waited until she was certain Sapphire was sound asleep. She then gathered everything she needed from her tote bag to finally prepare for bed. Unpacking her suitcase could wait until the morning. Tomorrow was going to be a long day, supporting Sapphire through her grief and Judith was ready for it. She sunk into bed with a quiet groan. Within minutes, she fell into a deep sleep, dreaming of the ocean, with warm breezes and turquoise water.

Chapter 11
The Phone Call

In the morning, Sapphire was not quite back to her old self, but she was centered enough to get dressed, do her Pilates, drink her mint water, and follow her usual routine. Coffee and breakfast fortified Sapphire to approach the day with energy and grace. By the time Judith emerged from her room, Sapphire had the box, the letter, the shawl, and the ring out to show her.

"Good morning, Judith. Did you sleep well?"

"Yes, I always sleep well in your home. The room reminds me of the ocean with the turquoise and white theme. Feels like home."

"Breakfast? The usual? I have my mint water out for you, room temperature, the way you like it. Coffee?"

"Yes, please. Black coffee, oatmeal, and mint water would be lovely. What's that on the table? The colors on that shawl are outstanding. Is it handwoven?"

"Aunt's Star's shawl. She always wore it. I inherited it. Isn't it beautiful?"

"Exquisite! Do you know where she got it?"

"I remember her wearing it before I came to Sedona. She seldom took it off. I think she was always cold, and it kept her warm. I don't know where she got it. It doesn't have a label, and I've never seen one like it. Maybe a gift. After you finish breakfast, I'll show you the other things that arrived from her estate."

"Who sent you these things?" Judith dipped her spoon into the homemade oatmeal.

"Her executor, a woman named Dani Lake," said Sapphire. "I never heard of her. I called her number but got voicemail. I was too upset to leave a message. Now that you're here, I want to call again this morning."

"Yes, of course, my dear. We'll call this Dani Lake together."

"Thank you, Judith," said Sapphire. "I feel better having you with me when I place the call."

Judith sat back. "Well, my dear, as soon as I finish my breakfast and wash my hands, I'd like to see what she sent you. Then we can place that call."

With clean hands, Judith sat on the chair in front of the box. It exuded an intriguing fragrance. "Lovely scent," she said. "I recognize mint and lavender, not sure what the other notes are." Gently, she lifted the shawl into her hands and studied it closely. "Extraordinary," she said. "I've never seen this stitching pattern before. This truly is a treasure, Sapphire. It suits you."

"Thank you, Judith. Here's the ring that Aunt Star always wore." Sapphire held out the gem for Judith to see. "It's a star-sapphire. Her parents had given it to her. They gave my mother a star- sapphire necklace. My grandparents. Never knew them. They died long before I was born. My mother gave me the necklace when I was fifteen."

"Yes, I've admired that necklace on you and have seen you holding the gem often. I can tell that you cherish it. You'll cherish Aunt Star's ring and shawl too. Let me see the letter now."

Judith squinted at the print. "I need to get my reading glasses. I'll be right back." She went into her guest bedroom and fished her jeweled case containing her reading glasses. As an afterthought, she grabbed her cellphone too. She wanted to take a photo of the stitching on the shawl but would ask Sapphire first. Weavers had their signature patterns, and Judith planned to examine the shawl more closely. She had an ancient textbook that described historical interpretations of particular weaving patterns. Maybe she could research the pattern and find out who the artisan was.

Sapphire observed the slow methodical way Judith read the short note. She could see her eyes move as she read and noticed a faint quiver on her lips. When Judith was finished, she stared at the letter for a long time. Why was she taking so long to respond? A tear fell from Judith's eye and ran down her cheek. Sapphire didn't understand this emotional response. She never even met her. Then, it hit her. Sapphire understood. Perhaps the letter is reminding Judith of her own mortality. She and Aunt Star were the same age. Sapphire couldn't imagine losing Judith as well.

Finally, Judith cleared her throat and said, "I wish I could've known your aunt. I'm so sorry for your loss, Sapphire." And with that, she went over to Sapphire and enveloped her in a tight hug. Sapphire didn't cry but did allow her grief to run through her, feeling like a cascading waterfall. She took a deep sigh and said, "I'm ready to place that phone call now. I'll put it on speaker phone."

Sapphire dialed the number again. After five rings, it was answered, and this time she did not hear the voicemail. "Hello, is this Sapphire Dover?" a voice answered in a British accent. "I saved your phone number in my contacts and have been waiting for your call. This is Dani Lake."

Sapphire had become very sensitive to voices over the years and developed an immediate impression from hearing a person's voice for the first time. Usually, her impression was right. Dani Lake's voice immediately provided comfort to her.

"Were you a long-time friend of Aunt Star?" Sapphire blurted out. "I'm sorry. I'm getting ahead of myself. First, I want to thank you for sending me Aunt Star's shawl and ring. They both mean a lot to me, and I'm sincerely grateful to have them."

Dani released her held breath and chose her unrehearsed words carefully. "Yes, I'd known your aunt for many years. I was a close friend of your parents as well." Straight out, no beating around the bush, right to the point. There, she said it out loud. The words she had been wanting to share with Sapphire since Jane and Andre died.

Complete silence met Dani on the other end. Did they get disconnected? "Are you still there, Sapphire?" asked Dani. "I'm sorry to surprise you like that. I think it would be best for me to tell you everything in person."

Sapphire's jaw had dropped. She blinked the stinging tears away. She had whipped her head around to Judith so quickly that she felt dizzy. Finally, she spoke. "Over the years, I've wanted to know so much more about my parents and thought I'd lost my final opportunity when Aunt Star died." She palmed her star-sapphire necklace. "I'm so excited that I can barely speak. Please give me a moment. My dear friend Judith is here with me." She motioned to Judith to please take over. Judith understood and cleared her throat before speaking.

"Hello Dani, please allow me to introduce myself. I'm Judith Saltan, a close friend of Sapphire. She's okay, just a bit overwhelmed with emotion. You're on speaker phone and Sapphire can hear you."

"Hello Judith, I'm so sorry to set Sapphire off balance. I've wanted to meet you Sapphire for many years and talk with you. I've so much to tell you. Out of respect for your parents and aunt, I waited until their death, as they requested. They loved you so much and were worried about your safety. Perhaps I was too hasty in mentioning your parents."

Sapphire nodded slowly and said, "I'm glad you mentioned them."

"She'll be fine," Judith said. "Sapphire's a strong woman. When can we meet in person? Would you like to come to Sedona, or shall we come to Asheville? I'll be accompanying Sapphire."

"I think it would be best if we met on the island of Kauai, Hawaii. This might sound a bit strange, but I have good reasons and will explain when you get there. I'm flying out tomorrow to visit our factory and will be staying for two weeks. The company owns a home there for associates to use when we visit. There's plenty of room for both of you."

Judith looked at Sapphire who was nodding her head up and down vigorously. Judith said, "we'll be there."

"Would you like for me to coordinate travel arrangements for you?" Dani's British accent sounded businesslike now. "I can—"

"I can handle the arrangements," Judith interrupted. "I'll let you know as soon as we book our flights. What's your cell number?"

Dani and Judith exchanged numbers. "American Airlines flies direct from Phoenix to Lihue," said Dani, "the only commercial airport on the island. I will send my driver to pick you up. The company home is only thirty minutes away on the south end of the island in Poipu." Dani was nervous and excited, and it felt like she was babbling. She made a dignified attempt to wind up the conversation gracefully. "I look forward to meeting you both in several days. Goodbye Judith. Goodbye Sapphire."

Dani Lake collapsed in her executive chair and welled up in tears. She pressed her palm to her heart to steady her breathing. Finally, she can tell Sapphire everything. Dani imagined Jane and Andre looking down with approval from the heavens.

Judith hung up the phone and sat quietly next to Sapphire, who had a soft smile on her lips. She felt hopeful she might learn more about her parents. She would give herself one more minute to take it all in. Then she would begin preparing for the trip. She accepted the glass of mint water from Judith and drank it down. Within moments, she perked up like a flower. "I'm going to ask Dani Lake how Aunt Star died," said Sapphire. "It just doesn't make sense. She would've told me if she was sick,"

Judith's suitcase was already packed since she hadn't taken the time to unpack. It was just as well since she would need to focus on booking their flights. She checked the app on her phone for American Airlines, silently thanking Taylor, Agent Silver's great-nephew, for installing it for her. Dani was right. American Airlines had a direct flight out of Phoenix to Lihue every morning. She must've checked ahead of time in hopes of Sapphire meeting her there.

Judith found Sapphire laying out clothing on her bed. "Sapphire, we can catch a flight tomorrow morning or the day after. Which would you prefer?"

"Tomorrow. The sooner, the better. I can't wait to hear what this woman has to say. Thanks for going with me. Wish Farrell and Sofia could go too."

"Well, maybe they can," said Judith. "You can bring whomever you want. We can arrange our own lodging if Dani doesn't have room for all of us."

"Really? It's a lot to ask someone to drop their lives at a moment's notice."

"Yes, really. Farrell looks like he needs some beach time. And Sofia can help us out with this Dani Lake."

"You mean like a profiler?" asked Sapphire. "I don't think that's Sofia's specialty. But you're right about her ability to read people. And you're right about Farrell too. I've noticed the heaviness he's been carrying around lately."

"Do you want me to call them for you?"

"No, thank you. They need to hear the request directly from me. It's a lot to ask. I'll call Farrell first."

"OK then, I'm on the app now. The remaining seats available tomorrow morning are in business class, is that okay?"

"Yes, fine. Business has been great lately and I can afford it," said Sapphire.

"As soon as you speak with them, I'll book the tickets. We'll need to leave at six am."

Chapter 12
All In

Sapphire had been thinking a lot about how she, Farrell, and Fisher had kept their past a secret from each other. It was time to come clean. She hoped Farrell understood and felt the same way. Sapphire took a deep breath and phoned him. Farrell picked up on the first ring as if he had been waiting for her call.

"Have you ever been to Hawaii?" she opened with.

"Uh, how are you today?" He rubbed the last remnants of sleep from his eyes and sat up straight in bed. He noticed the time and was surprised it was almost eight am. A restful sleep at that.

"I'm okay, better," Sapphire said "and I'm inviting you to join me and Judith to travel to Kauai tomorrow morning to be there when I meet Dani Lake. She was good friends with my parents as well as Aunt Star, and she wants to tell me about them in person. I'm inviting Sofia too." Sapphire ran her fingers through her long hair as she waited for Farrell's response.

"Wow," said Farrell. "Your parents. You've never spoken about them. In fact, neither of us have ever spoken about our parents. That was so long ago, why does it matter now?"

"Oh, Farrell, can't you see? It matters a whole lot. That's why I want you there with me."

"Yeah, sure, I'll go if it's important to you. Just gotta move my schedule around a bit. I can work remotely from anywhere. There's internet in Hawaii, right?" Sapphire giggled and Farrell's heart melted. He would do anything for his best friend.

"Thank you so much, Farrell. You know it's an island and there is a beach, a lot of beaches, I think. Pack your bathing suit. Be at my house no later than six am tomorrow morning. We're taking a shuttle to the Phoenix airport. Judith's booking our tickets. She has all your information. I don't know how long we'll be staying but we're going to book a week and extend our return flight if we need to."

"Yeah, okay. Sure. Pack a bathing suit and clothes for a week. I can do that. Be at your house by six am tomorrow to pick up the shuttle. Judith's getting the tickets now." Farrell repeated the plan to be sure he had heard it correctly. After he hung up, he wondered what had just happened. He was suddenly going to Hawaii! Time to rearrange his schedule.

Sapphire called Sofia next and told her about the call to Dani Lake. "I need my friends with me. Plus, we can swim in the ocean and see the sites. Think of it as a weeklong vacation."

"I love to travel. Sounds like an adventure. And I miss the beach." Sofia glanced at her full calendar, mentally groaning at her plan to cancel her week. It was a no-brainer when it came to priorities. Put the people you love first, including yourself, and all else will follow. Where had she heard that?

Sofia had come to love Sapphire, Farrell, and Judith as a genuine family. Families came in all shapes and sizes. Her friends were her family and therefore her priority. "Hawaii, with you, Farrell, and Judith? I'm in!" Sofia stood up and stretched. Time to pack her suitcase.

"Ok, Judith," Sapphire reported with a grin. "Farrell and Sofia are coming. Thanks for encouraging me to ask them. Go ahead and book the tickets." Sapphire handed Judith her Amex. "Charge my card. I like accruing the points. I'll start packing." Sapphire marveled at the range of emotions she could feel in a day. Grief was tricky.

Chapter 13
Ready, Set, Go

Sapphire emerged from her room at two-thirty that afternoon. "Packed and ready to go," she proudly declared. Judith turned in surprise, noting that Sapphire was freshly showered with her hair styled neatly in an updo, and she was wearing an ankle-length dress with a bold floral print.

"You already look like you've landed in Hawaii," Judith said. "Glad to see you're prepared for the trip."

"I've always found that dressing for my desired mood inspires my mind to follow suit. I found this at a local art fair and was drawn to the colors. Bright-colored flowers make me happy," Sapphire said. "And now, I want to phone Dani and apologize for becoming mute. Hearing Dani say that she had been good friends of my parents, well, it just stunned me."

"Oh, I'm sure she understood. It was a lot at once," Judith said. "She seems like an interesting woman. I look forward to meeting her."

Sapphire carried the box with the shawl and ring to the living room and placed it on the coffee table. The two women settled on the sofa. "I also want to let her know that there'll be four of us and offer to arrange our own lodgings," Sapphire said. "I searched through *Airbnb* and *Vrbo*. There are several homes we can reserve. Finding a rental car was a bit more difficult, but I found one. I placed a hold on both a car and a house."

"Wow! You packed, dressed, and searched reservations in record time. Good to see you're feeling more yourself."

"I had an overwhelming moment of sadness when Dani mentioned my parents," said Sapphire. "I never grieved my parents' deaths. I didn't know how. I was only fifteen and hidden away at boarding school at the time. Not only didn't I grieve their deaths, but I don't think I acknowledged it."

"Oh, my dear Sapphire," Judith said. "I wish I could've been there to comfort you so long ago." Judith remembered feeling maternal toward Fisher when he too became an orphan as a teen and was whisked away to boarding school.

"Aunt Star tried to stand in as a parent, but at first I kept her at a distance," Sapphire explained. "You know, being a teenager, I thought I didn't need anyone. It wasn't until I became an adult that we got close. I guess she was a surrogate parent to me once I was willing to accept her on my own terms."

"Oh yes," Judith said. "I remember how obstinate Fisher was at that age. I also remember how much he needed support and guidance. My boss, Mike Sandar, was like an uncle to him. I like to think Fisher thought of me as an aunt."

"Yes, Fisher spoke very highly of Uncle Mike and you as well, as I recall when we were teenagers at Wildhorse Academy boarding school," Sapphire said. She still missed him every day. He would have loved to go to Hawaii with them.

"I'd like to make that call now," said Sapphire. "It's two hours later in Asheville, right? I hope I can catch her before she boards her flight to Kauai."

Recognizing Sapphire's phone number from her caller ID, Dani picked up on the first ring. "Hello, is that you, Sapphire?"

"Yes, I got my voice back," Sapphire said. "I want to apologize for dropping off the call so abruptly. I lost my bearings momentarily. That's not like me. I was just shocked to hear that you had been friends with my parents. Their violent deaths were so tragic, and Aunt Star didn't talk about what happened. It's hard to explain. I haven't thought about them in a long time, but I feel them with me always."

Dani responded immediately. "Oh, no. There's no need for you to apologize. I'm the one who needs to apologize to you. I've been anxious to tell you about your parents for so long, that it just all came tumbling out too quickly. I'm sorry to have taken you by surprise."

Sapphire laughed in relief. She felt more comfortable with Dani now. "I'd love to hear everything about my parents from you and am looking forward to meeting you on Kauai. I've arranged a home and car rental."

Dani felt deflated at the thought of Sapphire not accepting her offer of hospitality. She started to object but Sapphire continued "Judith will be accompanying me to Kauai as planned. I will also be bringing two other close friends; Sofia and Farrell. I don't want to impose on you."

"Oh Sapphire, I'm delighted to meet your friends. Truly honored. You must stay at our company home. There is room for all of you, and I promise it is not an imposition. And don't worry about transportation. I have a vehicle and driver to show you and your friends around the island. He will pick you up at the airport. What time do you arrive?"

"Dani, you sound so much like Judith," Sapphire said. She quickly added, "That's a high compliment, I assure you." Sapphire smiled inside as she thought perhaps Judith might meet her equal.

Sapphire sensed how important it was for Dani to accept her hospitality. "Okay, Dani. If you insist. I appreciate you hosting the four of us. Our flight arrives tomorrow at two-thirty in the afternoon." Feeling more excited than nervous, Sapphire said, "I never dreamed I'd have an opportunity to meet someone who knew my parents. I'm truly fortunate Dani." She sincerely meant it.

Chapter 14
Up, Up, and Away

Early the next morning, just as daylight was breaking through, Farrell picked up Sofia on his way to Sapphire's home. He gallantly lifted her suitcase into the trunk and opened the car door for her. "Your journey begins," he declared with a wide smile. He clicked his seat belt in place, checked his mirrors, and drove off.

"You seem chipper this morning. I didn't imagine you being a morning person," Sofia said as she rubbed her eyes. Her nostrils flared as she inhaled the aroma of freshly brewed coffee and spotted the to-go container in the front seat cup holder. She had been too tired to prepare herself a cup before leaving.

"That's for you Sofia," Farrell said. "Black with no sugar, right?" He remembered her coffee choice from last summer when they all gathered for a week to solve Fisher's murder. Farrell also remembered asking Sofia if she thought he needed counseling when they had a private moment. He didn't want to talk to a counselor, but he knew he might need to. Maybe on this trip he could talk privately with Sofia about his struggles. He couldn't imagine talking to a stranger, but Sofia had become a close friend.

Sofia lifted the coffee to her lips. "Thanks so much, Farrell. Coffee is exactly what I needed and yes, I take it black with no sugar." The coffee was still hot, but not enough to burn her tongue. She relished it with slow sips.

Farrell was proud of himself for remembering to pick up coffee for Sofia when he bought his own, and even more proud to have remembered the way she liked it. Being a good friend had become more important lately. Helping others, no matter how small the gesture was, gave him a special feeling. A feeling he could not put into words. All he knew was that it rivaled the feeling he got from having a drink. He had learned that the satisfied feeling from helping others had a lasting effect. But the numbness from drinking soured quickly and drew him into despair. Farrell made a silent commitment to focus on helping his friends more often.

Farrell and Sofia arrived at Sapphire's home ten minutes early. Sapphire opened the door and ushered them into the hallway. Farrell placed his and Sofia's luggage next to Sapphire's and Judith's. "Mahalo my dear friends," chimed Sapphire, embracing each one with a long hug. "That's

Hawaiian for gratitude. I'm so thankful to have my three best friends join me in this adventure. I've found some great excursions on Kauai. And can't wait to go in the ocean."

Sofia and Farrell looked past Sapphire to Judith as both smiled in relief to see Sapphire's positive mood change. Judith nodded and said, "That's right, we're going to make this a memorable vacation." She was still shaking off the morning sleep and her achy joints. "I've been in the ocean in Florida, and years ago in St. Thomas, Key West, and Mexico."

Sapphire heard a car engine. "There's our limo, let's go."

"You booked a limo?" Sofia blurted out before she realized it sounded like a complaint. "I mean, wow, a limo, feels like a celebration." Why was Sapphire turning the trip into a vacation? Grief has many dimensions. Maybe this was Sapphire's way of celebrating Aunt Star's life. Certainly, Sofia was up for a Hawaiian vacation. She too had missed the ocean. Sedona was magnificent, but the ocean was a different kind of beauty, turquoise and salty.

Sapphire, Judith, and Sofia piled into the limo while Farrell insisted on helping the driver with the luggage. By the time he climbed into the back seat with the ladies, they'd already discovered the pastries, muffins, and large carafe of hot coffee prepared for them. "This limo is used for wine tours in the afternoons," Sapphire said. "They have it outfitted with coolers and tables for their tours. Judith booked it for us. The shuttle was full, and we were lucky to get the limo with such short notice. I know the owner of the company. I designed her home."

"Did everyone remember to pack a bathing suit?" asked Sapphire.

"I guess I'll buy one there," Judith said. "I wasn't thinking about the ocean when packing for Sedona."

"I brought two," said Sofia. "I love the ocean." She couldn't wait to plunge into the water and get the taste of the salty water on her tongue.

Farrell brought his bathing suit but wasn't interested in going swimming.

"I swam in the ocean with Aunt Star every year on Sanibel Island, and it was spectacular." Sapphire said. "I forgot how much I missed going to the beach. Kauai is home to some of the most beautiful beaches in the world, according to travel sites. Just thinking about the beach revived me." Sapphire took out a tube of mint lip gloss from her purse and applied it on her lips. "I'm intrigued to learn about my parents from Dani. I never imagined that I'd ever be able to learn more about them. She sounded interested to share everything with me. I want to know more about Aunt Star too. It all sounds so mysterious. I wonder what they were hiding?"

By the time they reached the airport two hours later, the four of them felt relieved to have escaped the worries each had been shouldering. "Let's go to the lounge," said Judith, after they entered the airport. "We can get a hot breakfast. I have a membership and can bring guests." Judith was proud to share her upgrade to enhance their trip. Since they always did what Judith said, they followed her lead.

An hour later, the four friends sailed through security and boarded their on-time flight fully satiated with freshly prepared omelets and fruit, courtesy of Judith's lounge passes. Sapphire sat next to Farrell and across the aisle, Judith sat with Sofia.

Judith and Sofia each took their iPads out of their tote bags, before stowing the bags under their seats. "I did some research about Aromaticus and Dani Lake," said Sofia. "I'm impressed with the direction Dani has led the company."

The plane began moving down the runway to prepare for take-off. Judith and Sofia continued their conversation, oblivious to the plane taking off. As soon as the plane was airborne, and passengers were permitted to use their electronic devises, Judith and Sofia opened their iPads and began reading aloud.

"I did some research too," said Judith. "Essential oils are a big business with lots of competition. Aromaticus stands apart from their competitors. And they avoided the court cases some of the other companies faced due to false advertising."

"Yeah, I'm not sold on the medical claims made by so many of those other companies," said Sofia. "Their research is sketchy. I like the scents of some and not others. Not sure if it helps me, but I use them when I remember."

"Essential oils aren't for everyone," Judith said. She took out her small vial of lavender oil and showed it to Sofia. "I like the way this smells, and it helps to calm me. Maybe it is just a placebo effect."

"Listen to this quote from Dani Lake when she was interviewed about Aromaticus," said Sofia. "Many companies claim their essential oils are therapeutic grade, which is simply for marketing. No government agency in the U.S. provides a grading system or certification for essential oils."

"And check out their business motto," said Judith. "It's from an interview with Dani just this year. Our success is based upon the simple fact that our customers like our products. It makes them feel good. Feeling good can inspire people to think differently and make better choices in their lives. For example, improving nutrition, exercise, and sleep habits naturally leads to improved health."

Sofia took her turn to read aloud to Judith from her iPad. "Please read our reviews from satisfied customers with caution. We do not endorse medical claims. Essential oils will affect everyone differently. We invite you to try our products to see if they are right for you."

Judith said, "Our Dani Lake sounds like one brave lady, taking on the entire industry and telling it like it is. I admire her."

"I agree," said Sofia. "It's not easy to publicly challenge big business. She certainly has chutzpa." She stifled a yawn as she noticed Judith's eyelids drooping. "I think we both need a rest. Are you able to sleep on a plane?"

"Just watch me," said Judith. "I'll be asleep in two minutes."

Sofia watched Judith close her eyes. She glimpsed Sapphire and Farrell holding hands, talking in hushed voices, and exchanging serious expressions. She looked back at Judith, and true to her word, she was sleeping soundly. Sofia leaned back in her seat, closed her eyes, and drifted off. Both ladies slept through half of the seven-hour flight.

Across the aisle, Sapphire squeezed Farrell's hand as the plane made its final approach. Landing was the only part of flying that made her anxious. Holding Farrell's hand helped her feel safe and calm. When the plane touched down, a sadness came over her. "Farrell, I wish Fisher was with us."

"I was thinking the same thing," said Farrell. He let out a deep sigh. "Having Judith and Sofia with us feels like he's being represented, but it's not the same. I miss him. I can't help but feel like we let him down in some way. We were his best friends."

Sapphire frowned. "We didn't know about his past and that he was in danger. We never talked about our past. We all kept secrets from each other. That's going to change beginning right now. The reason I want you with me is so there'll be no more secrets. I want you to know about my past." Sapphire studied Farrell imploring him to respond.

Farrell swallowed hard as he closed his eyes blinking away a single tear. Was his emotion his grief over Fisher's death or about his past? Sapphire didn't know. She sat with Farrell in silence.

Farrell wanted to tell Sapphire how he still obsesses over his regrets about one night as a teen. That regretful night led his father to promptly whisk him away to boarding school across the country. Farrell wanted to shout out loud how he has struggled with controlling his drinking his entire life to escape that memory and bury his shame. Instead, he simply accepted her comfort and hoped that one day he would find the courage to let it all out. Sapphire was his best friend and deserved honesty from him. Farrell made a solemn vow to find a way to tell Sapphire everything. No more secrets. No more desperate secrets.

Chapter 15
Aloha

Seven hours after take-off, the flight arrived on Kauai at Lihue International Airport. Through the windows, passengers viewed palm trees swaying in the gentle breeze. "The trees look like they're doing the hula," Sofia said.

"Set your watches back three hours," Judith reminded her friends. She stretched her limbs as they all deplaned. The nap on the plane refreshed Judith and she was ready to take charge. Sapphire, Sofia, and Farrell looked at their wrist, but only Farrell had worn a watch.

"I don't wear a watch when I'm on vacation," said Sapphire. "It's nice to get a break from following a schedule." She applied her mint lip gloss.

"I forgot to wear a watch, maybe my brain forgot on purpose," said Sofia. "We have our phones to tell us the time, so it's not necessary."

Farrell said, "Okay, I'll be the official timekeeper." He was glad to have the responsibility to keep him tethered. He was consciously striving to keep himself occupied. Having the simple task of keeping track of the time made him feel like the designated driver.

As they reached the luggage carousel, they spotted a tall, native-looking young man holding up a sign which read *Sapphire and Friends.* He smiled broadly as Sapphire approached him offering her hand for a warm greeting. "Hello, I'm Sapphire and this is Farrell, Judith, and Sofia. Thank you for meeting us."

"Aloha! I'm Kai, pleased to meet you." He accepted Sapphire's hand and shook hands with Farrell, Judith, and Sofia, greeting each by their name. "Allow me to help you with your luggage." Kai produced a large luggage cart.

Farrell managed to grab his suitcase just as it rounded the corner on the conveyor belt. He then chased after the other three pieces lifting them with ease. As he and Kai loaded the suitcases onto the luggage rack, the three women looked around in unison. "The ladies' room is that way," Kai pointed out, anticipating their need.

"I like him already," Sapphire said as she linked arms with Sofia and Judith, heading towards the ladies' room. "Look at all these flowers. I love the sweet smell."

"The air is more humid than we're used to in the Arizona desert," said Sofia. "Reminds me of

Florida." She smoothed her hair back with both hands.

"Much nicer than Florida," said Judith. "And I love the open-air concept. Did you notice that we're outside? Have you ever seen an airport with open walls?"

As the ladies met at the bathroom sinks, Sapphire said, "Even the soap smells like hibiscus. That's the name of the state flower. I looked it up."

Refreshed and fragrant, Sapphire, Sofia, and Judith walked back to Farrell and Kai. Farrell presented each of them with a lei and said, "Welcome to Hawaii." He had purchased the flowered necklaces from a vendor moments before the ladies returned. The smile on all three of his friends' faces made the impromptu gesture worthwhile. It was becoming more natural to help others, and Farrell welcomed his new pattern. Although, he couldn't help staring at all the large posters of Mai Tai's tantalizing him.

As the five of them exited the airport, Kai pointed to a white SUV shimmering in the parking lot. Sapphire immediately eyed the familiar script letters on the side of the vehicle, *AROMATICUS*. She picked up her pace with her long legs. "My parents worked for Aromaticus before their death, forty-six years ago," she told Kai. "Dani Lake was friends with them." Sapphire surprised herself with such candor toward a stranger. "I'm feeling closer to them already." She inhaled the aroma of the hibiscus flower necklace.

Kai said, "Yes, Miss Lake told me about your parents being here many years ago. Aromaticus has had a presence on Kauai since then and the community has welcomed the company to our island. They treat their employees well. Like family. Aromaticus built playgrounds, ball fields, and a park on the island. I'll show you later this week."

Farrell noticed how natural it had become for Sapphire to talk about her parents. Would he ever feel that way? *No More Secrets* was going to be very hard for him. He climbed into the front passenger seat after helping Kai load the luggage in the back.

Kai handed all four of them a bottle of cold water with *AROMATICUS* inscribed on the label. Sapphire, Sofia, and Judith got comfortable in the back seat. "The water is lightly infused with mint grown right here on Kauai," he said. Everyone donned their sunglasses adjusting to the bright sunshine.

Sapphire remembered the mint plants on her windowsill back in Sedona. Aunt Star had introduced her to the ritual of infusing water with mint when she was a child. Seeing the AROMATICUS label on the bottle and sipping her mint water gave her a feeling of familiarity. Sapphire was comforted with the memory.

"We're in Lihue now and we'll be driving south through Koloa to Poipu. It'll take about thirty minutes," Kai said. "I'll be taking you around the island this week. It'll be my pleasure to tell you all about Kauai." Farrell was glad to have another male around.

"This mint water is refreshing, thank you," said Judith. "Is the company home in Poipu? Will Dani Lake be meeting us there?" She tried not to sound too eager but found herself thinking more about Dani Lake. The more she researched about her, the more intrigued she became. Judith wondered if Dani looked anything like the photo on the internet as she absentmindedly smoothing her scarf. Why was she feeling butterflies in her stomach?

"Yes, of course," Kai said. "Miss Lake is waiting for you. I texted to say we're on our way. She has a light snack prepared for when you arrive and dinner reservations this evening." He smiled nervously. "I forgot to ask if any of you have special dietary needs?"

"We look forward to sampling the local cuisine," said Judith. "No special needs and we love to eat," she responded for all four of them. "I hear that your mangos are sweeter than sweet." Her stomach grumbled. She looked forward to the light snack awaiting them.

Chapter 16
Mango

Kai expertly navigated the traffic while his passengers observed the scenery. He opened the windows and a moonroof to let in the cool breeze. When the car slowed down, magnificent eucalyptus trees greeted them. "Behold our Tree Tunnel," Kai said as they drove through an archway of the tall trees.

As they drove through the mile-long Tree Tunnel, the four passengers looked all around. "What a welcoming archway," Sapphire said. "How long is it and how did it get here?" She had been deep in thought, unusually silent. Adjusting to a new atmosphere and climate always took some time for her. "It's amazing!" Her eyes were as big as the plumeria flowers.

"A cattle rancher gifted five hundred eucalyptus trees from Australia over a hundred years ago," Kai recited proudly. He enjoyed being a tour guide, especially when he could witness his passengers' reactions to the Tree Tunnel. "We call them swamp mahoganies, and they've survived two hurricanes. They're over a hundred feet tall, and the grand entrance goes on for a mile."

Sofia always felt a special connection with trees and the lush canopy touched a deep place in her heart. "Did you know that trees communicate with each other?" She asked the group. "I've been reading about how they signal danger and provide support within the forest network. The research is fascinating."

"Well, these trees must be having a major convention here," Farrell said. "Good luck getting this number of people to work together on a project. We could learn something from trees." Sapphire, Judith, and Sofia turned to face him all at once. Farrell pulled his shoulders back and sat up straighter. "Yes," he said. "I'm multidimensional and have studied the research on how trees communicate with each other too. You have no idea how much research goes into selecting socially responsible companies in which to invest your hard-earned money. My clients depend on me to vet the corporations they entrust with their savings."

"Yes Farrell, we do," said Sapphire. "And you fulfill your promise. You've earned an enviable reputation, and it's no wonder that your investment firm is successful. But I hope you don't plan on working this week." She folded her arms across her chest.

"Not unless you consider research work," said Farrell. "I plan on studying some possible interests here for future investments. You know I like to see businesses in person. Turns out Fisher and I visited the Aromaticus factory in Asheville when I first opened my investment firm forty years ago. We were on vacation. I'd completely forgotten about it. The name sounded vaguely familiar, but I couldn't place where I'd heard it before. For some reason, I kept connecting Fisher with Aromaticus. Finally, I checked my business records. Had to go back to my old logs. We had a great trip." The corners of his lips curled up in a smile. "We saw waterfalls, kayaked, and did a lot of hiking. Visited the factory on a lark one afternoon. Don't remember anything about it though."

"That's a synchronicity," Sapphire said. "I feel good knowing Fisher was connected somehow." She turned back to gaze at the trees as the archway faded in the distance. "Fisher loved trees and would've loved to see this canopy." Her eyes brightened. "I'm trying to imagine seeing it through his eyes. My heart tells me, however, that he's seeing it right now through our eyes."

"Almost there, just down this road," Kai said. "You can relax on the patio while I take your luggage upstairs to your bedrooms. If there's anything you need during your stay, please let me know. After you've had a chance to get settled, I'll tell you about the history of the island and let you choose from a variety of excursions for the week." He puffed out his chest. "My family has lived on Kauai for generations. Some of my cousins are tour operators, and I can arrange private tours for you."

"Thank you, Kai," said Sapphire. "First, I want to meet Dani Lake. I'm so excited to learn all about Aunt Star and my parents." She leaned forward in her seat. "I've always wondered about the mysteries surrounding my parents, "but Aunt Star was secretive."

"Here we are," said Kai. "We call this home Mango for obvious reasons." He gestured to the mango trees lining the long driveway as they approached the front entrance. "My grandfather is the groundskeeper here and sometimes I help him when I'm not driving." Sapphire inhaled the sweet scent through the open windows and knew she made the right decision to come to Kauai to meet Dani Lake.

Judith spotted a petite woman scurrying toward the car and was surprised to feel her heart beating faster. Was she sensing Sapphire's anticipation? Judith hadn't experienced this type of excitement in years. As their vehicle came to a stop, Judith shook herself out of her reverie, reminding herself that this trip was about Sapphire. She rearranged her scarf, draping it fashionably around her neck and down her blouse. Judith was here as Sapphire's supportive friend, and it was time to resume her role.

When the car stopped, Judith gently squeezed Sapphire's arm. "You go first. Take a private moment to meet Dani and we'll be right behind you." Sapphire bit her lip. Is this how adopted children feel when finally meeting their birth parents? She took a breath and glanced at her friends. Their compassion soared into her heart, giving her strength.

Dani Lake waited near the car as Sapphire gracefully stepped out of the vehicle. "Welcome to Mango," Dani announced in her clipped British accent, full of warmth. The feeling of family overwhelmed Sapphire and she ran into Dani's arms. The two women embraced briefly, stepped back to look at each other, and embraced again. From the car, Judith, Sofia, Farrell, and Kai observed in reverence as the shimmering sun cast a shadow of the embracing women. "Welcome to Mango," Dani said. "Welcome to Mango."

Chapter 17
The Marriage Proposal

After a long embrace, Dani Lake stood back and looked at Sapphire. "You're the image of both your parents. Simply enchanting. I'm so happy to see you in person, finally." Dani continued smiling, and warmth radiated throughout her body. She wanted to hold on to Sapphire forever. Instead, she reluctantly let go, took some deep breaths, and prepared for her role as hostess.

"How did Aunt Star die?" asked Sapphire. "She never mentioned feeling ill. She would've told me."

"I don't know, Sapphire," said Dani. "I was told her heart stopped. I didn't request an autopsy." Dani wondered if she should've. She had Star cremated, per her wishes. Now, Dani wished she knew more. She wouldn't tell Sapphire that she also found Star's death unusual.

"Her heart!" said Sapphire. "Aunt Star always had a strong heart. She went for annual check-ups and no heart problems were ever detected." She let out an exasperating sigh. "I don't understand," she said. "It just doesn't make sense."

Sapphire looked over at her friends, who had exited the car and waited patiently nearby. She almost forgot that she brought the cavalry. "Please come meet Dani Lake." She escorted her friends to meet Dani.

"You must be tired from your trip," said Dani, "so before introductions, please come sit on the patio." Dani led the group through an ornate metal gate onto the outdoor patio and into a garden bursting with color.

Farrell guided Judith to a chaise lounge. Judith no longer tried to hide her waning stamina, as she gracefully sat down, glad to have an opportunity to elevate her aching legs.

After Farrell, Judith, and Sofia sank into their deep-cushioned chairs, Sapphire took Dani around to meet her friends. "Dani, please meet Farrell Stanton. He's been my best friend since I arrived in Sedona." Farrell sat straighter and shook hands with Dani.

"Very glad to meet you, Dani. Sapphire's been my dearest friend since we first met at Wildhorse Academy. We were just kids then. We consider ourselves family."

Dani clasped both his hands. "Sapphire is fortunate to have a close friend. It is a rare treasure, and I understand how deep bonds of friendship can be."

"Thank you, Dani, for your hospitality. Kai is a great guide." He gestured to all the beauty surrounding them. "And this property is incredible."

"Thank you, Farrell. Meeting Sapphire's friends is my pleasure, a bonus."

Sapphire introduced Judith next. "Dani, please meet Judith Saltan. She's been like an aunt to me." Dani admired how Judith exuded confidence. This attractive woman appeared to be the same age as Dani. Maybe they'd have some things in common. "We've only known each other for a year." Sapphire continued.

Dani inhaled the strong scent of lavender wafting from Judith. Was this an essential oil from Aromaticus? "Judith was also like an aunt to my other best friend, Fisher," said Sapphire. She hadn't given thought as to how to explain Fisher's death. Some things were not explainable.

"Fisher Bond died last year, he was murdered," Judith said. "Sapphire and I became close as we helped the investigators solve the crime. Sometimes the grief feels fresh again. It was a gift of Fisher to bring Sapphire and me together in his death." Judith found herself babbling. What was it about this accomplished woman that intimidated her? "These young folks keep me feeling young. Although, it's so nice to meet a contemporary." She tried not to stare as she eyed Dani up and down. In person, Dani was more attractive than she envisioned and from the photos on google. Dani was pretty. Her skin was clear and had a youthful glow. Dani had a smile that went up to her eyes.

Dani noted that she and Judith were the same height. She admired Judith's stylish silver hair, her simple jewelry, and her colorful silk scarf. Judith was classy. It would be nice to spend time with another woman her age.

Sapphire brought Dani to Sofia next. "Please meet Sofia West. Sofia and I also met through Fisher. She moved to Sedona from Florida. It's complicated. Sofia has become my good friend and confidant over the past year. She's been a welcome treasure in my life."

"Glad to meet you, Sofia," Dani said.

"So glad to meet you too," said Sofia. "And thank you for hosting us. This garden is paradise. I love all the colors." Sofia felt very grateful to be on Kauai. The endless display of flowers took her breath away. She loved Sedona but forgot how much she missed the tropical Florida climate she left behind.

The fragrant air was inviting. Sofia continued to survey the garden, taking in each grouping of floral arrangements as if she were meeting each one. What a welcome!

"Would you all like a glass of mango iced tea?" Dani offered. The crystal pitcher was sparkling in the streams of sunlight that peeked through the array of flowers. Lemon, lime, and orange wedges floated among the ice. It looked too pretty to pour. Dani lifted the heavy pitcher with ease and began filling tall slim glasses. "Yes, please." Sapphire sank into her chair. "It looks divine."

"I love mangos," Judith said. "Can't wait to try your mango tea. If it's as good as it looks, I'll have two glasses, please." She eyed the platter on the table with bright orange mango wedges and juicy red strawberries garnished with fresh mint leaves. A silver tray alongside the fruit displayed a variety of cubed cheeses, macadamia nuts, and green olives.

"Please help yourself to some fruit and nuts," Dani said.

Judith stifled a yawn, then loaded up her plate for fortification. She hoped the mango tea was caffeinated. She also hoped a nap before dinner would refresh her.

Farrell, Sofia, and Sapphire also accepted a glass of mango tea and sipped it through their colorful straws. They each filled their plate with a hearty helping of fruit and cheese. The flowers and the mango tea reminded each of them that being on Kauai and meeting Dani Lake was a blessing.

Yes, being here was a blessing, but Sapphire felt perplexed. Why had Aunt Star kept Dani a secret for all these years? For a moment, Sapphire wondered if the secret was that Dani and Aunt Star were lovers. Surely, she would have known if Aunt Star was involved in a romantic relationship, wouldn't she? She shook her head slightly to brush off the thought. She had to know more. "Dani, I don't understand the years of secrecy. Why didn't Aunt Star introduce me to you?"

"It was for your protection, my dear. Do you remember anything about the abduction attempts before you were sent away?" Dani asked. "People were threatening your parents. I promise to explain it all to you." She wrung her hands, hoping that showing Sapphire places and photos would add dimension to the truth.

Sapphire said, "I remember some, not much." She palmed her star-sapphire necklace. "Mostly, I tried to forget about it." She took a sip of tea. "Mmm, this is delicious."

"This tea is made with the mangos from your trees?" Farrell asked. "You could bottle this and sell it. Folks in Sedona would love it," he continued. "I'll have another glass, thank you."

Dani was thrilled to please her guests. A smooth start was very needed given the difficult conversations ahead. But for now, she would enjoy being a consummate host. "I have some photos for you to see," Dani announced. She turned towards Kai who had reappeared as if on cue. "Please bring out the white bag on the table inside," Dani requested. She steadied her hands under the table.

The large drawstring bag was made of white velvet fabric, with the Aromaticus logo inscribed on top. The bag looked as elegant as a wedding gift. Dani wasted no time opening it and removing a photo album. "These are pictures of Sapphire's parents." She moved the album toward Sapphire, who gently began leafing through the pages. Judith craned her neck to see the photos.

Sapphire inhaled sharply as she viewed the grainy images in the photo book. "I've never seen these, or at least, I don't remember if I had. My parents look so young. And so in love. I do remember how much they loved each other. I don't remember much, but I do remember love. Where were these taken?"

"I will show you. We'll see the exact location sometime this week," Dani said. "Spouting Horn is nearby. It is a popular tourist spot due to the unusual way the waves crash into the rocks. People love to take photos there." She pointed to one photo. "Look at the waves in this photo crashing against the rocks behind your parents. They're shooting up through blowholes which are narrow openings in the rocks." A warm memory of that day settled in Dani's heart. "Your father proposed to your mother there."

Sapphire placed her hand on her heart. "Oh, my! A glimpse into their special moment."

"There's more photos of the proposal," said Dani.

Sapphire turned to the next page. "Look at this one," Sapphire said. "My father is down on one knee. The waterspout is shooting up right behind him. He timed it just right." She held up the album for her friends to see. Sofia's eyebrows shot up in amazement. Farrell gave an approving nod. Judith's face formed a sweet expression.

"I took that photo," said Dani, blinking away tears. "The happiest day of their lives."

Chapter 18
Hawaiian Siesta

The group consumed a second pitcher of mango iced tea as they relaxed on the garden patio. "Siesta time," announced Dani, much to everyone's relief. She stifled a yawn. "Kai will show you to your rooms where you can rest until dinner. I made reservations at Beach House, my favorite restaurant. We'll meet down here at 7:00. Dress comfortably. Everyone dresses casually here on our island."

Dani ushered the group inside. The home had uncluttered wide hallways with high arched ceilings. Muted tones of cool gray and mostly white gave a soft appearance. The furnishings were simple with sleek lines. Overall, the effect was elegant, yet warm and inviting.

Kai led the sleepy group upstairs with Farrell in back guiding Judith gallantly. He felt especially protective of her lately, noticing a decline in her strength. Farrell also noticed the mango tea was so refreshing he hadn't thought about alcohol. Still, he was glad Dani hadn't offered any.

"I know I've said it before, but I want to thank you again for coming with me," Sapphire told her friends. "It wouldn't be the same on my own. Did you see that photo of my father proposing to my mother? What a precious memory." Sapphire and the others continued up the stairs. "Dani said that she was gifting me the album. I'm going to frame that photo with one of Fisher's handmade metal frames. Love exudes off the photo. It'll make me happy to see it every day."

"What a sweet idea," said Judith. "It'll be heartwarming for you to have your parents in your home. They would have been so proud of you." She grasped the banister and as she continued to climb the steps.

"I'll check to see that you're awake by six-thirty," Farrell said to the group as they reached the top of the stairs. "Is that enough time? It's 4:30 now. That means it's 7:30 Sedona time."

"Thank you, official timekeeper," Sapphire chided. "I'm too excited to sleep. I might look around the house and the rest of the grounds." She went bouncing down the stairs.

"Please call me," Sofia said. "I usually don't nap, but the bed is calling to me. Thank you, Farrell." Her eyes drooped as she shuffled to her room.

"Two hours of sleep and half an hour to get ready is perfect for me," Judith said. "Looking forward to dinner. Thank you, Farrell, for watching out for me. I know you're trying to be discrete, but it's okay. I'm willing to accept help when I need it. I don't need it all the time, but I appreciate you being there when I do." She gave his arm a quick squeeze before entering her room.

Each room was bright and airy with white plantation shutters. The ensuite bathrooms had fluffy white towels and a robe, all with the *Aromaticus* logo. Mint scented soaps and shampoos added a warm welcome. Farrell's room had its own balcony facing the ocean. Wow! He watched the foamy waves crest over the deep turquoise water, feeling mesmerized by it all. Was this what mindful meditation was about? He'll ask Sofia later. Maybe she'll take a walk with him on the beach sometime this week. He felt hopeful about this time on Kauai. Maybe it would be a sober week for him.

Dani tried to take a nap in her room on the first floor. Her pillows were fluffed the way she liked them, but finding a comfortable position was difficult. She hoped her guests were comfortable in their rooms. They are sure to enjoy dinner at Beach House, her favorite restaurant. It was located on the water, had impeccable staff, and scrumptious local cuisine. Dani rearranged her pillows again, hoping to nap.

Dani shifted in the bed again. Would she be able to find the right words to describe the secret work that Sapphire's parents did? Would Sapphire understand? Finally, Dani's breath slowed. She thought she heard footsteps around the house before she drifted off to sleep. Dani dreamed of being at Spouting Horn, taking photos of Jane and Andre a lifetime ago. They would be with her in spirit this week as she held their daughter's hand and passed down the secret formula.

Sapphire noticed something strange about the house. She couldn't quite put her finger on it. Every room had familiar touches embedded in the architecture. Who designed it? She wondered. In the main room, Sapphire craned her neck to see the ceiling. The stained-glass skylight was a lot like a project she did in college. From that point on, the skylights became her signature in all the homes she designed. So did the rounded corners around the edges of the walls. Sapphire ran her hand along the smooth surface of the stone window ledges. They also resembled the work she did in college.

The unique niches throughout the house were the same as the ones she had designed for Fisher's home. The kitchen lighting, the dining room chandelier, and the recessed bathroom lights appeared to be identical to the ones she used in designing her later homes. Aunt Star had helped Sapphire fund her design firm when she first started. She had shown an interest in all of Sapphire's designs.

Although not formerly trained, Aunt Star had a natural design flair. Had Aunt Star helped Aromaticus design this home, using Sapphire's ideas? She would find the right time to ask Dani about it.

Sapphire wandered outside through the grounds and found a path to the ocean. Several beach lounges and deck chairs were lined up along the sand. Sapphire sank into a seat and stared at the water. Aquamarine, teal, azure, turquoise, and pale icy blue hues danced in front of her, changing colors as the sun created shadows from the clouds. Did the islanders stare at this magnificent site daily the same way Sedona residents honored their red rocks? Sapphire felt serene as she observed the shells washing up along the shore.

Sapphire thought of the proposal photo. Her parents were so in love, with their whole lives in front of them. Their faces were full of innocence and hope. What could their secret have been? Why were they in danger? Who was trying to hurt them? Yesterday, Dani reminded Sapphire of the abduction attempts. There were three before her parents sent her to Sedona. They wanted to keep her safe. Aunt Star wouldn't talk about it. Dani honored their wishes all this time. Sapphire was ready to hear the truth. With her friends by her side, she was ready as ever.

Chapter 19
Beach House

Dani missed Sapphire during the two-hour naptime. It'd been a long held dream to spend time with Sapphire and now she finally has the opportunity. She quickly dressed and headed to meet her guests. Sapphire, Judith, Farrell, and Sofia met Dani downstairs on the garden patio as planned at 7:00 pm. Each looked freshly scrubbed and rested, even Sapphire who hadn't taken a nap.

Dani greeted her guests one at a time with a smile that rose to her eyes. "Sapphire, you look radiant," she said. "Absolutely radiant."

Sapphire blushed. "Thank you. I'm feeling very content and especially at home here. Dani, I'm wondering about some of this home's architectural features. Who was the designer?" She hadn't planned on blurting out her question, but her curiosity got the better of her. Dani nodded. The car pulled up, and Kai exited the car with a flourish, opening the doors for his passengers.

"Here's Kai," Dani said. "Let's go and I will tell you about the house on our way to dinner." The five of them arranged themselves in the vehicle, with Farrell sitting up front. As they drove off, Dani turned to Sapphire. "I'm so glad that you noticed the home's design, I was hoping you would. Your Aunt sent me photographs of your early designs when I was remodeling." Dani tilted her head toward Sapphire. "She said that one day you would visit Mango, and she wanted you to feel at home here. Aunt Star was very proud of you and your design flair."

Sapphire felt a warmth within her heart and clasped her star-sapphire necklace. "I'm touched. And still confused as to the secrecy." Sapphire wiggled her foot impatiently. She had so many questions. How long would it take for Dani to explain everything? She let out a deep sigh, resigning herself to waiting for Dani to tell her story at her own pace.

"I noticed the stained-glass skylight in the main room," Farrell piped up from the front seat. "Sapphire, those were drawings you did in college, remember?" He turned to Dani. "All the homes Sapphire designed in Sedona are known for her signature stained-glass skylights. You should see them, they're stunning."

The gleam in Sapphire's eyes appeared to light up the inside of the vehicle. "I love my stained-glass skylights and Aunt Star was right. Seeing one here at Mango does make me feel more at home. I can't wait to see the design they cast on the stone floor when the sun is directly above."

"That's what happens in Fisher's home," Sofia sat up straighter. "I run to the dining room at noon each day just to see the display of colors projected on the table. It's magnificent."

"And ingenious," added Judith. "Clients recognize a Sapphire Designs home from that unique feature alone. Her business needs no advertising."

"Yeah, word of mouth is the best advertisement," said Farrell. He turned to Kai, wanting to include him in the conversation. "Our Sapphire is a truly gifted artist."

"I can tell by the design features at Mango, the company home," Kai responded. "I wondered where the ideas came from. No other home on Kauai looks like Mango." The car came to a stop as Kai announced, "Here we are. Beach House. Enjoy your meal and our sunset."

Beach House sat high on a hill, the best view to welcome the nightly sunset Tonight was no exception. True to form, the Hawaiian sunset radiated blazing streaks of light shimmering on the turquoise ocean. Islanders and tourists gathered on the plush lawn adjacent to the restaurant as they treasured the breathtaking view. Sapphire, Judith,

Farrell, and Sofia stared at the ocean reverently before willing their legs to move and step out of the car.

Dani exchanged a knowing glance with Kai. "Thank you, Kai." He nodded with admiration and warmth.

Farrell noticed the close connection between Kai and Dani. Kai was like a devoted grandson to Dani Lake, who clearly loved and appreciated him. Feelings of despair stirred in Farrell. He never felt appreciated or loved by his parents. Suddenly Farrell wanted to drink. Quickly, he remembered his newly discovered antidote to quash the urge and walked over to Judith offering his arm. "Judith, let's go inside, shall we?"

Judith accepted Farrell's assistance disguised as a courtly gesture. "I can get used to being treated this way," she told him. From behind, Dani admired Judith. How wonderful to see a woman her age conduct herself in such a stately manner. Judith was the epitome of grace and ease, moving through life, adorned with a flowing silk scarf along the way. She seemed to leave a trail of invisible stardust in her wake. Dani hoped they'd get some time alone.

Chapter 20
The Research Grant

Makani, the maître d', recognized Dani immediately and greeted her with a hug and air kisses. "As always, a pleasure to see you, Miss Lake." With a flair, he gestured for her to follow him as he escorted the group to their table. "Your usual spot, the best seat in the house." The casually dressed diners at the tables nearby glanced at Dani and the others, smiling in greeting before returning to their conversations and meals. "Enjoy your evening," Makani added before waltzing away tuxedo tails trailing behind him.

"Makani likes to dress formally," Dani explained. "He loves his job here since he gets to model his tux. He's been the maître d' at Beach House for as long as I can remember, and he's considered an institution at the restaurant." The group settled in their seats and opened their menus but remained captivated by the unobstructed views of the sunset. "I don't drink," said Dani, "but feel free to order wine or champagne. They also have a selection of unique cocktails."

"I'll pass on the alcohol tonight," Sapphire said. "Water for me, with mint please," Sapphire said to the waiter who had quietly appeared at their table. Each of the diners mumbled "same here," as he looked around. The waiter left them with their open menus, still unread.   Farrell was grateful that everyone made the decision easier. If they weren't drinking tonight, then he wouldn't either. He spied Sapphire darting a glance at him and Farrell smiled.

"Dani, why don't you order for the table?" Judith suggested as she looked around for confirmation from her friends. They all eagerly nodded their heads. Admiring the spectacular sunset took all their attention, and they were grateful for a reprieve from ordering food. "We would love to sample the local cuisine and we all have large appetites, I assure you," Judith said. She opened her decoratively folded napkin and placed it on her lap.

Dani sat up a notch taller. "They source local produce," she said, "and buy their fish directly from island fishermen. I will order their well-known watermelon salad, macadamia nut butter sauteed fresh Hawaiian catch, and tiramisu for dessert. How does that sound?"

Judith said, "Sounds great. I think we'll all enjoy that." The sun was about to disappear as it dropped into the ocean like a blazing ball of fire.

Outdoor revelers whooped and hollered while applauding the spectacular scene. Sapphire and her friends were too enthralled to notice that Dani had produced another large white velvet drawstring bag with the *Aromaticus* logo inscribed in silver thread. She gained their attention with a light ting on her water glass, and announced, "I have another memory for show and tell."

Dani opened the bag and ever so delicately lifted an old wooden frame, weathered with age, encased around a scratched pane of glass. The news clipping under the glass had yellowed giving it a battered appearance. Dani held it up for all at her table to see and pointed to the headline. *The Winner of the Aromaticus Summer Internship is Jane Ceres.* The name of the company newspaper was *AROMATICUS*, printed with the same recognizable calligraphy currently in use.

Sapphire squealed, "My mother, my mother! She won a contest? What date was that? How old was she?" Squinting her eyes to see the tiny numbers, she answered her own question. "Nineteen hundred and fifty-eight." She tried to do the math in her head, her eyes looking up as her lips mouthed the calculated numbers.

"She was twenty-one years old," Dani said. "Her winning proposal was *Here Comes the Judge:*

Take it Directly to the People. Jane's proposal was creative and clever. It caught the attention of the contest judges. They liked her out-of-the-box thinking, and it came at a time when Aromaticus was in desperate need of creativity."

Sapphire tried to imagine her mother at twenty-one. She barely remembered her mother at all, but *creative* and *clever* fit her few memories. She reached for her star-sapphire necklace while waiting to hear more. "Your remarkable mother proposed to do field research to test the public's reaction to essential oils," Dani said. "She developed a simple questionnaire to survey groups of people who were not accustomed to using essential oils. Your mother was amazing, far ahead of her time." The judges were dazzled. Dani put her hand to her heart. "Aromaticus continues to use Jane's unique research conclusions as the cornerstone of our motto: *People like our products.*"

"May I see the article?" Sofia asked. Dani gently handed it to her. Sofia put on her reading glasses and read aloud. "Jane proposes to field test lavender essential oil and peppermint essential oil, our two most popular products. Rather than present the public with medical research and unsubstantiated claims, Jane will simply report how the public liked it." Farrell, Sapphire, Judith, and Dani listened in rapt attention. Sofia continued. "A high school football team, an office of postal workers, a construction crew, and federal IRS auditors will try the products and tell us what they think. Six questions would be presented to those folks after a week of use: 1. Did you like the scent? 2. Did it help to calm you when feeling stressed? 3. Did you notice improved sleep? 4. Did you notice an improvement in your attention and focus? 5. Did you notice an improvement in your performance? 6. Would you purchase and use these products?"

"It was fun to develop the proposal," Dani blurted out. "Andre and I encouraged her to create the proposal, but never imagined she would win." She smiled. "Lucky for us, she did win and convinced Aromaticus that she needed to bring us along as research assistants." She reached her hands out with both her palms open toward the ceiling. "That's how the three of us wound up on Kauai. Aromaticus had a small research facility here, right on the grounds of The National Tropical Botanical Gardens. We're all going there tomorrow morning. I want to show you where it all began."

Just then the food arrived. In unison, five servers placed iced cold watermelon salads in front of their patrons. Sofia handed the framed article back to Dani who placed it back in its velvet bag. She stowed the bag under the table. The five of them had forgotten they were in a restaurant and suddenly remembered how hungry they were. Sounds of *mmm* were all they uttered as each began piercing bits of watermelon with their forks and savoring the sweet flavor.

Sapphire now understood Dani's plan of unfolding each new part of the puzzle encased in Aromaticus bags. She found herself looking forward to the next white velvet bag like a child opening birthday presents. Sapphire loved hearing about her parents but when will she be told about the years of secrecy?

"I read about the National Tropical Botanical Gardens," said Judith. "Don't they also have a site in Florida? The Kampong, in Coconut Grove. That's Miami. I've been there." Judith added, "I can't wait to see the site on Kauai. The Miami gardens were fascinating."

"I've been at the Kampong too," said Sofia. "My friend Lena took me there for my birthday two years ago." Sofia missed sharing special occasions with her best friend and wished Lena was on Kauai to experience its magical charm. "I loved learning about the local flora and fauna." Sofia enjoyed studying nature and felt a connection to others who shared her passion. She took another bite of watermelon from her salad.

"Yes, that is their sister site," Dani said. Whew. Her guests were enthralled so far. But how would they be once she unveils the story of the secret formula. She needed to present Sapphire's parents in a positive light, which would be tricky, given the circumstances. *You promised*, she reminded herself. Of course, Dani would keep her promise to Star, Jane's sister. It was Star's mission to pass the formula on to Sapphire for safeguarding until the world was ready.

The salad plates were cleared, and the mint water refreshed. Sapphire gazed around the restaurant noticing the other guests for the first time. Judith noticed how patrons were a mix of couples, families, and groups. They all dressed casually. There was no glamour, fake looking faces with plastic surgery, or designer clothing, yet everyone looked grand. Judith smiled. Kauai was magical. It brought out the best in people, islanders, and tourists alike.

Farrell felt restless as they waited for their main course. "What is the Pono Pledge?" he asked Makani, their maître d', who stopped at their table. "I saw the words hanging on a plaque when we entered." Farrell had tucked away his question for a time when he needed a distraction from thoughts of drinking.

"Yes," said Sapphire, "I spotted that too."

Makani assumed an even straighter upright posture. "I pledge to be *pono*, which means righteous," Makani recited. He cleared his throat and continued louder, "on the island of Hawaii."

Lifting his chin and peering out to the dark ocean, Makani continued, "I will mindfully seek wonder, but not wander where I do not belong." Two children from the table next to them stood up and recited along with Makani. Their parents nodded in approval.

"I will not defy death for breathtaking photos, or venture beyond safety." Three more children from tables also stood up and added their voices. Makani's eyes misted.

"I will *malama*, which means care for, land and sea, and admire wildlife only from afar." An elderly gentleman rose slowly from his chair and stood next to Makani and joined the chorus.

"Molten lava will mesmerize me, but I will not disrupt its flow." By this time, the patrons in the restaurant stopped eating and remained still in reverence. Makani thrusted his tuxedo-vested chest out further as he motioned for the children to stand next to him.

Two teenagers ambled over, joining the ensemble, tattoos, face piercings, and all. "I will not take what is not mine, leaving lava rocks and sand as originally found."

The children, the teenagers, the older man, and Makani all continued. Everyone who was seated remained transfixed. "I will heed ocean conditions, never turning my back to the Pacific."

Tears filled Sapphire's eyes as she remembered Fisher Bond's allegiance to the land of Sedona. The pledge continued. "When rain falls *ma uka,* which means inland, I will remain high above the ground, out of rivers and streams."

Sofia had never seen such a display of loyalty to their land, and she had seen a lot throughout her life as a therapist. It stunned her.

"I will embrace the island's aloha spirit, as it embraces me."

Finally, like a conductor, Makani locked eyes with his chorus, took a deep sigh, and nodded his head to continue. Each child, including the teenagers and the older man, put their hand to their heart and recited the final verse in Hawaiian. "Lawe I maalea I kuonoono." They looked around the restaurant and in English pronounced, "Take wisdom and make it deep."

Patrons, waiters, busboys, and kitchen crew applauded those who recited the Pono Pledge. He took a bow with aplomb and motioned his entourage who took bows too.

Makani and his companions gave each other a final hug. "That was amazing," Sapphire said. "I've never seen anything like that."

"Such devotion to their homeland is heartwarming," said Sofia.

Farrell said, "That was so moving to hear it recited spontaneously. Glad I asked about it."

"I like the sound of the Hawaiian language," said Judith. "It's melodic."

"I am always touched by the Pono Pledge, no matter how many times I hear it," said Dani.

The restaurant staff resumed their duties, and within minutes, the main course arrived. Judith, Farrell, Sapphire, Sofia, and Dani admired the assortment on their plates, artistically presented, complete with an edible flower. Judith was the first to dive in and take a bite. "Delicious, as promised," Judith looked at Dani. "Thank you for sharing your favorite restaurant with us." The others nodded happily.

Not one morsel of food remained on any of their plates. After the main course was cleared, Dani noticed her guests were beginning to fade. "Do you want to skip dessert?" she asked. "It's getting late, and we have an early start in the morning."

"Yes, please Dani," said Sapphire. "I'm too full for dessert, I hope you don't mind. This evening has been magical," Sapphire assured Dani. "But I think we're all fading fast. We're still on Sedona time and that's three hours ahead. So, it's late for us." Sofia gave Sapphire a knowing glance, silently thanking her for speaking up.

"Yes Dani," Judith said. "I think we're all tired and ready for bed." Sofia and Farrell nodded their heads. "What time should we be ready tomorrow morning?"

Dani mentally reorganized her plan. "Let's all sleep as late as we can, and go to the National Tropical Botanical Gardens in the afternoon, how's that?"

Sapphire murmured, "Sounds good." The others appeared relieved.

Dani would ask Kai to set up the umbrellas, lounge chairs, and towels in the morning, in case any of them would want to sit out on the beach.

A wave of exhaustion finally hit Dani and she was relieved to receive a text from Kai. *Waiting out front.* "Let's go, Kai is here." She gave a quick nod to Makani on their way out, which was their usual signal to put the bill on Dani's tab. He flashed a warm smile in return as he held the door open for his guests.

Farrell shook hands with the proud maître d'. "Thank you very much for reciting the Pono Pledge for us, Makani." The ladies made a big fuss, each hugging Makani, to his delight. The air outside had become cooler, though still pleasant. Kai exited the vehicle and swiftly opened the doors.

Dani, Sofia, and Sapphire climbed into the car, while Farrell helped Judith into a seat. "We'll be back home to Mango in ten minutes," Dani said. Judith's eyes drooped as she struggled to stay awake during the drive. She didn't want to embarrass herself, especially in front of Dani. All remained silent, satiated, and lost in their thoughts.

When they arrived at Mango, the group shuffled out of the car. Sapphire watched Kai unlock the front door and disarmed the alarm. Why would a home alarm system be needed on the island? Was it safe? Dani kept alluding to danger in the past, but what about now?

Sapphire hugged Dani tightly, no longer a stranger. The others thanked her profusely as they staggered up to their rooms. It had been an exhausting day, physically and emotionally. But so far, the trip had been successful.

Despite the day's excitement, no one had trouble falling asleep. Deep gratitude ushered calm slumber for each one of them. Mango was filled with peace that night, with love surrounding each room.

Mango had many guests over the years. Mostly business executives and their families. Lots of relaxing beach vacations, sandy memories with water sports, board games and quiet meals. The atmosphere was always peaceful. A business trip combined with a family vacation at Mango was a perk that company employees looked forward to.

Serenity was the only mood Mango had experienced. No drama had ever transpired during the calm paradise Mango had offered its guests. But now the unveiling of a dark mystery hid behind its walls. Long hidden secrets about to be revealed.

Chapter 21
Walk and Talk

Early the next morning, Dani enjoyed her morning coffee on the garden patio. To Dani's surprise, Judith strolled in. "Good morning, Judith, you're up early," Dani said, warmly. "May I pour you some coffee?"

"Yes, please. It smells wonderful," Judith said. "I always wake early. Old habits. I've been retired for over a decade, and I like my relaxing mornings." She took a sip of the coffee. "This coffee is superb, what brand is it?"

"Kauai Coffee Estate has a plantation right here on the island," said Dani with pride. "It's the largest coffee farm in the United States, and it's not far from here. Their beans are grown and roasted right on the premises, and they give tours. You're drinking their chocolate macadamia nut blend."

"I'd love to see a genuine coffee farm and take their tour." Judith's voice was as strong as her coffee. She had been looking forward to spending some time with Dani alone and was glad the opportunity presented itself naturally. No stirring noises could be heard upstairs. Maybe the others will sleep late. "Are you also an early riser?"

"Oh, yes," Dani said. "Have been my whole life. I was born and raised in London. My parents woke up early and expected me to follow suit. I was their only child and they treated me more like an adult." Dani didn't usually share things about her life so easily. But she felt at ease with Judith. "How about you? Where were you born?"

"Miami, Florida," said Judith. "The sunshine state. Just the opposite of London with all your rain. Not unlike Kauai, but more humid." She savored another sip of coffee. "How hot does it get here?" Judith kicked herself for talking about the weather. She wanted to know more important things about Dani but was too polite to ask. Does she get lonely? Is she healthy? Does she worry about a legacy? Who will run Aromaticus after she's gone?

"The high temperatures are usually in the seventies, but it feels hotter in the direct sun," Dani said. "Would you like to go for a walk? It is so much more pleasant this early before the sun gets too warm. There's a lovely path just out back leading to the ocean." Was she being too presumptuous or making Judith feel pressured? Dani hoped not. It simply felt like a nice idea to walk along the beach with a companion. She had become accustomed to walking alone in the morning, yet it felt natural to be with Judith. "I have an extra hat by the front door."

"A walk sounds perfect." Judith stood up, emptied the last drop of her coffee, and grabbed the extra hat. "Shall we?" She wanted to reach out and clasp Dani's arm as they began walking, but didn't dare. "Do you usually walk alone?" she asked. Judith looked directly at Dani as she asked the question, really wanting to know if Dani ever married.

"I go through life alone," Dani responded, as if reading Judith's mind. "Never married, never found anyone who could keep up with me." What would Judith think if she told her that she was gay? She hadn't had a relationship in so many years. Would it even matter?

"Neither did I," said Judith. "Look at us, a pair of fabulous single ladies, daring to enjoy life on our own. I lead an active life and being single hasn't stopped me from traveling or doing anything I want."

Dani said, "I love to travel, it's one of the best parts of leading Aromaticus. Being single has advantages. I do not have to compromise with anyone. I get to go wherever I want and do whatever I want, whenever I want. Although sometimes I argue with myself." Dani had never felt this comfortable with a stranger. She's also never met someone with whom she had as much in common. Is it possible that Judith is gay as well? She spotted an unbroken shell and picket it up. Absentmindedly, Dani handed the sandy shell to Judith who accepted it with a smile.

"Ever come close to getting married?" Judith asked. So much for being polite. At her age, she had no time to beat around the bush. Besides, being direct was her nature, and she was not about to try to be someone she was not. If her question was too direct, then Dani could say so. She examined the shell before pocketing it.

"Well, once I lived with someone," said Dani. "Many years ago. It didn't work out. She left. Had some other relationships over the years. Women only. Men don't appeal to me." Dani looked sideways at Judith who had a soft smile on her face. Whew. Being gay hasn't disturbed Judith in the slightest. "My career and the company have kept me busy. No regrets, especially since I see so many unhappy marriages."

Maybe when they knew each other better, Dani would reveal more about the lack of romance in her life. The real reason why Dani's relationships didn't work out over the years was because she couldn't be totally honest with a partner. She couldn't share the major focus of her day-to-day thoughts. Partners found her to be distant. Dani couldn't reveal her excitement about the formula. It was too dangerous to acknowledge it even existed.

Dani picked up another shell. She examined it and threw it into the ocean. A foamy wave rushed up to greet Dani, stopping inches before drenching her shoes. She reflexively jumped to her side, bumping into Judith, almost knocking her down. The two women grabbed hold of each other for safety as they regained their balance.

In the early days of the secret formula, Dani, Jane, and Andre lived in fear. It would have been irresponsible to include another person, exposing them to danger. Now it was different. Judith was about to learn everything. She looked at the horizon in the distance. Dani felt comforted that Jane and Andre would guide her.

Chapter 22
A Walk on the Beach

Sapphire woke to the sounds of birds chirping outside her window. For a moment, she forgot she was on Kauai. Her vague dreams slipped away as she tried to grasp the pleasant visions before they evaporated. Sapphire remembered the inviting ocean out behind Mango. Maybe she was dreaming about walking on the beach. She hoped Sofia remembered to bring a bathing suit. They had a walking date several mornings each week in Sedona. No reason to skip it now.

Sofia had just put on her bathing suit when she read a text from Sapphire. *Our usual walk this morning? And a swim!* Just what she was hoping for. She gathered her hat, sunscreen, and beach shoes. She texted back. *Meet you downstairs in five.*

The ladies followed the aroma of freshly brewed coffee waiting for them on the garden patio. Farrell was finishing his coffee and croissant. He was dressed in shorts and a flowered Hawaiian shirt that Sapphire had never seen.

"I'm going to Princeville this morning," he said. "Hope you don't mind." Sapphire and Sophia hadn't thought to include him in their morning plan, and both were relieved. "Kai is driving me. I want to check out an investment property on the market. Judith and Dani went for a walk," Farrell said. "You two are on your own."

"Of course," Sapphire said. "Go ahead, it's okay." She had expected Farrell to do some work during their trip. Property on the island was probably a good investment. "Where did you get that shirt?"

"A gift from a Hawaiian client years ago," Farrell said. "I found it in the back of my closet. Never wore it in Sedona, but it's perfect here." Sapphire was impressed. Farrell's always dressed right for every occasion.

Kai stepped onto the garden patio and smiled at the trio. "Good morning, Sapphire. Good morning, Sofia." Kai was looking forward to the drive up the northernmost part of the island before the traffic got heavy. He couldn't wait to tell Farrell all about Princeville. "Let's go," Kai said to Farrell.

Sapphire and Sofia waved goodbye as they poured their mint water and coffee. "We'll be back this afternoon to go to the National Tropical Botanical Gardens. About three o'clock," Kai said as they walked to the car. The ladies were already nibbling on fruit and croissants.

Sofia and Sapphire ate in silence, then began their descent along the path to the beach. "Shall we walk barefoot?" Sapphire asked. She applied her mint-flavored sunscreen lip balm. "Aunt Star and I walked barefoot on the beach on Sanibel Island."

"Yes, if the sand isn't too hot, it'll feel good between our toes," Sofia said. "I liked walking barefoot on the beach in Florida." She hadn't been on a beach since she moved to Sedona last year. Both kicked off their beach shoes and left them next to the chaise lounge chairs on the sand behind Mango.

"Do you ever miss your home in Florida?" Sapphire asked. It was refreshing to spend time with Sofia. "Have you decided to sell your condo there?" They walked side by side, escorted by seagulls and the warm ocean breeze.

"Yes, it's time." Sofia had struggled with the decision. "I moved to Sedona so suddenly, it took me a while to catch my breath. The move felt surreal. I closed my private practice, so I guess I'm retired." The word *retired* didn't feel like it belonged to her. "I was winding down my practice when I inherited Fisher's home, but it was still an adjustment." She hadn't planned to talk about it but was relieved that Sapphire asked. As a therapist, Sofia knew it was important for her to hear herself express her words.

Sofia stopped momentarily and sighed. "I had such passion for my work as a therapist, so it was difficult to retire." She stared off into the horizon. An unplanned move and a somewhat planned retirement had taken their toll and Sofia felt overwhelmed with confusing emotions.

Sapphire listened intently to her friend who was a decade older than her. She stopped next to Sofia and gave her a quick hug. "You always seem so relaxed." Sapphire shook her head. "It had to be stressful to move across the country at seventy years old." Sapphire hesitated before continuing. "I suspected you held a lot inside and was worried about how you were adjusting to your new life."

"Well, Sedona feels like the right place for me to be, but I miss my friend Lena," Sofia said. "Establishing new friendships was not something I planned." She turned to look at her new friend. "Our friendship means a lot to me, Sapphire."

Sapphire beamed as they resumed walking. They edged toward the ocean and watched the gentle waves come to shore and wash over their toes. It felt tingly.

"The feeling is mutual," Sapphire said. "After Fisher died, I had a hole in my heart." She could finally say that without crying. "Your connection to

Fisher was a healing comfort." A larger wave splashed up their legs and both women squealed in delight.

Sofia and Sapphire were catching their breath just as another wave hit them, sending them both tumbling on the sand. The sun warmed them. Both women closed their eyes and slid under the water before jumping up, bursting through the surface in unplanned unison.

"What do you think Dani is going to reveal today?" Sapphire said as they sun grew stronger. They stood up to their necks in the cool water.

"Haven't a clue," said Sofia. "But it must be important. "Feels like she's leading up to something intriguing."

"This is glorious," Sofia said. They bobbed up and down, rode the waves, and floated on their backs. "Feels like we've been in the ocean for hours and the sun is blazing hot." She wanted to remain in the ocean all day but worried about sunstroke and dehydration. "We should get back to shore." Her eyes stung from the salt, and she was parched.

"What a perfect morning," Sapphire said. "The ocean here is not as calm as the gulf off Sanibel Island but delightful." Her body felt heavy as they trudged in the sand. "I wonder if Aunt Star swam in this same place."

"I see our lounge chairs and Mango up ahead," Sofia said. "Now I know why the beach towels are bright turquoise. Helps to spot them." They continued along the wet sand until they reached the chaise lounges. Then they collapsed onto them and wrapped themselves with the thick terry towels.

"We need water," Sapphire said. She traced the Aromaticus logo on the towel with her fingers. "I'll go up to the house and get some." Sofia turned back toward Mango and squinted at two figures in the distance approaching them. They were dragging something.

"Look, it's Judith and Dani," Sofia said. "It looks like they're rolling a cooler through the sand." Sapphire smiled at the thought of Dani and Judith becoming friends.

"We saw you two young'uns frolicking in the ocean and thought you might be thirsty," Dani said. It sounded odd to hear Dani relax her formal speaking voice for the first time, although her British accent remained. "Mint-infused water, courtesy of Aromaticus." She handed Sapphire and Sofia a bottle each from the cooler and watched them gulp quicker than they could swallow. "Take it easy, I brought you three bottles each."

"Thank you, Dani," Sofia said between swallows. The cold water streamed down her chin and felt cool as it dripped on her lap. She held the bottle up to her forehead.

"We loved swimming and floating in the ocean," Sapphire said. "Thank you for the water. We were parched."

Judith removed a container of mango slices from the cooler and scooped some on small plates for Sapphire and Sofia. "These are sublime," Sapphire cooed. She practically gobbled up her plateful, enjoying every bite.

"We're having lunch on the garden patio before going to the National Tropical Botanical Gardens," Dani said. Sofia noticed a more relaxed air around her. "Looking forward to showing you the gardens and our first lab."

The sun moved higher in the sky as noontime approached. "Let's go," Sapphire said. The four women made their way through the sand and meandered along the path back to Mango. They brushed the dried sand off their feet. "I'm going upstairs to shower and dress," Sapphire said as they reached the entrance. "What time is lunch?"

"Me too," said Sofia. "And I might rest a bit."

"Oh, just come down when you're ready," Dani said. "We're not on a schedule here." She was in no hurry. Dani was relieved that they were enjoying Kauai and their stay at Mango. Would they still be carefree after hearing the story she was about to tell them? There was no way to lighten the epic narrative. She had to tell Sapphire everything. She owed that much to Jane and Andre.

Dani took a deep sigh, wishing Jane and Andre could witness how extraordinary their daughter was. She knew in her heart that their spirits were here on Kauai with Sapphire and her friends, and it gave Dani courage. She glimpsed over at Judith and her courage blossomed. Judith glanced back. Their new friendship sealed; the two octogenarians shared a conspiratorial smile.

Chapter 23
National Tropical Botanical Gardens

Judith helped Dani set out platters of assorted salads, cheese, meats, fish, fruits, and root vegetables on the garden patio. Sapphire and Sofia sauntered in just as all the food was ready. Farrell and Kai arrived as the ladies were filling their plates. Dani motioned for Kai to join them for lunch. "Thank you, Miss Lake, I'm starving, and this looks great," he said.

"What an incredible island," Farrell said. He piled his plate with nourishment. "Hanalei Bay had dramatic views of the mountains." He ate forkfuls of food, trying to talk between swallows. "The fog over the mountains looked like a mythical scene. I took photos." He swallowed and took a breath. "Kai showed me one of the children's playgrounds built by Aromaticus, a lighthouse, and we passed by Limahuli Garden and Preserve."

"Limahuli has endangered plants and birds found nowhere else on earth," Kai told the group. "It's affiliated with the National Tropical Botanical

Gardens where we'll be visiting after lunch. The taro you're eating now still thrives there."

"Are those the crunchy things that look like potatoes?" Sofia asked as she held up a slice on her fork.

"Yes, it's an ancient root vegetable native to Hawaii, and the Hanalei Valley has the largest taro-growing area," Kai added proudly. He loved sharing the culture and history of his beloved island. "It's a staple here."

Sapphire scrunched up her face at the untouched taro on her plate. "I guess it's an acquired taste," she said. She finished her mango slices and sipped more mint water.

Dani noticed all had finished their lunch. "Ready to go everyone?" she asked. "It's just a short ride from here. Make sure you have a hat; the sun is strong this time of the day." She surveyed the group. "I'll be right there. You can all start getting in the car." Judith brought the remaining platters back to the kitchen, acting more like a friend than a guest. Seeing the comfortable rhythm between Dani and Judith made Sofia miss her best friend, Lena, even more.

Kai opened the doors to the vehicle and the group piled in. Sapphire spied the familiar-looking white velvet drawstring bag tucked under Dani's arm as she entered the vehicle. She couldn't wait to see what was inside. She clasped her hands in her lap, trying to wait patiently.

After a short drive, Kai motioned to a large estate off the road. "That's the Kauai Coffee Company." Judith and Dani shared a glance at each other, both recalling their discussion that morning. Sofia craned her neck to get a better view.

Dani said, "We won't have time today, but later in the week we can go there. They grow and roast their own beans."

Kai checked his guests through the rearview mirror. He wanted to show them everything on the island. But would there be enough time? "You've been drinking their brand."

"Here we are," Kai said as they pulled into the elaborate entrance of the National Tropical Botanical Gardens. Every time he entered the gate, Kai experienced a swell of pride driving the long winding road leading to the gardens. He slowed down to enjoy the moment and allow his guests to admire the beauty through their windows. Kai spied Dani tapping the side of her hand, a sign she's tense. Sofia witnessed it too but remained silent. As a therapist, Sofia had taught many of her clients *tapping,* a highly effective strategy to calm one's nerves and relieve anxiety. Why was Dani so nervous?

Kai returned to narrate. "The work here has restored hundreds of acres of Hawaiian habitat and advanced plant conservation on a global level." He checked in his rearview mirror. All eyes were on him as they listened with rapt attention. "You're about to see many rare and endangered species of plants." They parked and exited the vehicle. As they walked along the path to the entrance, a sign reading *People Need Plants ~ Plants Need You* greeted them.

Kai continued his presentation as he pointed out further signs along the way. "There are five botanical gardens and research facilities that make up the National Tropical Botanical Gardens, with over two thousand acres of living laboratories and classrooms. Staff scientists, researchers, students, and visitors from all over the world gather to learn, restore habitats, and save plants facing extinction. McBryde Gardens and Allerton Gardens are right here, Limahuli Gardens is in the northern part of Kauai, Kahanu Gardens is in Maui, and the Kampong Gardens is in Coconut Grove near Miami, Florida.

Dani waved to the entrance attendant, and he waved back. After she nodded goodbye to Kai, Dani took over as tour guide. "The Allerton Gardens were once a retreat for Queen Emma of Hawaii. All these deep purple bougainvilleas cascading along the valley were her favorite." Sapphire kept her eyes on the white velvet bag, as Dani moved it from under her right arm to under her left. What was in it? She tried to pay attention to Dani as she continued. "The McBryde Gardens has a laboratory where scientists are still discovering the secrets of our native and exotic plants. *Jurassic Park* and other movies were filmed there." Sapphire heard the words *lab* and *secrets* making her even more impatient.

The group reached the end of a fragrant meandering path lined with flowers exploding in color. Dani said, "We can tour the gardens another time if you wish." Judith and Sofia appeared confused. Farrell rubbed his chin. Sapphire glanced around. Weren't they there for a tour? Kai and Dani had built it up. Now what?

Dani's tone turned somber. "Now I want to show all of you the lab where Sapphire's parents worked." Sapphire heart skipped several beats. This is where her parents had worked! They all entered a quaint-looking older building covered in ivy. Dani led them single file through a maze of hallways. When they reached the last room, Dani ushered everyone inside, then turned to Sapphire. "This is where it all began." Sapphire surveyed the entire room. It looked like a high school science lab with rows of high tables, sinks, and assorted ancient equipment. Paint was peeling from the walls, but otherwise, the room was spotless. There was a whiff of must in the air. Sofia rubbed her eyes. Judith coughed.

Farrell's brow formed deep creases. He was triggered back to a memory of the day he met his high school girlfriend. She was his chemistry lab partner. They were in love, but it didn't end well. Farrell was abruptly shipped off to boarding school in Sedona without getting to say goodbye. The circumstances still tormented him. He shook off the memory and followed the group into a small adjoining office.

"Aromaticus has been permitted to use this space. We have a partnership with the gardens, sharing the same goals for promoting the protection and nurturance of plants." Dani placed the white velvet bag under the table located in the center of the room. A tray with the Aromaticus logo held tall glasses and a large pitcher of mint water. Five modern office chairs circled the table. A cross breeze circulated through the open windows. The sun shone through, bathing the room in natural light. Dani gestured for them to sit. Judith caught sight of Dani's hands shaking as she poured herself some water. Hmmm. Why is she so nervous?

"Your parents worked in this lab when they were not out in the field," Dani began. She took a deep breath. "I worked side by side with them exploring the native plants. We were mesmerized by their wonderous mysteries. Sapphire's mother, Jane, asked one of the caretakers to save samples of leaves from their pruning. Many were endangered species, now thriving in the gardens. We studied them for hours through the lens of those ancient microscopes you saw in the lab." Dani had a wistful expression on her face. "We were so innocent and carefree, back then." Judith reached out and gently patted Dani's hand. Dani's eyes misted with tears, then she fell silent.

Farrell adjusted his position in his chair. Sapphire placed her hands on her cheeks as imagining her mother peering through the very microscopes on the other side of the door. Sofia poured mint water for everyone to fill the silence. Waiting out silence had become second nature to her throughout her years as a therapist. They all waited for Dani to continue.

After a few moment, Dani cleared her throat. "We were quite fascinated with photosynthesis. The process by which plants use sunlight to synthesize foods from carbon dioxide and water." She didn't want to insult her new friends but was hoping that she wasn't getting too technical. "Have you ever noticed how the veins on plant leaves resemble the veins in human beings?" Dani delicately ran a finger along her smooth skin of the top of her hand. Thoughts of Jane and Andre comforted her. In solidarity, Judith mimicked Dani's motion and traced a finger along the blue veins on the top of her hand, visible through her porcelain-colored skin.

"I'm getting a bit ahead of myself," Dani said. "Outdoors, the forest was our original lab. The three of us observed insects, especially butterflies fluttering through the gardens. We were captivated, noticing which plants they were drawn to. The three of us became so engrossed in our butterfly observations that the activity absorbed entire afternoons." Dani noticed Sapphire eyeing the bag below the table. "I brought along some photos." She lifted the bag and removed a large envelope containing about a dozen photographs. The enlarged pictures of vibrantly colored butterflies had not faded over the years. "We had these processed with high-resolution color saturation, and I've kept them out of sunlight to remain preserved." Dani passed the photos to Sapphire who admired them one by one before passing them around to her friends. "Sapphire's father, Andre, was the photographer. And an excellent one at that." Sapphire spotted more items peeking out of the bag.

While everyone admired the photos, Dani continued. "We selected sample cuttings of the same flowers and plants that the butterflies were drawn to and brought them into this lab." She took another sip of mint water. "Jane learned how to extract oils from those plants and flowers to process them into essential oils."

Sapphire beamed. "Wow, my dad was a photographer, and my mom was making essential oils? Impressive."

Farrell said, "Now you know where your creativity came from, Sapphire." She nodded appreciatively. Judith, Dani, and Sofia nodded too. The sun streaming through the windows cast long shadows around the indoor potted plants. The group could see butterflies flitting around the outside blooms. Everyone sat in silent reverie, honoring the cherished memory of Sapphire's parents.

Dani broke the silence. "Sapphire, the story about your parents must be kept private."

"Of course," said Sapphire.

Dani looked intently at each of Sapphire's friends. "I was prepared to tell Sapphire this alone. But I can see how close you all are. So, I will share the story with all of you. I am trusting you, Farrell, Sofia, and Judith, to keep what I am about to share, completely confidential."

"Certainly," said Judith first.

"I'll keep everything private," Sofia said.

"I won't share this with anyone," Farrell said. "I'm a very private person, so I understand. You can count on me."

"You can trust me," Sapphire said. "You can trust all of us."

Dani felt renewed energy to continue. "Jane stumbled upon her discovery by accident. She began refusing the usual cup of coffee Andre had been bringing to her every morning ever since they started living together. He didn't think much of it until he noticed Jane's uneaten lunches." Dani pursed her lips. "Five days had passed before Andre and I realized that Jane had stopped eating." Dani's brows knitted. "We would have noticed earlier if Jane had been lethargic, pale, or had any other side effects. She appeared healthy and energetic. Her skin glowed."

Farrell piped up. "What do you mean, stopped eating?" He had gone days without food during his younger drinking binges. Did Sapphire's mom have an addiction?

Sofia wondered about anorexia but remembered that Jane had appeared to be of normal weight in photos. Perhaps she was taking diet pills that were popular at the time.

"She was healthy," Dani stated emphatically. "We made her go see a doctor to be sure." Dani pulled out a folder from the white velvet bag, then she removed a sheet of paper from the folder and handed it to Sapphire. "This is a copy of your mother's bloodwork seven days after having no food." Sapphire didn't know how to interpret the results. Her eyes glided down the final column on the right. *WITHIN NORMAL RANGE* was listed next to each entry.

Sofia wondered if Sapphire's mother knew enough to stay hydrated. People could live without food but not without water. "Was she drinking water?"

"Plenty of mint-infused water," Dani said. "The same variety of mint you are drinking now. She was well hydrated, and it was medically verified that she was very healthy." Dani removed a second sheet of paper from the folder. "Here's a copy of her bloodwork, a week later." She slid the results to Sapphire who quickly noticed the *WITHIN NORMAL RANGE* listed down the far-right column identical to the first copy. She passed the pages to her friends. Sofia noticed that the second page of results came from a different medical lab and was ordered by a different doctor.

Judith put on her reading glasses and scanned the report. "What did the doctor make of this?"

"Jane didn't tell the doctor about her mysterious lack of appetite. She simply asked for a routine physical with bloodwork."

"How was she living without food?" Sapphire asked.

Dani allowed silence to let the question sink in. She already had a guess who would be the first one to understand. "What about the plants Jane was working with?" Judith blurted out in a high-pitched excited voice. "Weren't they rare and exotic varieties?"

Bingo! "YES. THEY. WERE," Dani said slowly emphasizing each word. "Jane's skin had absorbed small quantities throughout the day, as she mixed a variety of essential oils." Everyone had leaned forward as Dani continued. "She was experimenting with different formulas. The first group she surveyed responded positively to lavender essential oil and peppermint essential oil. Jane wanted to try different essential oil combinations with a new group." Dani quietly rested her hands on her lap.

"Wasn't she also inhaling the fumes?" Farrell asked. He was still thinking about the addiction angle. "Wouldn't the chemicals have entered her system that way?" The others looked at him, and he reddened. Did the term *chemicals* make it sound like he was accusing Jane of being a drug addict? "I mean, are essential oils more potent inhaled through the lungs or absorbed through the skin?"

"That's a good question, Farrell," Dani said. "As scientists, we knew that inhaling essential oils was as powerful as applying them topically. The difference is that the topical absorption time is only a few seconds, so the active ingredients begin working immediately." She hadn't intended to give them a science lesson, but they needed to understand how the development of the formula transpired. "There was no protocol for wearing gloves or a mask since these oils were not being developed for commercial use."

"So, Sapphire's mother stumbled upon a formula to dull hunger?" Judith asked.

"More than dull hunger, it replaced nutrition," Dani said. "Disbelief would be an understatement. We were stunned." She opened her eyes wide. "Plants use sunlight, water, and carbon dioxide to create oxygen and energy. We humans have a lot in common with plants."

"How long did this go on?" Sapphire asked. What was it like for her mother to unintentionally stumble upon a formula that replaced nutrition. It sounded incredulous.

"We wanted her to stop," Dani said. "Andre and I were worried. "She was excited about her discovery and wanted to study further." Dani looked at Sapphire. "We argued. Your mother was determined to continue her research as her own guinea pig." Dani stopped talking, took a breath, and continued. "Finally, we compromised and agreed to look at this as scientists. We devised a plan and assigned tasks."

"You let her continue?" Sapphire said accusingly. "You were her best friend." Sapphire glared at her.

Dani felt stung. She looked down and talked to the floor. "We even threatened to share the information with the head of the research department at Aromaticus. Your mother was stubborn and determined to continue," Dani said flatly. "We had no choice." Sapphire remembered her mother's stubbornness. She bit her lip. "Please go on," Sapphire said. "I'm sorry to judge you. It was so long ago. My friend Fisher was stubborn as well. I understand what it's like to try and reason with someone you love who is like that."

Dani wasn't sure if she should feel relieved. The rest of the story would likely elicit more judgment and emotions. Sh had been her only judge over the years, and now it felt like she had a jury. She noticed Judith squirming in her seat. Sitting that long was difficult. "Let's take a break," she finally said. No one really wanted a break, but they did as Dani instructed.

Sofia got up to stretch. Judith went in search of the restroom. Dani followed behind to show her the way. Farrell picked up the butterfly photos and studied them. Sapphire sat missing her parents, Aunt Star, and Fisher. Farrell put down the photos. He walked over to Sapphire and put his arm around her. She rested her head on his shoulder, closed her eyes, and allowed herself to be comforted.

Chapter 24
The Secret Plan

Ten minutes later, the group had reassembled in their chairs, ready to hear more. Two bowls of macadamia nuts had appeared on the table. Little place cards with the Aromaticus logo rested in front of each bowl. One was labeled *natural macadamia nuts* and the other *caramel sea salt macadamia nuts.* An iced-filled pitcher of freshly brewed mango tea with the familiar fruit wedges glistened invitingly. Thinking about her mother on the formula and not eating reminded Sapphire that she was hungry. Her stomach grumbled.

Finally, Farrell began spooning some nuts on a napkin and poured himself a glass of tea. He offered to pour each lady a glass by tilting his head. "Dani?" "Judith?" "Sofia?" and finally "Sapphire?" Judith noted the age order he placed them in going from oldest to youngest. It privately amused her. Each accepted a glass and scooped some nuts on their own napkin with the Aromaticus logo inscribed. Farrell wondered how many items the logo could be stamped on. It was an effective advertisement, he had to admit.

Dani waited for everyone to serve themselves some snacks and ice-tea, then continued with her story. "Jane went for two full weeks of not eating at all. She continued to drink water, a lot of mint water. When she finally did begin to eat, we were worried about how her digestive system would react." Dani instinctively placed her hand on her stomach. "We closely monitored Jane as she ingested small amounts of food at first. Everything was fine, there was no problem. Jane said the food tasted good, but that she hadn't missed it."

"I remember not eating for two days after a bout of food poisoning," Sofia said. "It felt weird to chew, swallow and digest food after that." She gripped her stomach with one hand.

Dani returned to her narrative, relieved to have gotten through the first part. "There was no internet to help us back then. So, we researched ancient uses of plants in the public library. The gardens here also had an extensive collection of books detailing medicinal uses of plants over history." The group listened while sipping their tea. "Much of our findings were anecdotal descriptions of herbal nutritional practices handed down through generations. Indigenous tribes and ancient peoples did not formally record their traditional remedies." Sofia nodded her head. "Some of the cuttings that were brought over here were from South America and Central America, indigenous to the Amazon Jungle. These rare species were endangered, and we ran out of specimens."

Dani said. "Your parents wanted to collect more specimens and interview the natives about their traditional uses. Aromaticus hired all three of us as a team, after the summer internship on Kauai ended. Once we returned to Asheville, I stayed at the lab whenever your parents traveled. You went with them to different locations near the Amazon Rainforest. When you were ten years old, all three of you moved to Columbia full time. By that time, you had traveled with them to nine different countries bordering the Amazon Rainforest." Dani held up her fingers as she counted. "Bolivia, Brazil, Columbia, Ecuador, French Guiana, Guyana, Peru, Suriname and Venezuela."

"Wow," said Sapphire. "I remember some of those places. How did you get Aromaticus to hire the three of you once the summer internship ended?" Sapphire asked. The others held back their questions, allowing Sapphire to set the pace.

"That was your brilliant mother again," Dani said. "She proposed to continue her survey of the public. This time, the proposal was to survey observers instead of the individuals who tried the peppermint and lavender oils." She sipped her tea. "Teachers would observe students' behavior, prison guards would observe inmates, counselors would observe addicts in rehab, coaches would observe professional athletes, and nurses would observe hospital patients. Aromaticus welcomed the idea and hired the three of us as a team. They also loved the results, all extremely positive."

Judith discreetly tried to remove a piece of nut that got caught in her teeth. She hoped no one noticed as she held one hand over her mouth. All eyes were on Dani as she spoke. "Every one of the observers reported a measurable difference in performance and relaxation. Test scores and medical records documented the improvement." Sofia nodded in agreement. She had seen a variety of clients respond favorably to the use of essential oils.

Dani continued. "Technically, the secret nutrition formula belonged to Aromaticus since it was developed while working for them and in their lab. Legally, we could not claim ownership if we left the company."

Farrell nodded in understanding. He was familiar with corporate structures.

"As the years went on," said Dani, "we continued to work for Aromaticus while secretly experimenting with our formula in the lab during off hours. Jane and Andre also formulated some of the popular scents in the company's current catalog." It was a point of pride for Dani to report a high work ethic. "Researching new plants in different countries was a part of their job description, so our secret work went undetected. Or so we thought."

A breeze sent a cluster of leaves dancing just outside the windows.

"I remember a trip to Vancouver Island," Sapphire said. "We visited a lavender farm and learned how to distinguish the different varieties of lavender."

Judith smiled. She knew from her trips to Europe that there were hundreds of varieties of lavender, with the more common ones used to manufacture soaps. The rarer varieties were distilled into expensive perfumes. She ordered hers from Paris.

"Lena and I went to Bouchard Gardens on Vancouver Island one year," Sofia said. "The most stunning display of roses I've ever seen." She remembered the High Tea at the Empress Hotel. A surprise from Lena for her birthday. "We visited a lavender farm not far from there. It was the highlight of the trip."

"I know the one you are both referring to," Dani said. "We import their lavender for our products at Aromaticus. And yes, Sapphire, your parents discovered that farm when you were just a child." Sapphire smiled as she fondly recalled the memory.

"The three of us kept a journal at first," said Dani, "writing in code to document our observations of Jane's health. We took turns trying out the formula, only one of us at a time so the other two could observe." Dani sat back in her seat. Sapphire peered at the folder and wondered if the coded journal was there. As if reading her mind, Dani said, "We destroyed our coded journals but kept these." Dani removed the final stack of papers and handed them to Sapphire. She leafed through pages of bloodwork and medical reports from different names and cities. Then she handed them to Farrell who briefly skimmed them. Sofia studied the records next.

"Whoever was trying the formula had weekly medical check-ups," said Dani. "We used assumed names and visited different doctors. Using the same medical facilities might have aroused suspicion, so we often took day trips to nearby towns. When living on Kauai that summer, we hitched boat rides to the other Hawaiian Islands."

Dani sipped water. "We all returned to Asheville after the summer. It was several years before your parents began traveling to South America. Back in Asheville, we took day trips throughout the Carolinas, Tennessee, and Georgia." Dani recalled those fun trips with great pleasure. Sofia handed the records to Judith who perused them perfunctorily.

Dani held one final page in her hand. "After a year, we ran low on funds. We were also having difficulty finding new medical facilities to monitor our health as we continued to try out the formula without eating. We were paying in cash, and it was expensive. Your mother selected a Planned Parenthood clinic since it was free." She handed Sapphire the final document. "That's how your mother learned she was pregnant with you." Sofia stretched her neck to read the POSITIVE pregnancy result on the document.

Dani remembered how astonished she was. "I didn't know your parents were trying to conceive."

Sapphire gasped with horror. "You mean my mother was trying to get pregnant while NOT EATING AND TAKING THE FORMULA?" That would have been terribly irresponsible. What if it impacted Sapphire's health? She had enjoyed excellent health throughout her sixty-one years. Were there lurking medical issues?

"NO, she was NOT," Dani said. "It turned out your parents were using birth control. They weren't trying to get pregnant. We thought perhaps the formula counteracted the birth control pills." She patted Sapphire's hand. "You were unexpected, but they considered you a blessing." Had Dani revealed more than Jane and Andre would have wanted? Sapphire didn't know she was unplanned. Dani gestured emphatically. "Your parents were elated, over the moon!" Sapphire sat motionless, trying to wrap her brain around this new revelation. "You were a miracle and brought more happiness to your parents than anyone could ever imagine," added Dani.

Sapphire let out a sigh while experiencing a myriad of reactions. *Unplanned. Unexpected. Miracle.*

Judith tilted her head and smiled at Sapphire. She never wanted children, but if she had, she would've wanted a daughter like Sapphire. Reading Judith's thoughts, Dani said, "Sapphire, you brought great joy to both of your parents."

"I remember a happy childhood with loving parents," Sapphire said. "I felt privileged to travel to so many countries and live abroad." Most children who moved a lot resented it and felt ungrounded. But not Sapphire. "Home for me was wherever my parents were."

It was getting late. The sun had set, and the moon was rising. It was time to leave and save the rest of the story for tomorrow. Dani texted Kai letting him know they were ready to go. "I know that you have a lot to think about and I want to tell you more. I need to explain why Jane and Andre decided to keep the formula hidden." She still hadn't revealed the danger nor described the countless hours of agonizing soul-searching Sapphire's parents had experienced. "Thank you for coming to Kauai to meet me in person, Sapphire. And thank you for bringing your friends. No one outside this room knows of the existence of the secret formula. I know I can trust you all to hold our secret."

Sapphire's impatience returned. Why was the formula so secret? Why was Dani, her parents' best friend, kept secreted? She let out a long breath. She would have to wait until tomorrow to find out more.

Chapter 25
Sapphire's Questions

The group remained seated in the office at the gardens while they waited for Kai. Sapphire shifted in her chair. "I have so many questions, Dani." She wanted to know more than the medical effects, although she was interested in that as well. Dani was the only person alive who had experienced using it. She tried to put her thoughts into words. Her friends listened as Sapphire listed her questions for Dani.

"Were you able to eat at all while on the formula?" Sapphire asked. "Could you alternate days? Like taking the formula one day, then eating the next, then back to the formula again?"

"We were not hungry at all when taking the formula," Dani said. "There was just no desire to eat. We didn't try to alternate days. That might've been part of the research had we continued."

Sapphire couldn't stop her questions. "When it was your turn to try the formula, what was it like for you to not share meals with others? Did you miss the social aspect? I mean, what did you do when other people were having meals?" She finally took a breath.

"I think I understand what you're asking, Sapphire," said Dani. "Your parents and I had many medical-related observations, but that is different than the social aspect. Very astute of you to ask." Dani took a moment before continuing. "Physically, I felt fine when taking the formula. Your parents did too. Surprisingly, the only remarkable observation was that we remained healthy. But socially, yes, it was weird. We hadn't thought about how much everyone's days and socializing are structured around meals."

Sofia nodded briskly. She had seen clients with eating disorders struggle with those same aspects. It was difficult to help them develop healthy social habits around eating. Same with most addictions. "Kind of like cigarette smokers who quit and miss their smoking routines, their smoke breaks, and their smoke break buddies," she said.

"Yes, Sofia," Dani said. "Exactly!" She wished Sofia would've been available to address those aspects back at that time. "I missed the routine of drinking coffee to start my day." Dani's eyes looked up as she retrieved further memories. "I didn't feel comfortable joining others for meals if I wasn't eating." Dani recalled how awkward she felt the first time she met friends at a restaurant, planning on just drinking water and socializing. "Others don't feel comfortable being around someone who is not eating when they are."

"That's what I meant, Dani," said Sapphire. "So much time is spent shopping for food, preparing meals, eating, cleaning up and even thinking about food." What it would be like to not do any of that? "What'd you do with the extra time you saved? Were you more productive?"

"Well, I know it sounds like I should've been more productive, adding more time for work," Dani said. "Instead, I tried to spend more time outdoors, walking, observing animals, and breathing the fresh air." Dani remembered setting up a schedule for herself to do something she enjoyed when she skipped meals. "Much later in life, I was forced to find a similar substitute when I stopped drinking."

Farrell's ears perked up. He had been daydreaming about a house he wanted to purchase on Kauai and was only half listening to the conversation. Did Dani struggle with a drinking problem? He hoped she would say more about it.

As if reading his mind, Dani did share more. "I'd been sad and lonely after your parents died. They were my best friends." She had felt all alone in the world. "I sought solace in the bottle." Her cheeks turned red. "It began with just one martini at the end of the day." Dani recalled the relaxed sensation she looked forward to. "One led to two, then three each night. I lost count after three. Soon, I began drinking at lunchtime." It had happened so gradually. "Lunchtime got moved up earlier and earlier each day. I'm ashamed to admit that there was a time in my life when I was inebriated all day long." Dani closed her mouth and looked down at her lap. Had she said too much? How did the conversation turn from the formula to her drinking?

"I understand," said Farrell, fixing his eyes on Dani. "I've had to search for new habits and routines to substitute for my drinking." He couldn't believe he was talking about it. He never wanted to attend an AA meeting because he didn't want to share his private struggle. "I admire your honesty Dani," Farrell said. "Thank you." How did she manage to stop drinking? Farrell didn't want to ask her directly.

"Thank you, Farrell," Dani said. "I appreciate that, especially coming from you." She had suspected Farrell struggled with a drinking problem. She couldn't quite put her finger on why, but it takes one to know one. "I went to one of those treatment programs for a month to dry out," she said. "In Florida. Jane's sister Star encouraged me to do so.

She arranged the whole thing." Dani had resisted at first. She was so full of dreadful shame. "I haven't touched a drop in forty-five years." Dani didn't celebrate her sobriety anniversary and didn't experience a sense of pride in becoming sober. She still struggled with the shame, although talking about it now was a bit of a relief. Maybe she would talk privately with Farrell some more.

Judith reached over and held Dani's hand. It felt so natural for Dani as she clasped Judith's hand in both of hers. Her face returned to its natural color.

Dani suddenly felt exhausted. Would her guests be hungry for dinner? The last thing she wanted to do was to play hostess tonight. She needed to be alone. She decided to set out some platters of light dinner for her guests to help themselves. "Just got a text from Kai. He's waiting outside for us. I hope you don't mind if we stop for now and take this up tomorrow."

"Of course not, Dani. I'm sorry to go on with so many questions and keep him waiting. Thank you for telling us more about yourself," said Sapphire. "And about your experience with the formula." Sapphire went over to Dani and hugged her. "And for telling me about my parents. And giving me the photos. And for this beautiful week on Kauai."

All five were quiet during the ride back to Mango. The full moon highlighted pensive expressions. Kai remained silent as he drove. Being intuitive, he noticed a strange vibration between his passengers, almost electric. Each appeared on the outside to be lost in their thoughts, yet subtly bonded together as a group, including Dani. Shared energy pulsated rhythmically as the tires crunched on the gravel road to home.

Chapter 26
Tea Time

Once Dani felt assured that her guests were properly fed, she cleared the left-over trays of food and finally retired to her private suite. She sat lost in thought about preserving the formula and worried about the danger. As Dani prepared her evening tea, she heard a knock at her door. "Come in," she said, not knowing who it might be. "Oh, Judith, please come in."

"I hope I'm not intruding," Judith said. "I thought maybe you could use some company." She glanced at the tea set up. It was an English routine Judith recognized, down to the crustless cucumber sandwiches. Usually, an afternoon custom, but Dani clearly made it her evening ritual. "I can leave if you prefer to be alone."

"Oh, no," Dani responded immediately. "Please stay and join me for tea." Dani had wanted to be alone but seeing Judith brought a smile to her face. "I enjoy your company and I'm glad to see you." Did she sound too forward? But then again, it was Judith who came knocking at her door.

"I'd enjoy tea," Judith said. "Thank you." She recognized the imported Earl Grey, her favorite. "No cream or sugar, just black, please."

"That's good because I don't have cream or sugar here," Dani said. "I take it black too." Both women were transported back to early childhood memories where it was thrilling to find something in common with a new friend. Dani found it comforting to have Judith by her side. "I'm not used to company when I have my evening tea," Dani said. "But, well, this is nice, having you here." They smiled at each other as they drank their tea and nibbled on their sandwiches. Dani felt a longing for companionship that she had long forgotten. Her body relaxed in a state of peace.

After a long silence, Judith said, "My entire career with the Witness Protection Program involved keeping people safe and guarding secrets." She held Dani's gaze. "The Witness Protection Program was my life." Judith had not discussed her job with even her closest friends but talking to Dani felt different. "I was a secretary, more like a personal assistant to one of the best US Marshalls. We were a team. That's how I came to know Sapphire this past year." It was a confusing story to tell but Dani seemed interested.

"One of Sapphire's closest high school friends had been in the Witness Protection Program. Fisher Bond. You've heard her talk about him this week. He was murdered last year. The investigators tracked me down to explain his history as the authorities were investigating his murder. None of his friends knew that he had been relocated. A year ago, I told the entire story to Sapphire, Farrell, Sofia, and the investigators."

Dani felt honored to have Judith share a personal experience. "Much like I am telling my story," she said. Judith nodded. "I've guarded Sapphire's safety by keeping secrets," Dani continued. "I'll be explaining more about Sapphire's parents tomorrow. It's not easy, but it's time for me to tell Sapphire everything. I'm glad you understand how it feels to share long-kept secrets."

They fell into an easy silence as they drank their tea. Both tilted their heads back on their chairs as their eyelids drooped. Judith reached over and placed her hand on Dani's. Dani enveloped Judith's hand into both of hers. The warmth permeated Dani's heart. A soul-to-soul connection imbued the room. Moonlight shone through the lacey curtains that danced gracefully in the warm Hawaiian breeze.

Chapter 27
Betrayal

The next morning, Sofia and Sapphire found two thermoses next to the coffee urn on the garden breakfast table. A note from Dani said, *Lets meet up this afternoon to continue. Enjoy your morning.* From the neatly piled used dishes and lipstick marks on two coffee cups, they knew Dani and Judith already had their breakfast. A second note from Farrell was placed next to the thermoses. *I'll be back at noon. Kai and I are up in Princeville this morning. Mahalo, Farrell*

After breakfast, Sofia and Sapphire took their thermoses on their usual morning walk. "I wonder what Dani will reveal today," Sapphire said. "I can't imagine what my mother was thinking and how she felt about her discovery." They walked barefoot on the early morning cool sand, knowing it would be burning hot by afternoon. Neither wanted to go into ocean as it appeared choppy. Swimming against the tide would exhaust them and they wanted to be alert for Dani in the afternoon.

After lunch, Farrell, Sofia, Sapphire, Judith, and Dani gathered indoors for their continuing discussion. Each relaxed in a comfortable swivel club chair in the den, arranged in a circle around a large coffee table. Assorted macadamia nuts, mint water, and two large pitchers of mango tea rested on platters. Dani had two white velvet drawstring bags at her side. "I found more photos," she said as she removed a large album from the first bag. "They are of you as a baby, Sapphire."

"I've never seen these," Sapphire said smiling as she studied each large eight-by-ten professional-looking portrait of herself. Why had they been hidden away for so long? "Hey, look at this one. I'm building a house with blocks. My first venture into architecture." Dani felt glad the mood was light. For now. Sapphire held up some of the photos for everyone to see, then she passed the album around.

"You look like you were about five here, Sapphire," Farrell said. "What a cute child." Farrell never had children of his own, yet they always brought a smile to him. "Dani, did Sapphire's father take these photos?"

"Yes, Andre took each one. He was a proud papa," Dani said. "And very protective, especially after what happened next." The mood turned serious as they all focused on Dani. "Your dad had to stop taking photos of you, Sapphire, and asked me to store these away for safekeeping."

"Why?" Sapphire asked. "What happened? I don't remember."

"You were about five at the time and your parents shielded you," Dani said. "There was nothing for you to remember. From your point of view, everything was normal. We should've noticed what was happening but brushed off a colleague's infatuation as harmless. His name was Duke." Dani took a deep sigh before continuing. "Jane was a very beautiful and accomplished woman. Others in the company took notice. Some were impressed. Some were proud. Some were jealous. All to be expected as she rose through the company ranks. Many men were attracted to her, but Andre was her only interest. One man was relentless in his efforts to spend time with Jane. He followed her around, asked her out for lunch frequently, and brought her snacks. He was infatuated. Duke was his name." Dani bit her lip. "He didn't like being rejected. Your babysitter found him watching you play on the playground, Sapphire. She didn't know who he was and was concerned." Everyone had concerned looks as they listened.

"When he approached you on the swings, the sitter noticed from her park bench and was alarmed," Dani continued. "Fortunately, you didn't go with him, and she scooped you up and whisked you away immediately." Dani spoke louder and more quickly. "When the sitter asked you what the man said, you told her that he said he was a friend of your parents and wanted to take you to see them." Sapphire's eyebrows shot up. She didn't remember that, yet she felt fear hearing it. "When the sitter told your parents, your dad showed her a company photo of Duke and she identified him." Duke. Sapphire felt a chill every time she heard his name.

"Did they report it to the police?" Farrell asked. He felt a fatherly sense of protection toward five-year-old Sapphire.

"No," Dani said. "Your parents chose to give him a warning instead. When they went to his office, he wasn't there. While waiting for Duke, Andre spotted photos peeking out of a folder on Duke's desk. There were dozens of photos of Jane, all candid and some close up in her lab." Sapphire's hands flew to her face. Farrell's brows knitted together. "There were also some of you, Sapphire, taken from a distance." They were horrified. "Andre kept his cool. He had Jane lookout in the hallway to intercept Duke if needed, while he searched Duke's office for more evidence. He found some mini tapes and a recorder in one of the drawers."

Dani continued. "They took the evidence before Duke returned to the office. Jane didn't want to call attention to her secret lab work. She and

Andre decided to have Aromaticus handle the situation without police involvement. In today's climate, that would not have been an option." She crossed her arms in defiance.

"I can't believe they didn't press charges," Farrell said. His fists tightened. "Stalking is illegal."

"Aromaticus confronted Duke and accepted his resignation with the stipulation that he leave town," Dani said. "From then on, Jane and Andre felt they were being watched. Jane was determined to continue her work and Andre took more safety measures. When you weren't at school, Sapphire, you came to work with your mother or father. Sometimes I watched you."

"Did he leave town?" Sapphire asked. "Did they ever see him again?" She flashed on a memory of Fisher, who lived with the fear of being stalked for most of his life.

"Oh, yes," Dani said. Duke left Asheville, and we never saw or heard from him again." She sighed. "Not directly."

Alarmed, Sapphire asked, "What do you mean, *not directly?*"

"We heard about him from others," Dani said. "Duke had bragged about his suspicions. Probably exaggerated what he knew. The idea of an essential oil as a nutrition substitute piqued a lot of interest."

Judith squirmed in her seat and said she would be right back. Dani looked at Judith's empty tea glass and knew she needed a bathroom break. Dani realized she needed one too. "I'll be back in a moment," she told the others. Sofia, Sapphire, and Farrell gave each other quizzical expressions. How could Dani just stop in the middle like that.? Five minutes of waiting in silence felt like an eternity.

After they all settled back in their seats, Dani continued. "Andre listened to the tape-recording Duke had made of their private conversations. It was apparent he knew something about the secret formula. Duke would have heard enough to glean the general idea of a nutrition substitute being developed. One of the tapes recorded us talking about the millions of dollars the formula was worth. That was why he was bringing Jane snacks and asking her to lunch. He wanted to test out his theory. We missed the boat entirely. Duke was interested in your mother's lab work, not in her." Dani shook her head. "We later suspected that kidnapping you, Sapphire, might have been a plan to ransom you for the formula." Dani felt enraged all over again as if it was yesterday.

She sipped some tea to gather herself. The next part of the story would be more complicated to explain. She lifted the second white velvet drawstring bag ready to unveil more.

Chapter 28
The Telegrams

The white velvet bag rested on Dani's lap while she adjusted herself in her seat. "Several months after Duke resigned and left town, Jane and Andre relaxed and fell back into their usual routine. We only kept coded notes regarding the progress of developing the formula. We didn't consider the larger picture." She took a sip of tea before continuing.

"Jane received a job offer with a larger company. It was for a higher position with an increased salary. Not a surprise. Scientists often changed jobs for promotions." Farrell nodded. He understood the way promotions worked in various industries.

"Jane and Andre were comfortable in Asheville and loyal to Aromaticus," continued Dani. "The company's values aligned with theirs, and Aromaticus supported Jane by forcing Duke to resign. Plus, the three of us worked together as a team."

A sweet scent from plumeria blooms drifted through the open windows. "Jane showed the job offer to the head of Aromaticus and he blanched," said Dani. "Turns out Duke was working for the company that tried to recruit Jane. They were a competitor in California." Dani pursed her lips. "Aromaticus hadn't told other companies about the issues with Duke. He had threatened to sue if they provided an unfavorable reference. Instead, Aromaticus simply shared a description of the work he did and reported satisfactory job performance."

"That still happens all the time," Sofia blurted out in exasperation. "Teachers, university professors, and doctors get shuffled around as employers fear lawsuits if they report problems. Not to mention clergy." Sofia had counseled many victims who were traumatized by serial predators who could have been stopped if reported.

"Jane and Andre were confused and worried," said Dani. "We'd suspected all along that Duke knew about the formula. Now, we wondered if he tipped off his new employer, and that was why they wanted Jane. So, she politely refused the offer. We thought that was the end of it."

Dani smoothed a strand of hair off her face. "But that wasn't the end of it by far. Jane began receiving letters from pharmaceutical firms. They courted her with offers of expensive dinners and trips to exotic locations." Her voice quickened. "These companies had deep pockets and boldly expressed an interest in new formulas they heard

Jane was developing." All eyes stayed riveted on Dani as she continued. "Prescription medications are mostly synthetics copied from naturally occurring plants and herbs. Scientists compete to bring new medications through the governmental approval process. There's a lot of money to be made so corporate espionage is rampant and pure greed is the motivation." She grimaced. "The public is the loser."

Sofia, Farrell, Judith, and Sapphire all nodded in agreement.

"It was a bidding war," continued Dani, "as the competing offers kept escalating. Jane refused them all." Dani removed a folder from the velvet bag. "Andre kept all the correspondence." She held up a stack of papers. "This was just a minor distraction. We were amused, but not worried." Dani handed the letters to Sapphire who leafed through them.

Sapphire squinted at the letters and regretted leaving her reading glasses upstairs. "I recognize some of these names. They're still in business today." She handed the letters to Farrell, who shook his head while scanning the papers.

"I don't include these companies in my portfolio," Farrell said, "even though they're money makers." Farrell's clients only wanted his investment firm specifically for his highly scrutinized socially conscious investment opportunities. "People can acquire and build wealth while supporting companies that align with their values. Like Fisher. He insisted on investments with environmentally responsible corporations."

Dani's ears perked up. "Perhaps you will consider adding Aromaticus and The National Tropical Botanical Gardens to your portfolio."

Farrell smiled. "I've been considering that." He grabbed a handful of macadamia nuts. "Let's talk more about it later. Sorry I interrupted, please continue Dani."

"Let me get some fruit first," she said. "I have mango sherbet in the freezer. Anyone interested?" Everyone nodded. Judith rose to help Dani. Both stretched their limbs before walking into the kitchen.

Sapphire stood. "I'm getting some lemon water. Anyone else want some?" Farrell and Sofia shook their heads as she headed into the kitchen.

Farrell scanned the letters more closely and grimaced. The companies in the letters were responsible for polluting the earth, causing environmental harm far into the future.

Sapphire returned from the kitchen sipping her lemon water. Judith and Dani followed with bowls of mango sherbet. Farrell's eyes hungrily followed each bowl as Dani and Judith passed them around. "Yum," said Sofia, after her first taste. "This mango sherbet is amazing. Did you make them from the mangos you grow here, Dani?"

"Yes," Dani said. "We have so many mango plants on the property that we don't know what to do with them all." She ate a spoonful and let out a sigh of satisfaction. "Kai's mother Pearl made this for us. She's coming by later to cook dinner for tonight."

After everyone gobbled up their sherbet, they leaned back in their chairs. "Well," Dani said. "That was refreshing." She delicately wiped her mouth with a napkin before continuing. "Back to the job offers. First, was the company that was Aromaticus' competition. Next, the pharmaceutical firms. All very forceful, but still civil as you can see from the letters."

Dani put on the reading glasses that were attached to a delicate chain around her neck. She removed another folder from the velvet bag and produced another stack of papers. "Andre intercepted a telegram addressed to Jane but was unable to track down the source." Dani read aloud, "We are a group of investors interested in buying the formula. WE STRONGLY ADVISE YOU TO CONSIDER OUR OFFER. We will be in touch very soon." She passed the telegram to Sapphire.

"Was my mother afraid?" Sapphire asked. She checked out the telegram with wide eyes and passed it on to Judith. Judith stared at the telegram. She recognized the familiar veiled threat from her years at the Witness Protection Program protecting witnesses from criminals.

Clouds covered the sun and the mood in the room grew darker. Dani passed five more telegrams around the room. Each one contained vague threats with increasingly greater demands. The last one was the most disturbing. *YOU WILL DEEPLY REGRET IT IF YOU REJECT OUR OFFER.* A photo of Andre, Jane, and six-year-old Sapphire was attached. It'd been taken with a telephoto lens. The happy family was sprawled out on a blanket in a park having a picnic. Sapphire gasped. She suddenly felt unsafe even though the danger was fifty-five years ago. Deep breaths brought her back to the present.

"Your mother was frightened for her family, especially for you, Sapphire," Dani said gravely. "After Jane recovered from her initial shock, Andre and I helped her evaluate options. We approached it scientifically, considering all possible and likely outcomes."

Sofia nodded. She had used this technique with clients who struggled to make important decisions.

"Jane suspected these threatening parties would approach her in person. We agreed Jane would categorically deny the existence of any secret formula," said Dani. "It was the best decision at the time, and it turned out to be the right one."

Sapphire stared into space. Why were her parents so desperate to keep the formula secret?

Dani looked directly at Sapphire. "Your mother was very brave. She maintained her usual routine." She turned to the others. "Jane felt calm as soon as she made her decision. She was resolute. Andre and I were on pins and needles. Three weeks after the final telegram, Jane was approached by the so-called investors."

A light drizzle turned into a loud thunderstorm. The faint smell of rain mixed with the fragrant flowers. Farrell helped Dani close the windows as the rain began to come inside.

"I left my windows open upstairs," Sofia said. The others turned their heads towards the stairway. Farrell bounded up the stairs. Sofia followed behind him, not quite as quickly. "I'll get yours closed, Judith," said Sapphire as she trailed behind.

The group reassembled in their chairs several minutes later. Farrell, Sofia, and Sapphire were out of breath from their sprint. "Please continue, Dani," Sapphire said. "Did my mother convince them that no formula existed?"

"Your mother wove a believable tale. Could've been an actress." She chuckled at the memory. "Jane was beautiful. You look so much like her, Sapphire."

Sapphire blushed.

"In preparation for the approach from the threatening parties," said Dani, "your mother dressed provocatively She had decided a sexy look would be best to throw off those who approached her. Do you remember push-up bras? She looked very sexy in her miniskirts and long legs. Not like your typical scientist. She even teased her hair and wore make-up. Andre didn't like it, but Jane convinced him that it was the right costume for the situation."

Sapphire smoothed her short sundress with her hands. She suddenly felt self-conscious.

"Jane was ready for her major role, the performance of a lifetime," Dani said. "Three men approached her one day on her lunchtime walk. Although she had no clue what to expect, she recognized them by their tailored suits. No one in Asheville dressed like that. Jane feigned surprise when the men inquired about the formula. She played a defenseless maiden. The men gaped at her cleavage as she wove a timeless tale. Jane tearfully admitted to leading Duke on. She had flirted with him to get back at Andre who cheated on her. After she and Andre made up, she dropped Duke, and he was angry. Jane convinced three men that Duke lied about the secret formula for revenge." Dani laughed out loud. "Men can be so fickle." She quickly glanced at Farrell. "Not you, Farrell, you're a gem."

"No offense taken," said Farrell. "I know how men can be, when it comes to women." He shook his head. "They lose their sensibilities. Seen it over and over."

"Incredible," said Judith.

"Yes, and ingenious," said Sofia with a pained expression. "Unfortunately, that would work, even today."

Sapphire's brain couldn't wrap itself around her mother dressed up in a sexy outfit and performing a flirtatious role. Her mother was graceful with a natural beauty. She never wore make-up. Never needed to. Clearly her mother was motivated to protect her family and keep control of her professional career.

"Since she didn't hear back from them, we thought Jane convinced them that there was no formula." Dani frowned. "Another five years passed before Jane was contacted again. You were ten years old by then."

The rain stopped, and the sun shone through the windows. "I hear Pearl coming in," Dani said. "I hope she didn't get caught in the thunderstorm. The weather changes so unexpectedly here." She left the group to greet Pearl, finding Kai shaking out a wet umbrella outside.

"Miss Lake, quick, come outside," Kai said. "A double rainbow. You must see it." Dani never tired of witnessing Hawaii's magnificent rainbows. She ran outside and smiled.

"Kai, please tell Sapphire and her friends to come outside to see this," Dani said. "They're in the den. Quickly, please, before it disappears." The magnificent Hawaiian rainbows often disappeared in the time it took to find one's phone and snap a photo.

Kai ran to the den. Sapphire, Farrell, Sofia, and Judith sat silently in their chairs, trying to absorb Dani's story. "Come outside to see the beautiful double rainbow," he said. When they didn't move immediately, Kai added, "Hurry, before it disappears." His urgent words brought each of them back to the present. They quickly followed Kai outside where they stared in awe at the vivid double rainbow.

"Stand right there," Kai said to the group. "I'll take your picture with the rainbows behind you."

Dani, Sapphire, Judith, Farrell, and Sofia gathered close. Kai positioned his iPhone horizontally, then vertically, clicking away. "Perfect," he said. "I'll send you each a copy."

Pearl joined everyone outside. "This is Pearl, my mother," Kai told the group. She smiled demurely as Kai put his arm around her.

"Thank you for the amazing sherbet," Sofia said. "Nice to meet you." The others greeted her warmly.

All eyes remained fixed on the rainbows. Miraculously, they were still there. Everyone stood still as the double rainbow gradually faded away, leaving no trace of having graced the sky.

Chapter 29
It Feels Right

The group wandered back inside after the rainbows disappeared, feeling blessed for having seen them. "Dinner will be ready in two hours," Dani told her guests. "You can rest or walk on the beach or do whatever you like."

Sofia turned to Dani. "Do you think Pearl would mind some help in the kitchen?" She had no idea what Pearl was cooking but loved the process of preparing fresh food. Chopping vegetables was her meditation.

"Oh, that would be lovely," Dani said. "I'm sure Pearl would appreciate the help and enjoy the company." Sofia happily made her way to the kitchen.

Sapphire announced, "I'm going upstairs to rest." She had a lot to process and wanted to be alone.

Farrell knew she meant it. They shared the comfortable secret communication established as teenagers and carried out through their long friendship. "I'll be in my room doing some work," he said. "Let me know if you want to take a walk on the beach in a little while." Sapphire nodded at Farrell with a weary smile as she labored up the stairs.

Kai had already left. Judith and Dani were the only two remaining in the foyer. They looked at each other exchanging silent thoughts. "Let's walk on the beach," Dani finally offered. Judith nodded and they gathered their hats on the way out the back. They walked side by side with arms locked loosely, crooked at elbows. The seagulls escorted them, honking in welcome.

In the kitchen, Sofia smiled at a colorful display of vegetables lined up on the counter, waiting to be chopped, sliced, diced, and julienned. The tomatoes looked juicy. There were plump peppers in three colors, large onions, shiny purple eggplants, fresh arugula, and several vegetables that Sofia had not seen before.

Pearl's calm energy permeated the kitchen. She appeared to be about fifty years old, and Sofia calculated that would be the age of her daughter, if she had one.

"Mind if I help?" she asked Pearl.

"Sure," said Pearl. "I'm cooking Miss Lake's favorite. She checked with Judith, and you all enjoy eggplant parmesan, right?" Sofia nodded. "You can begin by cutting up those vegetables for the salad," said Pearl. She pointed to the butcher block and handed Sofia an apron. "The knives are sharp. Be careful."

Sofia washed her hands and donned the flowered apron. She sliced the peppers, carefully removing all seeds and pulp. The two women worked silently, listening to the rhythmic sounds of *chop chop* as they prepared the meal. Sofia quietly reflected on how generations of women in various cultures enjoyed this bonding tradition. Occasionally, Pearl and Sofia glanced at each other and smiled. It was divine, being in Dani's kitchen, slicing vegetables next to a sweet Hawaiian woman. Sofia sent a message of gratitude to the universe.

Resting in her room, Sapphire sensed she should check her emails. Her laptop was left at home to avoid doing work while on Kauai. She had set up an automatic response on her business email indicating she would be unavailable for the next week. Same with her voicemail. Yet, the sensation to check emails tugged at her. When the temptation could no longer be ignored, Sapphire pulled her hair back into a scrunchie, sat crossed-legged on her bed, and opened her emails on her iPhone.

She scrolled through the list until she found an email from a vaguely familiar name. *Betsy.* Sapphire clicked on the sender's address. *Betsy, Aunt Star's Neighbor* was the description on the contact card. If she opened just this one email, maybe the annoying tug would go away.

Sapphire read the message silently, then aloud. It was a method she employed when she struggled to comprehend the meaning behind the words. Sapphire learned the strategy in school from one of her beloved high school teachers at Wildhorse Academy. Hearing her voice, with added inflection, aided her comprehension.

> *Greetings from Betsy, Please accept my sincere condolences on the passing of your Aunt Star. As you know, we were not only good neighbors, but we were also good friends.*

Sapphire recalled Aunt Star referred to her neighbor as Nosey Betsy. She continued reading.

> *You might remember playing with my daughter Cindy when you were a child. I've attached a photo of you and Cindy building a sandcastle on the beach, with your aunt helping.*

How sweet of her, thought Sapphire. It'd be heartwarming to see a photo of Aunt Star when she was younger. She would open it after reading the rest of the email.

> *I noticed an older man go into Aunt Star's home last week. When I went to talk to him, he said he was a realtor from Ft. Meyers. I didn't realize that you would put the home up for sale so quickly.*

Sapphire checked the date of the email. It was sent the day after Aunt Star died. Dani had a realtor go to the house that soon?

> *Since Cindy is now a realtor on Sanibel Island, I hope you will consider giving her the listing.*

What? A solicitation for business in a letter of condolence! Sapphire abruptly closed the email before she completed reading it, never bothering to look at the photo. She pulled the scrunchie out of her hair and chastised herself. That's what she got for checking her emails. Sapphire threw her phone in a drawer and decided to keep it out of sight for the rest of her trip. She put on her bathing suit and beach shoes. She would go for a quick swim in the ocean to wash away the disturbing email.

An hour later, Sapphire knocked on Farrell's door. He opened it immediately, not surprised to see her. Farrell had become accustomed to his good friend's pattern of taking time to herself to absorb and process before sharing her experience. Sapphire appeared refreshed, with her hair still wet from the shower. She was wearing her favorite jean shorts and a long white tee shirt.

"Hi, Sapphire." He motioned her to the small sitting area in the corner where large brightly colored cushions rested along a window bench. Both made themselves comfortable on the cushions. Sapphire sat cross-legged like she always did as a teen.

"Do you believe that my mother dressed up like an actress, all sexy with teased hair and make-up?" she said. Farrell shrugged his shoulders. "You'd never fall for that act, would you?"

"I hope not," Farrell said, "but I know lots of guys who have." He shook his head. "Your mother sounds like a person I'd like to have known." He thought for a moment and added, "Your dad too."

"I miss them both," Sapphire said. "And Fisher." Sapphire gazed around the room. Something was missing. Ahh, there're no bottles. She gazed out the window at the ocean waves, took a deep breath, and let out an audible sigh. "Can I ask you something, Farrell?"

"Of course," he said. "Anything." He eyed her cautiously. Why would she ask permission first? They told each other everything and never requested permission to ask a question.

Sapphire tried to find the right words. When she couldn't figure out how to say what she wanted, she blurted out, "You haven't been drinking, Farrell." It'd been a constant concern of hers over the years as she watched her friend struggle to control his alcohol consumption. "I haven't seen you drink one drop." Sapphire had been so wound up in thoughts about her parents, Aunt Star, and meeting Dani, that she hadn't thought about anyone or anything else. Until now.

"Yeah," Farrell said. "I haven't." And for the first time, he didn't resent Sapphire bringing up the topic. He let out a sigh of relief. Farrell wanted to talk about it with Sapphire, but he was a man of few words. "Something about being here on Kauai. I don't know, but I feel good here and don't need it." Farrell also attributed feeling good to his new custom of helping others. He didn't quite know how to explain that. A tear ran down Sapphire's cheek. She had been worried, Farrell realized. The tear plopped onto her bare leg. She had become quite tan. It must have been all those morning beach walks while he was scouting property with Kai up in

Princeville. "I've been thinking about purchasing property here," Farrell said.

"Yes, I know you've looked for investments," Sapphire said. "It does seem like a wise business plan." Sapphire and Farrell's conversation had gone from talking about her parents, to his drinking, to business ventures in a matter of moments. It was always like that with them. No need to belabor any one topic. It amused Sapphire that they covered more ground in several minutes than most people did in countless hours. Farrell appreciated that quality in Sapphire, quite unlike the chatty women he had known throughout his life.

"I'm thinking about more than a business investment, "Farrell said. "I'd like to buy a home here." There, he said it. The thought had been floating around his mind for the past week, waiting for an opportunity to express it out loud. Sapphire had always been his trusted sounding board. "Maybe live here?" he added. It came out as a question, and Farrell realized he wanted Sapphire's blessing. "If I don't feel like drinking here, then maybe this is the right place for me."

Sapphire thought about the simple solution Farrell had stumbled upon to manage his drinking. Was it truly that simple? There had to be more. A person doesn't simply stop drinking because of a location change. "Wow, Farrell," she said. "That's a big move." She didn't want to be selfish but was beginning to panic at the thought of not having Farrell nearby. Losing Fisher was hard enough. She was already missing Farrell. Sapphire willed herself to be the supportive friend that Farrell deserved. "If you feel good here, I understand." She couldn't help herself as her words slipped out. "It's just that I'll miss you."

"Oh, Sapphire," Farrell said. "I didn't mean year-round." Sapphire looked up at him. "I meant maybe for the winter or vacations. I could work here, remotely. So could you." His tone was pleading. Farrell had gotten ahead of himself, presenting his ideas out of order. "If I did purchase a winter home here, maybe you'd like to visit." He hoped she would. "You've been uncomfortable in the cold Sedona winters lately, and you love the beach."

Sapphire thought about how she had just gone for a quick swim in the ocean when she felt overwhelmed. She hadn't thought about returning to Kauai, but hearing Farrell's plans to return got her thinking. "I do love the beach and I do feel good here," she said. "I love my work, but I could take a break from design contracts when I come here." The image of bathing in the ocean with Sofia flashed in her mind. "Maybe Sofia would come here too."

Farrell let out a breath, not realizing he had been holding it in. "And Judith too," Sapphire added. "She and Dani have become close."

Sapphire had said *when I come here,* not *if I came here.* And just like that, Farrell's mind was made up. He already knew which home he planned to show Sapphire before placing an offer. There would be room for all of them. Sapphire would relish decorating this unique Kauai home. Farrell smiled widely. In his mind, he had already moved into his new beach house, furnished, and decorated by Sapphire.

Chapter 30
Bon Appetit

Pearl and Sofia proudly served steaming plates of eggplant parmesan along with crusty Italian bread and a large colorful salad. Two places at the table were empty. "Aren't you and Kai joining us for dinner tonight? Dani asked Pearl.

"Kai wants to take his dad and me out to dinner. He has important news to discuss with us," said Pearl. Farrell smiled knowingly. "I hope you don't mind, Miss Lake." She clutched her apron. "I'll come back tomorrow morning to clean-up."

"Of course, Pearl," said Dani. "Go enjoy your family. No need to return in the morning. We'll take care of the dishes."

"Thank you, Miss Lake," said Pearl. "And thank you Sofia for your help." She smiled sweetly at Sofia.

"It was *my* pleasure to meet you, Pearl," Sofia said. "I hope to see you again before we leave."

"What a lovely woman," Sofia told the group once Pearl left. "At first, we just worked quietly side by side. Then we talked as if we'd known each other forever."

"The entire family worked for Aromaticus many years," Dani said. "Pearl, her husband, her father, and Kai. Her father is now the full-time caretaker and gardener. Sometimes Pearl and Kai help at Mango too."

Dani tossed the salad, filled the salad bowls, and passed them around the table. "Here's the mango vinaigrette dressing," she said, handing the bottie to Farrell. Then she twisted the mahogany peppermill, sprinkling freshly crushed black peppercorns on her salad. She passed the peppermill around the table. Next, she sliced the crusty bread. Steam escaped in the air.

"Kai is a very intelligent young man," said Farrell. "He is ambitious and energetic. With his college degree, he could've left the island for work but stayed close to home to help his family." Farrell twisted the peppermill and coarsely grated pepper fell to his salad.

"That's right," said Dani. "Strong family values and loyalty permeate the Hawaiian culture." She turned to Sapphire. "Just like the family you have here, Sapphire. Your loyal friends are your true family."

Sapphire put her hand to her heart. "Yes, Dani, and I couldn't ask for a better set of friends to be my family." Her stomach grumbled. "Now, let's eat!" Sapphire had a nagging thought. "Did my mother miss being a part of family meals?"

"Yes, Sapphire," Dani raised her brows. "Your mother did miss family meals and many other things. Your parents had long discussions about that tradition. Meals are bonding experiences as well as significant rituals in every society. Even the act of lovingly preparing a meal brings people together. Like you and Pearl this afternoon, Sofia."

"Yes, I was thinking about that," said Sofia. "Family recipes are handed down through generations and traditional foods are symbols of individual cultures." Sofia held up a piece of crusty Italian bread. "Food is more than nutrition. Food represents love." The others nodded at the bread in her hand.

"Farming and growing fresh produce are cornerstones of our society," said Judith. "And let's not forget the fishing industry, dairy farming, poultry farming, meatpacking, and grocery shopping." She shook her head.

Farrell said, "If the nutrition formula replaced the need to consume food, then hundreds of industries would die. Restaurants, factories, trucking, the entire production line would cease to exist."

"I didn't think of the wider implications with the formula," said Sapphire. She eyed her delicious-looking forkful of eggplant parmesan, holding it midstream between her plate and her mouth. "And baking. I would miss birthday cakes, cupcakes, cookies, and pie. Was my mother tempted to eat while taking the formula?"

"Jane didn't experience hunger when taking the formula," Dani said. "Neither did Andre. I didn't either. It was an odd sensation to have no desire to eat." She put her fork and knife down on her plate, remembering how it felt to have no hunger.

"If the formula helped people avoid junk food and too much sugar, we would all be a lot healthier," Judith said. "And maybe live longer."

"And think about the medical breakthroughs for people with cancer and eating disorders," Sofia said. "So many lives could be saved."

"And the problem of world hunger could be solved," said Farrell.

Dani nodded. "On the other hand, consider the environmental impact if industries travelled to the Amazon Jungle to secure the plants for the formula. They could destroy sacred lands in search of the rare plant leaves and the plants could be driven to extinction." She was worked up. "We've already lost a large portion of the Amazon jungle to deforestation."

Farrell winced. "It must have been agonizing for Jane and Andre."

Tears slipped down Dani's cheeks. "I'm sorry," she said. "It is just that this reminds me of the same conversations I had with Jane and Andre so many years ago." Judith reached over and patted Dani's hand. Sapphire handed her a tissue. "I miss them," Dani said. She lifted the napkin from her lap and placed it on the table. "Excuse me," she said. "I'll be right back."

After five minutes, Judith stood up. "I'll go check on her," she said. "This week has been so joyful, but also so emotional for Dani." She left the dining room.

Sapphire and Sofia looked at each other. Should they continue eating or wait? "Well, this eggplant parm is amazing, Sofia," Farrell said. "Did you get the recipe from Pearl?" He took a large forkful to his mouth. Sapphire stared at Farrell. "What?" he said. "I don't want to let this great meal go to waste."

Chapter 31
The List

Dani and Judith returned to the dining room with their arms loosely linked. Dani carried a new white velvet Aromaticus bag. Both ladies sat, and Dani placed the bag under the table. "Let's finish this lovely dinner and enjoy dessert, the way food was meant to be enjoyed," she said. "Jane didn't want her discovery to deprive people of the joy of food."

Farrell gave Sapphire an *I told you so* look. He wiped his mouth after finishing every morsel on his plate, mopping up the last bit of sauce with bread.

"Dessert?" asked Farrell. "What's for dessert?" Thoughts of food replaced thoughts of drinking, and Farrell was ravenous. He'll have to up his exercise routine.

"Does anyone want tiramisu?" asked Dani, hoping to resurrect the happy mood before her tearful outburst. "It's really delicious."

Sapphire and Sofia exchanged a glance. It was a challenge keeping up with Dani's rapid mood change.

"Tiramisu?" asked Judith. "I was looking forward to that dessert the night you mentioned it at Beach House, but then we were all too full and so tired."

"Yes," said Dani. "It can't be missed. You now have another opportunity to sample it."

Sofia sat lost in thought. Her time cooking with Pearl was so special. A world without the need for food was overwhelming and sad to imagine. She heard Dani and Judith speak a familiar word and was jarred back to her surroundings. "What?" asked Sofia. "Did someone say tiramisu?"

"Yes," said Dani. "We are having tiramisu. Remember Makani, our maître di from the Beach House restaurant?"

"How can we forget him," Farrell said. "He recited the *Pono Pledge* and the children joined in." Sapphire smiled.

"Well," Dani said. "He sent over their tiramisu since we missed ordering it our first night out. Makani didn't want you to leave Kauai without tasting the best dessert on the island."

"I'll have a serving," said Farrell. He turned to Sapphire. She loved tiramisu.

"Okay," said Sapphire. "I turned it down once. I was so tired that night. I don't want to miss out this time."

Sofia pushed her chair back and rose to go to the kitchen. "I'll bring it in and serve," she said. "I knew about it all along." She smiled slyly. "I was in the kitchen with Pearl when the caterer from Beach House delivered it."

As Sofia returned with five small glass bowls balanced evenly on a large tray, all eyes followed her. "I worked as a waitress through high school and college," she said. "That's where I learned how to balance serving trays." The stemless goblets with the tiramisu contained layers of espresso-dipped ladyfingers, and mascarpone cream, topped with a fine dusting of dark chocolate. No one could resist.

"This is heavenly," said Judith. "Thank you, Sofia for helping to prepare such a lovely meal." The others uttered sounds of *ah* and *mmm* as all bowls were emptied.

Sapphire and Sofia stood up simultaneously. "We'll clean up," Sapphire said. They gathered the plates, bowls, and silverware.

"I'll help," Farrell said, collecting the remaining glasses and napkins. "I'll do the dishes too."

"I knew you were a gem," Dani said with a smile. Judith felt relieved. Dani had resumed her steady calm. "Please come back to the den when you're all finished, I have something to show you," Dani said.

After the dishes were done, the group settled into their comfortable seats. Dani removed a three-ring binder from the white velvet bag. The binder contained pages encased in clear plastic sleeves. Each sleeve protected an official-looking document with the name of an organization and its accompanying mission statement.

Dani lifted the binder and slowly turned the pages for all to see. Everyone could see the names in large, bold letters. There were about twenty-five in all. The names included: National Restaurant Association, the United Farm Workers of America, the American Trucking Associations, the American Dairy Association, the National Fisheries Institute, and more. Sofia recognized the symbols for The American Medical Association and The American Cancer Society.

"These are organizations that would have had a vested interest in seeing the nutrition formula destroyed or produced. The idea of a nutrition substitute became an urban legend, as it circulated throughout various industries. For almost five years, Jane had received no contact from anyone expressing interest in the formula. Then the contacts resumed. We couldn't figure out why. Representatives of these associations and institutes approached Jane. It was a fishing expedition. Jane held steadfast to her claim that there was no such formula being studied or produced. Dani paused and glimpsed outside. Moonlight cast long shadows as the palm trees gently swayed.

Sofia fidgeted in her seat. "How did Jane know that the approaches were from these companies? Did they just hand her their business cards and introduce themselves?"

"Not at all," said Dani. "They claimed to represent a wealthy investor or an anonymous philanthropic group." Dani closed her eyes briefly, remembering. "Jane, Andre, and I were suspicious and researched each person who approached her." Dani smirked. "Jane was creative and sly. She followed these unsuspecting goofs, sometimes sitting at hotel bars. She resurrected her sexy damsel-in-distress costume to blend in. In that way, Jane went unnoticed as she overheard conversations from her barstool."

"Were they dangerous?" Sapphire asked. "Did any of them threaten her or our family again?" Sapphire remembered her childhood as normal and safe. Her parents called her their little star. That is until they sent her to boarding school and changed her name to Sapphire. The star-sapphire gem hanging on a necklace close to her heart always reminded Sapphire that she was both Star and Sapphire.

"Yes," said Dani. "There was danger. Not initially, but some of them became demanding when Jane was resolute in her insistence that no such formula existed." Dani wrung her hands. "That's why Jane and Andre severed ties with Aromaticus and removed themselves from the scientific community. If they continued their scientific careers, they would continue to be surrounded with suspicions about the existence of the formula." Dani covered her mouth as she yawned. "I will tell you more about that tomorrow. But there's one more thing I want you to see tonight. I remembered it during our earlier conversation."

Dani turned to the final page in the binder. It was a handwritten list. Sapphire recognized her mother's delicate handwriting, even though it had been forty-five years since she had last seen it. Dani opened the rings on the binder with a loud click. Sapphire flinched at the sound. She carefully removed the page with Jane's list and handed it to Sapphire.

THINGS I WOULD MISS was the title at the top of the page. Listed neatly below were items that filled the entire sheet. Sapphire read aloud to the rest of the group.

> *Blowing out candles on my birthday cake.*
> *Drinking chicken soup when sick.*
> *Picking fresh strawberries.*
> *Butterscotch ice cream dripping down a cone.*

Sipping hot chocolate on a cold day.
Melting marshmallows for s'mores.
Grocery shopping with Andre.
Baking fresh bread.
Tending to my herb garden.
 Morning coffee.
Ordering a pizza with Dani.

Sapphire stopped reading. There was one more item on the list highlighted in bold letters. She' had not seen her birth name written in her mother's distinctive handwriting in decades.

Dani already knew the last item by heart. She had read the list repeatedly over the years. First with Jane and Andre, then alone after they died. She took a slow deep breath, and Dani spoke the words Jane had recited over and over again.

BAKING COOKIES WITH STAR.

Overcome, Sapphire sat in silence.

Chapter 32
Waimea Canyon

The group sat in silent reverie with Sapphire. Finally, she said, "I remember baking chocolate chip cookies with my mother. She let me lick the spoon." She smiled contentedly. "It's a sweet memory." The others smiled back. "Thank you for sharing that with me, Dani." Sapphire stifled a yawn and said, "I'm tired. Ready for bed. What's planned for tomorrow?"

"Tomorrow's Wednesday," said Dani. "Kai's taking us to see Waimea Canyon in the morning."

"I can't believe it's only been three days since we arrived on Sunday," said Sapphire. "I'm looking forward to seeing Waimea Canyon tomorrow."

"Kai's picking us up early in the morning before the afternoon fog settles in and clouds all views," said Dani. "Let's get some sleep and meet down here at 5:30 am."

Judith said good night to Dani with a hug. Then she retreated upstairs with Sapphire, Sofia, and Farrell. Dani fell asleep, too exhausted to prepare her evening tea.

That night, Sapphire dreamed about baking chocolate chip cookies with her mother and woke with lingering warm feelings. She held the star-sapphire necklace in her palm and cherished it close to her heart. Her mind was filled with questions. What type of danger surrounded her parents? Why didn't Aunt Star tell her about her parents' best friend? Will Dani finally share that part of the story today? She looked at the pile of white velvet bags in the corner of her room. At the end of each day, Sapphire found a new one at her door as Dani gifted her with the memorabilia shared that day. It was her treasure trove.

After an early breakfast of oatmeal, coffee, and croissants, the group headed out as the sun rose. Kai drove along the south shore of Kauai, then headed north following the highway to Waipo'o Falls. "We'll stop at some vantage points along the way. The canyon is ten miles long and three thousand feet deep." Kai loved his tour guide role. "It was formed by a deep incision of the Waimea River. Mount Wai'ale'ale rises from the island's central peak. The extreme rainfall makes this canyon one of the wettest places on earth." He glanced in his rearview mirror. His passengers sat upright in their seats, keenly attentive.

"Waimea Canyon is one of the most remarkable geological formations in Hawaii," Kai continued. "It's known as the Grand Canyon of the Pacific."

Farrell said, "I wonder how it compares to the Grand Canyon's south and north rim in Arizona."

"I've never seen the Grand Canyon," said Kai. "Heard it's incredible."

Soon Kai inched the SUV along the canyon road providing great views of Waimea Canyon. "Truly magnificent," said Sofia. "I've seen the Grand Canyon once. This is more vibrant and closer."

"How was this canyon formed?" ask Farrell.

"Erosion and collapse," said Kai. "Just like the other Hawaiian Islands, Kauai is the top of an enormous volcano rising from the ocean floor." He adjusted his sunglasses. "Four million years ago, while Kauai was still erupting, a portion of the island collapsed, forming a depression which then filled with lava flows."

"I'm glad we have a clear morning to experience the vivid colors. The bright red you see is basalt that was originally black," Kai explained. "Check out the red sand and look up there at the waterfalls. Waimea in Hawaiian means reddish water." Farrell snapped photos with his smartphone.

"Look at the canyon's spectacular colors," Sapphire said. "Reminds me of the red rocks in Sedona." Had her parents viewed this magical canyon when they were on Kauai? Was that why they chose to send her to a school in Arizona, to be near another magical canyon?

"You can see Ni'ihau Island from this viewpoint," Kai said as they parked. He was prepared to hand out bottles of cold water when he noticed that each had brought their own Aromaticus thermoses. After their brief stop, he continued driving the final section of the winding road, slowing down around the sharp switchbacks.

"We can get sandwiches up ahead at the park," Kai said. He couldn't wait to make his announcement.

Sofia heard the word *sandwiches* and looked forward to their lunch. Food always tasted so good at a picnic. No more picnic lunches if the formula substituted for food, she lamented.

The air at Koke'e State Park felt refreshing and cool. Everyone selected a sandwich at the rustic market and settled down to eat their picnic lunch. "Thank you, Kai," said Sapphire. "You've been the quintessential tour guide."

Kai looked at Farrell, who nodded. "I'm applying for a master's degree with a joint major in tourism management and business administration," Kai announced proudly. Farrell tilted his head toward Kai, encouraging him to continue. "Farrell will mentor me and I'll manage his Kauai investment properties he plans to purchase."

"Wonderful!" said Dani. "You're a perfect candidate." She patted his shoulder. "Farrell is lucky to have you here on the island. Where is this program located?"

"That's the beauty of it," said Farrell. "It's an online program, so Kai can remain right here." He didn't share that he'll sponsor Kai by paying his tuition. Investing in people with ability always paid off for Farrell. Not only was it a sound financial investment, but a rewarding personal experience.

"I talked to my parents last night and they're on board," Kai said. "They're looking forward to working for me." Kai's smile was as wide as the brim of his big straw hat. "I'm so grateful to have met all of you," he said. "Mahalo nui loa."

Chapter 33
Farmers

On the drive back to Mango, Kai stopped at Spouting Horn. He led Dani and the others on the short path to the edge of the railing overlooking the geyser. Mist rose from the ocean. "Every several minutes," said Kai, "with only a tiny spritz of warning, the ocean sprays high into the sky, like Yellowstone's Old Faithful."

Suddenly, the mist shot upwards, startling Sofia. "That happened fast," she said.

"How long does it last?" asked Judith.

"Several seconds," said Kai. "Keep your eye on it, or you'll miss it."

The group watched the waterspout in awe. Nearby, children squealed in delight, and a dog barked. Farrell grabbed his hat just as the strong breeze threatened to steal it right off his head.

Dani never tired of seeing the water spray high into the air. It brought her back to happy memories with Jane and Andre.

The gust of wind whipped Sapphire's long hair across her face. She barely noticed, lost in thought. "Oh," she said. "This is where my father proposed to my mother. Right?" She brushed the hair away from her face. "Dani, it looks exactly like the photos you showed us. Thank you for giving them to me. I'll cherish them."

Dani smiled. "I remember taking the photo of their marriage proposal, timing the exact moment to snap the geyser at its highest point."

Sofia wrapped her arms around her body as the wind picked up. Judith tightened her scarf to cover her neck. Both observed in pure delight, despite feeling chilled.

After Kai delivered everyone back to Mango, he shook hands with Farrell. "Thank you again for offering to mentor me." Farrell smiled as he watched Kai drive away. He felt confident that he had made a good decision, bolstered by the encouraging reaction of his friends earlier that day. He marveled as he fine-tuned his newly developed attribute of helping others. The joy it brought him far surpassed the fleeting numbness he experienced with alcohol.

"I'm ready to share more of the story," Dani said. "Let's gather in the outdoor patio garden in about fifteen minutes."

The afternoon sun warmed the colorful garden as the group gathered around the table. More flowers appeared to have blossomed since the group arrived. Mango iced tea with lime slices glistened in the sunlight. Rivulets of condensation ran down the outside of the glass pitcher. Familiar bowls of macadamia nuts in a variety of flavors sat on the table invitingly.

Dani poured everyone a glass of mango tea. Then she spoke. "Jane and Andre decided that it had to appear that they severed all ties with Aromaticus." She clasped her hands in her lap. "If they no longer worked for Aromaticus, and were no longer scientists, maybe the unwanted interest in the secret formula would disappear."

"Really?" Sapphire said. "It must've been a difficult decision. Sounds like being scientists was their passion."

"It was a loss for all of us. But it felt like the only option. Your parents hoped it would dispel all rumors about the existence of the formula," said Dani. Sapphire felt sad that her parents lost their careers they were so passionate about. Was the formula worth it?

Farrell grabbed a handful of nuts, then passed the bowl around.

Dani took a breath then continued. "They planned on buying a farm to grow herbs and plants. Andre agreed to use the inheritance from his parents. Since Andre and Jane grew up on farms, both had the needed skills. They would combine their farming experience with their scientific knowledge of plants."

"You mean like for medicinal purposes?" asked Sofia. "Drugs used to treat many diseases are derived from plants found in the Amazon Rainforest. It's known as the pharmacy of the world."

"Yes," said Dani. "They wanted to pivot from producing essential oils to producing plants for use in medicines." She took a sip of tea. "Jane and Andre were passionate about contributing their scientific knowledge for a better world." All nodded in appreciation.

"We had to make their departure from Aromaticus look convincing. Jane even wrote a script," Dani laughed. "I was such a poor actress; I couldn't play a believable role. Instead, I was instructed to stare blankly at the floor, as Jane stormed out of the lab in Asheville, screaming 'I QUIT!' She could have been an academy award-winning actress." Sapphire's eyes widened, as Dani continued. "Everyone heard her outburst, which was the plan."

Dani remembered the shocked faces of other Aromaticus employees. No one expected that from Jane. "The gossip mill churned through the company and throughout the scientific community. Andre also submitted a terse letter of resignation. Jane and Andre published a brief farewell in one of the scientific newsletters. *We thank the scientific community for your collegial support over the years.*

It is time for us to transition to new careers. We will miss you all."

Judith nodded. "Throughout my career with the Witness Protection Program we often faked altercations, sometimes even deaths. People are easily deceived into believing what they think they see."

"But did they really quit?" Sapphire asked. "Or was that just for appearances?"

"They officially resigned from their jobs at Aromaticus. You all moved to Columbia."

"I remember," said Sapphire. "I was ten years old and just completed elementary school in Asheville." She smoothed her hair back with both hands. "I thought it would be exciting to live in another country."

"That's right, Sapphire," Dani said. "They first selected an American school for you to attend and then searched for an existing farm to purchase. "By that time, I'd risen through the ranks of the company. During the transition, I paid them a temporary salary as consultants under assumed names." Dani still felt proud of her sly tricks in massaging the budget.

"Within a month, your parents purchased their farm and reinvented themselves. They hired migrant workers to help." Dani had been amazed they were able to create these new careers. "Their farmland was close to the locations of the rare indigenous plants they were collecting to produce the formula. It also kept them close to ancient clans to learn more from the elders about traditional medicinal uses of herbs and plants." Dani turned to Sapphire. "Your parents rented an apartment in town to be near to your school since the farm was further away in a rural location."

"I visited the farm with them sometimes on weekends," Sapphire said in an exited voice. "It wasn't that far away. It had a lot of open space, very different from the village we lived in. I played with the migrant workers' children and got to practice my Spanish."

"Your parents were fluent in Spanish," said Dani. "Both studied the language in high school. They were comfortable with the language from their college days in Albuquerque when they often took trips to Mexico."

"We spoke English in school," said Sapphire. "But I picked up Spanish quickly while living in Columbia."

"Yes, Sapphire," Dani said. "I heard from your aunt that you acclimated very well." Dani had been so relieved. "Once your parents were satisfied that you adjusted to living in a new country and were happy at your new school, they attended to their work. Your mother was passionate about studying the effects of the formula, and your father shared that passion. They continued to create the formula when they accumulated enough of the endangered plant leaves."

The sunset was turning to twilight. Another beautiful evening.

Dani repositioned herself in her chair. "Down in Columbia, Jane and Andre secretly studied further effects of the formula. They took turns using it and recorded their observations. Andre set up a make-shift medical lab to analyze blood and tissue samples. They sent me coded messages about their discoveries."

Dani took a sip of her tea, although she would need a bathroom break soon. "I secretly continued to study the formula back in Asheville. Aromaticus still had the original equipment from Jane's lab. That enabled me to examine the properties of the formula over time and evaluate its stability under different temperatures."

"You produced and studied the chemical properties of the formula in Asheville?" asked Sofia, "While Jane and Andre produced and studied it in Columbia?"

"Yes," said Dani. "That is exactly what happened." She squirmed in her seat. "Honestly, I can't believe their plan to become farmers and continue their research on the formula worked out."

She looked at Sapphire who was also shaking her head in disbelief. "Your parents established a profitable business by selling their produce to local distributors."

Dani couldn't wait any longer. "Excuse me," she said. "I'll be right back. Nature calls." She scurried to the bathroom as quickly as she could.

"I'll be right back too," said Judith. She had been waiting for a good time to excuse herself for the same reason. The others stood up to stretch. Farrell munched on more nuts.

When Dani and Judith returned, Dani continued. "Jane and Andre were desperate to dispel all suspicions of the existence of the secret formula. Since I continued to work for Aromaticus, their fictitious clean break included ending ties with me. To be convincing, it had to appear that I severed my relationship with them. It was not easy." Dani frowned. "We kept in contact with telephone rings and teddy bears."

"Telephone rings?" asked Farrell. "Teddy bears?"

"Jane and Andre called the lab every day around noontime, using the secret code we had agreed upon. One ring meant *all is well*. Two rings meant *we are making progress*. Three rings meant *wait for instructions on where to meet us*. Four rings meant *destroy all research and shut down the lab.*

Five rings meant *it's safe to pick up the phone.*" Dani only received one or two rings daily, until the fatal day when she received four rings. To this day, Dani maintained the habit of waiting for five rings before picking up calls around noontime.

Dani turned to Sapphire. "Your parents would send stuffed teddy bears to Aunt Star, with more detailed messages inside. Since you visited every summer, Aunt Star set up a bedroom for you. She kept the teddy bears on your bed."

"I remember," Sapphire said.

"The first teddy bear had a note revealing that Jane and Andre were studying the effects of the formula on muscle mass and fat distribution." Dani looked at Sapphire. "You remember Aunt Star's teddy bear collection?"

"Yes," said Sapphire. "I thought she was collecting them for me. I liked them when I was ten, but by the time I got to be a teenager, I outgrew them. I couldn't understand why Aunt Star kept getting new ones. Every year I visited, she would have three or four new teddy bears. I told her I wasn't a baby anymore. Then, one year when I visited, they were all gone." She palmed her star-sapphire. Her voice cracked. "Oh, that's when my parents died."

Dani nodded sadly. "Before they died, your aunt saved each teddy bear your parents sent. I could only visit Star two or three times a year, otherwise we might have aroused suspicion." Dani thought it all sounded so silly now, but there were times when she felt like she had been followed. "I carefully deconstructed the seams of the teddy bears which held folded-up papers inside. The papers had information from your parents updating me on their research."

Dani had waited with excitement to learn of Jane and Andre's observations through the teddy bears. "One note described the effects of the formula on the digestive and elimination system," Dani said. "All were found to be normal."

"Mom told me that mint helped with digestion," Sapphire said. "I thought it was Aunt Star, but now I remember it was my mother who introduced me to mint and taught me how to infuse it in water. She also taught me how to grow mint."

"One of your mother's discoveries," Dani said, "was that a certain variety of mint activated an essential oil from a rare plant, which enhanced the formula." She turned her head to stretch her neck and winced at a creaking sound. "Old age is no fun. We hoped that mint activated a natural response in the body to regenerate youthful cells."

"Ah, the elusive fountain of youth," Sofia said. "Essential oils have a lot of anecdotal reports of improved health. The western medical community has begun to publish documented evidence of their benefits." She looked at Judith, remembering her use of lavender oil for calming.

"So, you severed contact with my parents since you worked for Aromaticus, and it needed to appear that they no longer had anything to do with the scientific community?" Sapphire asked. "But they still secretly continued to study the formula, and you secretly maintained a lab at the Aromaticus factory in Asheville?"

Dani nodded, but Sapphire wasn't sure it made sense. She had to ask more. "And this was to dispel dangerous investors who believed there was a money-making formula, and stop them from threatening my parents?" That's a lot of effort to keep something secret. Was the formula that important? Maybe it did make sense. "Did the plan work? Did people believe that you were no longer in contact with them? And that there was no secret formula?"

"We thought so," Dani said. "For almost five years, there were no approaches. Then one day, governmental officials came to their farm to verify compliance with agricultural regulations. When they saw their make-shift lab, they questioned your parents. The inspectors were suspicious of the explanation that it was for studying the soil composition. Soon after, the telegrams and threats began again. Finally, it escalated to kidnapping attempts."

"Kidnapping?" said Farrell. "Was that a typical tactic of pharmaceutical companies?" He scrunched his face in disbelief. "Judith, what about your experience with the Witness Protection Program during that period of time?"

"That sounds more like the work of a criminal organization," Judith said, "or a corrupt sector of government."

Dani didn't know what Sapphire remembered. "There were two attempts, despite your parents hiring a security guard for you." It shocked and frightened Dani when she heard about it from Star. "The second failed kidnapping attempt was followed by a threatening telegram to your parents. The threat warned them to finally release the formula." Dani hoped Sapphire didn't recall much about it, but the pained look on her face revealed otherwise.

"Oh, I remember a little, mostly I tried to forget." said Sapphire. "That's when they sent me to boarding school in Sedona and changed my name to Sapphire." She wrung her hands nervously.

Sapphire's stomach twisted. Sounded like her parents were trying to protect the secret formula more than their child.

Dani squeezed Sapphire's hand from across the table. "I looked forward to the day that I could see you again and tell you about your parents." A wave of exhaustion overcame Dani. "Please excuse me now, I didn't realize how draining this would be." Dani rose slowly. "I hope you don't mind but I'll continue to tell you more tomorrow." She walked back inside the house, leaving the others sitting in the garden. It was dark now, except for the moon and the twinkling stars.

"What a time to leave!" said Farrell. The rest were also taken aback at Dani's abrupt departure. He let out a long sigh. "We'll just have to wait until tomorrow to hear more."

Sofia yawned and said, "Well, I guess she was too tired to continue." She looked at the others. "We're all looking tired." She yawned again.

Sapphire sat silently looking like a lost child. Judith did not get up to follow Dani. She could feel the tug on her heart. Sapphire needed her now.

Chapter 34
Kidnapping Foiled

Farrell, Judith and Sofia remained with Sapphire. "Let's go back inside," Judith said, "It's dark and getting cold out here." The four friends went indoors. The women sat on the couch in the den and Farrell sat on the lounge chair opposite them. Sofia recognized that Sapphire was remembering and processing her traumatic memories. Judith sat next to Sapphire and held her hand.

Farrell felt out of place, not sure how to be helpful. He needed to grasp the dire situation Sapphire had been in. "You were in so much danger that your parents hired a bodyguard to protect you?"

Sapphire no longer appeared like a lost child. Her jaw was tense. She was simmering. Her friends waited.

Finally, she spoke. "My parents were *not* protecting me the way parents should protect their children!" Sapphire's voice rose in anger. "My parents' *secret formula* was my *secret competition*."

Farrell's jaw dropped. He had never seen Sapphire this angry. She was justified, but it still surprised him. At least she's not holding it in.

Sapphire's eyes turned cold as she spoke louder. "Dani keeps saying how much my parents loved me, but I think she's blinded by her admiration of them. Why didn't they just remove the formula from their lives and focus on raising their child?" She turned to Sofia. "Do you consider that a *normal* parenting response to attempted kidnappings?"

Sofia was taken aback by Sapphire's outburst. She had never seen Sapphire blow up before. Maybe it was a good for her to express her anger with comforting friends. She had the same thoughts about Jane and Andre's choice to prioritize the formula over their only child. "I'm not going to defend your parents, Sapphire." The pregnancy was a surprise. Did Jane and Andre truly consider placing the well-being of their child ahead of their careers? "It sounds like they loved you but didn't know how to juggle their professional ambitions with parenting. You should've been their first priority."

Sapphire jumped out of her chair. "What's to juggle! I was their *child* and should have automatically come *first!*" Sofia, Farrell, and Judith grimly nodded. Sapphire fell back into her chair. Her lips quivered.

A lump formed in her throat. She gulped before speaking.

"I was fifteen and so tired of wearing my boring school uniform," Sapphire said with tears in her eyes. No one asked her what she meant. "I went into the ladies' room. I was with my friends. At an ice cream parlor. After school. An elegant woman followed me inside. Asked if I wanted to be a model." Sapphire spoke in a flat cadence. "Her clothes were fashionable. So elegant. She said that since I was tall, slim, beautiful, and moved gracefully, I'd be a perfect model. I was thrilled at the prospect of wearing stylish clothing."

Judith poured a glass of water and handed it to Sapphire, but she was too upset to drink. "The woman invited me to meet the modeling scout. He was just outside in his car." Sapphire stared straight ahead, almost unaware of her friends next to her. "I stepped outside with the beautiful woman's arm around me. She led me to the dark sedan with tinted windows. The woman opened the car door. Started guiding me inside. My driver, Mr. Lorenzo, was parked and waiting outside for me. He saw the whole thing. Ran over, grabbed me. Pulled me away just in time."

Sapphire glimpsed Judith on one side of her, Sofia on the other, and Farrell sitting across the room. "I didn't realize the serious danger. My parents warned me that I should never go with strangers." Sapphire recalled feeling disappointed at the time with not getting to model fashionable clothes. "I was too naïve to understand the horrifying fate I narrowly escaped." Her face turned pale.

"Take a deep breath, Sapphire," said Sofia as she held her hand. Farrell watched. The moment felt like a women's circle with no space for a man, even a close friend.

Sapphire took some deep breaths and sipped water. "Details are coming back now," she said. "The second time was a month later. My neighbor, an older woman, Miss Ana, was walking her dog. I was less than one block from my home. The dog was very large. A German Shephard. His name was Guarda. A loud motorcycle spooked him. Guarda pulled away abruptly from Miss Ana." Sapphire's words came out faster. "Miss Ana couldn't run to chase him. I ran down the block to catch his leash. Two large men appeared out of nowhere. They grabbed me. Guarda heard me scream. He charged us. The men let go. Ran into a car." She took a trembling breath. "If it wasn't for Guarda, those men would have kidnapped me."

Sapphire looked down at her star-sapphire necklace resting on her chest and held it tightly. "I was shaking and couldn't move. Mr. Lorenzo lived on that block. Heard my screams. Came running. He grabbed my hand. Practically carried me back home. Guarda, on his leash, followed behind. I was so scared." Sapphire shuddered.

"After that close call, my parents hired Mr. Lorenzo to be my bodyguard. He was a retired military officer, very muscular and protective of me. I was already six feet tall at age fifteen and he was a head taller than me. His mere presence was intimidating. I felt safe." Sapphire swallowed hard. "Only two weeks later a third incident occurred. It was the deciding factor. The desk clerk at my school delivered an envelope to me in my classroom. She thought it was dropped off by a friend of my parents. It was an innocuous white envelope with my name written on the outside." Judith leaned forward as Sapphire continued. "Inside the envelope was a note. It wasn't a note from my parents. It contained a message to my parents. I never understood what the words meant. Until now." Sapphire paused and her dazed look returned. Sofia, Judith, and Farrell waited for Sapphire to continue.

"I remember the message to this day. *Tell your parents to give it up or else their star will vanish.* It was written in English." Sapphire blinked several times. "It didn't occur to me that their *star* was me. I was their *Star*. That was my name, before I was sent away to boarding school."

Farrell stared at Sapphire. This happened right before they met. How could he help her now?

"When I showed the note to my parents, they both turn as white as the envelope. I didn't think their work was *dangerous*. I couldn't understand their over-the-top reaction. I was sent to Wild Horse Academy in Sedona with a new name a week later." Sapphire's speech quieted down to normal. "I trusted my parents knew what was best. Now I wonder if the note was referring to the secret formula. *Give it up* meant *give up the formula*?" Sapphire stopped talking. Her brow formed a deep crease. "They chose the *formula* over *me*!"

Farrell couldn't restrain himself any longer. Women's circle or not, he wanted to be present for Sapphire. He kneeled in front of Sapphire, so they were at eye level. " I'm so sorry that this happened to you. I wish I knew about it when we first met. You seemed so serene. I had no idea what you'd experienced right before arriving at our new school."

Sapphire saw a tenderness that Farrell rarely displayed. He had always shown he cared for her. They were pals right from the start. This was different. This was a deeper connection based on her raw honesty. Sapphire collapsed into his arms and wept.

Sofia and Judith quietly carried the food and drinks to the kitchen, allowing the two friends a sphere of privacy. Farrell didn't notice. He was viscerally feeling Sapphire's emotions. His eyes became misty as his shirt soaked up Sapphire's tears.

Chapter 35
Flashbacks

Memories of the attempted kidnappings flooded Sapphire's brain as Farrell held her in his arms. Terror rose from her chest. Why was her heart beating so rapidly *now* when she was no longer in danger? She repeated to herself: *I'm safe now, I'm safe now.*

After a good cry, Sapphire pulled back from Farrell. Her heartbeat returned to normal. "Sorry I soaked your shirt. I feel a little better now. I hadn't thought about the kidnapping attempts in so many years. Guess I blocked them out soon after they happened."

"Don't worry about my shirt," Farrell said. "I'm grateful that Mr. Lorenzo and Guarda were there to protect you." Sapphire silently thanked her guardian angels. She hoped that she had expressed sincere appreciation at the time.

Sofia and Judith were already in their rooms with lights out by the time Sapphire and Farrell went upstairs. Sapphire assured Farrell that she was fine and just wanted to go to sleep. But when she got into bed, she felt afraid to fall asleep. Would she have nightmares? When she finally fell off to sleep, dreaded images flashed in her mind. She tossed and turned until she startled awake.

Sapphire sat up in bed and took deep calming breaths. Her nightshirt was drenched with sweat, and she felt chilled. She wrapped her long hair in clips and tucked it under a shower cap. Then she stepped into the hot shower and inhaled the steam. The lavender-scented soap calmed her nerves. As soon as she had enough, Sapphire wrapped herself in the plush white terry robe to keep her warm.

When she emerged from the bathroom, Sapphire noticed a folder had been slipped under her door. She smiled at Farrell's colorful business logo. She had designed it for him. With folder in hand, Sapphire crawled into bed.

The note inside simply said, *Something to distract you. Design ideas?* Sapphire found a floor plan for a house and two dozen large glossy photos. The photos displayed different angles of the rooms, along with close-ups of some of its unique architectural features. Must be the house Farrell planned to show her. She leafed through the photos and smiled again. It certainly was a distraction. Just what she needed. Farrell knew her well.

Where would she place her signature skylight? She selected the bedroom she hoped would be hers. Visions of fabric swatches pushed away images of kidnapping attempts.

Sapphire fell asleep that night with the folder open and the photos sprawled over her bed. She dreamed of decorating each room with whitewashed walls, pale aqua tones, and rich turquoise shades, reflecting the Hawaiian ocean and sky.

Chapter 36
Celestial

The next morning, Sapphire, Sofia, Farrell, Judith, and Dani gathered for breakfast in the outdoor garden. Each one of them had awoken early.

"How are you feeling this morning, my dear?" Judith asked Sapphire.

"I had a good night's sleep and pleasant dreams," Sapphire said with a reassuring smile.

Farrell sat next to Sapphire. Was she okay after the previous night's memories? Did she like the house photos? She hadn't mentioned anything yet. Should he ask her?

Dani said, "How about we go for a walk this morning before it gets too hot, and then we can gather inside. She turned to Sapphire. "I'd like to finish telling you more about your parents."

"I look forward to hearing more this afternoon," Sapphire said. "I had something different in mind for this morning." She glanced at Farrell, as if she had read his mind. She wanted to see the house as much as he wanted to show it to her.

"Farrell, how about you and I take a drive this morning?"

Farrell grinned. Just what he hoped for.

"Dani, would you mind if Sapphire and I took the vehicle out on our own?" He wanted private time with Sapphire, so didn't want Kai to be their driver. "I have a valid driver's license and know my way around the island, thanks to Kai."

"Sure, go ahead," said Dani. "The keys are in the bowl by the doorway." Judith was already holding her hat and water. Both locked arms at the crook of their elbows in their familiar grasp as they headed towards the beach.

Sofia said, "I'll clean up out here and then I'll go sit by the beach." She was glad to have time to herself. She had become accustomed to having more alone time back home in Sedona and missed it.

Farrell adjusted the driver's seat, then the rearview mirror. Next, he adjusted the side-view mirrors while the air conditioning kicked in. His first time driving on Kauai. Sapphire sat in the front seat for the first time. It felt like they already lived there. Farrell felt like they were teenagers, getting a taste of freedom.

Before they reached the end of the driveway, Sapphire had already opened the folder from the night before. She leafed through the pages. "So," she said. "Take me to our new home."

Farrell glanced at the markings on the pages when he halted at the first stop sign.

"I have some color ideas and I know which room I want." She quickly added, "If it's okay with you?"

Farrell laughed as he drove north toward Princeville. "That depends on which room it is. Don't I get the first choice?"

Sapphire giggled. "We'll see about that."

Farrell felt ten pounds lighter enjoying the banter they've had since high school. "I haven't put an offer in yet," added Farrell, "so maybe we should wait for room assignments." That was partially true. Farrell hadn't submitted his written offer, but the realtor assured him that the sellers were eager and willing. His signature was already attached to the offer, ready to be sent through email with the click of a button. All he wanted was Sapphire's approval.

Farrell had scoped out various neighborhoods and seen a dozen homes. He selected this one based on its unique design features he thought Sapphire would like. Plus, he felt as if the home had selected him from the moment he entered it. He had Kai take him back there three times just to be certain. He was more certain each time. Farrell's heart beat faster as they got closer.

"I've thought a lot about my parents," Sapphire said. "There's so much about them I didn't know." She gazed out the window at the deep turquoise ocean. "They were devoted to bringing a vital formula to the world. I wasn't neglected but they didn't prioritize me." Her throat felt tight. "Their reaction to the kidnapping attempts, well, I still can't understand. Last night it was difficult for me to accept. I felt hurt and angry." She took a deep breath. "I have a better perspective now. They were scientists and discovered the formula before they became parents."

"So, just like that," Farrell said, "Your anger evaporated?"

"It didn't evaporate, Farrell," said Sapphire. "I looked beneath it." She put her hand to her heart. "My parents *did* love me very much, of that I'm sure of. They were imperfect. I think of them now as obsessed scientists who lost sight of their priorities. I think that's what Dani has been trying to convey. It doesn't excuse them for not prioritizing me. But I understand."

"In the end," Farrell said, "they *did* secure your safety by sending you to Sedona." Farrell thought about his father. "That's more loving than my experience. My father shipped me away to avoid having his political career ruined by his son's scandalous actions." Once he said it, he couldn't take it back.

Sapphire's jaw dropped. "I had no idea. You never mentioned anything. I want to hear all about it. We learned about Fisher's history after he died. You know my history now. It's time I know yours."

Farrell felt Sapphire's imploring eyes even though he was focused straight ahead on the road. "I'll tell you the whole sordid story when the time is right." No more secrets. "Anyway, I'm glad you have perspective. Maybe I'll get perspective someday regarding my parents as well. Right now, I want to see my future, not my past. The house is just up ahead."

"I still want the first choice of rooms," Sapphire said. She playfully punched his arm. Both let out a sigh of relief.

Out of the corner of his eye, Farrell watched Sapphire's reaction as they pulled into the long winding driveway. "Weeping willows!" she cried out. "These trees are ancient, I love them." Sapphire took in the long span of drooping branches. They sat in the parked SUV and absorbed the trees and front of the home, before stepping out into the warm ocean breeze.

Farrell was so excited about the house that he had the urge to scoop Sapphire up and carry her across the threshold. He never had romantic feelings for Sapphire. Sure, she was gorgeous, but his feelings remained platonic. Hers seemed platonic too. Farrell and Sapphire were great pals, like close siblings. Neither ever married. Many times, they were mistaken for a couple. They often remarked how their friendship endured longer than most marriages. Instead of scooping her up, he held her hand as they entered the home. White-washed oak hardwood floors had been newly installed throughout the entire house. The view was breathtaking from almost every room, with huge ocean-facing windows. The four full-sized ensuite bedrooms would be plenty for Farrell and Sapphire as well as Judith and Sofia. The bedrooms and main living area had curved walls, which Farrell knew would delight Sapphire. The domed ceilings had unique archways connecting the rooms. Sapphire sat cross-legged on the floor of each room, looking around and making further notes in her folder.

Finally, Sapphire stood in the entry foyer and looked up. Yes, she could install her stained glass hexagon skylight right above where she was standing. After a long moment, she said, "I name thee Celestial."

"Huh?" said Farrell.

"All stately homes have a name," she said. "The rounded walls and circular structure look like a spaceship from above." Farrell smiled. "Plus, it feels heavenly," Sapphire added.

Next, they stood in front of the floor-to-ceiling windows in the family room and gazed at the ocean. The back of the house was raised on piers, offering a view beyond the ocean and far into the horizon. The sand along the shore was pristine. Mountains could be seen to the far left, looking toward Hanalei Bay.

Behind the house, a set of stairs led down to the beach. On an earlier visit, Farrell noticed the creaky wood structure needed repair. The bathrooms also required upgrading. Other than that, no major renovations would be necessary. Even the kitchen was a state-of-the-art chef's kitchen. Sapphire wondered about the stability of the structure. Hawaii had suffered several hurricanes in the last decade. "Have you had an inspection yet?"

"That'll be done after we have a contract," Farrell said. "Kai will oversee the process." Kai was already researching inspectors and contractors to do the needed repairs and upgrades.

"I say you should go for it, Farrell." Sapphire gave him a tight hug. "It's perfect." He let out a huge sigh and pulled his phone out of his pocket. "Okay, Celestial." Farrell retrieved the signed document he had saved. "Here it goes," he said as he clicked send. *Whoosh.* The invisible internet carried his intention through the universe. He stared out the window, looking toward the beach, and said, "Welcome to the family, Celestial."

Chapter 37
A Fateful Tuesday

It was lunchtime when Sapphire and Farrell pulled up to Mango. Sofia, Judith, and Dani were already on the garden patio, helping themselves to assorted salads lined up in large wooden bowls on the table. "This is mango salsa dressing," said Dani as she spooned some onto her plate piled high with colorful vegetables.

"Sapphire. Farrell. Just in time," said Dani. She motioned towards the salads and handed them plates. "I hope you're hungry." Sapphire and Farrell smiled at Dani and the others.

"How was your drive?" asked Judith.

"Princeville is so different in the northern part of the island," said Sapphire. "And Hanalei Bay looks mythical, with mist rising from the mountains." She wasn't going to share Farrell's plan to buy a home. That was for him to tell. "That looks scrumptious, I'm hungry, thank you. I'll be right back." Sapphire took her folder full of photos and notes to her room and quickly returned for lunch.

"There wasn't much traffic," said Farrell. "Glad we made it back in time for lunch." He scooped some salad and mango salsa dressing onto his plate and sat down.

As Sofia munched on her salad, she realized she wouldn't be enjoying this meal if the nutrition formula was the norm instead of eating. Would people be able to eat while taking the formula if they wanted to? Could they go on and off each day at will? Dani said that they hadn't tried that back then.

After the group finished eating, Sofia gathered the dishes to bring to the kitchen. She liked anything to do with kitchen work. Sofia added *doing dishes* to her mental list of things she would miss if the nutrition formula substituted for food in the world.

"Let's stay out here today," said Dani. "The air feels lovely and there's enough of a breeze to keep us cool." No one minded or objected. When Sofia returned from the kitchen ten minutes later, Dani was ready to begin. She had another white velvet bag in her lap and her reading glasses hung on a chain around her neck. She remembered to wear them as she got dressed this morning.

"I told you about the coded telephone rings," Dani began. "Every day, like clockwork, I received one or two rings at noontime. The only exception was the few times I visited Aunt Star. I would go into the office on Saturdays and Sundays briefly, just to wait for the call." Dani didn't have much else to do on weekends since she kept to herself after the fake blow-up. She hadn't wanted to face gossip and judgment from her Aromaticus associates, or questions from her friends. "There were always one or two rings. One ring meant *all is well*. Two rings meant *we are making progress*." Dani felt the anticipation build up each morning until the rings confirmed that Jane and Andre were okay.

"Three rings signaled *wait for instructions on where to meet us*. I never received only three rings." She had hoped to but never did. Dani never received five rings either. That would have meant it was *safe to pick up the phone*.

"Four rings meant *destroy all research documents and shut down the lab*. I was in the lab when the dreaded four rings signal came in. It was a Tuesday. About five years after they moved to Columbia. One ring, two rings, three rings, and finally four. Then nothing. The ringing stopped."

"That must have been terrifying," said Sapphire.

Danni nodded. "I hoped I had counted wrong. Then, it happened again, exactly five minutes later. Four rings, then silence. And finally, one last time, ten minutes later. Jane and Andre knew that I'd need the four rings to be repeated to be sure."

Sapphire, Farrell, Judith, and Sofia sat slack jawed.

Jane and Andre had instructed one of their trusted friends to place the call in the event of their deaths," said Dani. "The same friend destroyed all records from the lab at their farm, as they had previously requested." She took a sip of tea. "He thought he was destroying business records so the corrupt government inspectors wouldn't find them, never suspecting that the top-secret documents held information about a miracle nutrition formula."

"Mr. Lorenzo?" Sapphire asked. "Was he the trusted friend?" She was remembering more. Hushed conversations between Mr. Lorenzo and her father floated around her mind. She recalled hearing whispered words like, *risk, protect* and *danger.*

"You *remember* Mr. Lorenzo?" Dani asked, clearly surprised. "He was your driver and then your bodyguard."

"Yes," said Sapphire. "I remember him with gratitude. He saved me twice from kidnappers." She could now state that as a fact without feeling an emotional disturbance. "I felt safe with him looking out for me."

Dani smiled. "Your parents trusted Mr. Lorenzo. He was the one who called with the four rings. After the third round of four rings, I shut down the lab at Aromaticus and destroyed all of my research, along with the only other written copy of the formula. I informed the product safety department that the plants and herbs became contaminated with mold." It was an easy lie to believe. "I warned them that the contamination could lead to a highly contagious bacteria which would damage the products in the entire factory." Dani had been a good actress like Jane had taught her. The deception worked. "The company president thanked me." She was promoted for her astute find. "They fumigated my lab and wrote off the loss." Dani rubbed her temples.

"Jane and Andre Dover's deaths were reported in the Columbian newspapers," Dani said. "They were allegedly killed in an explosion during a failed coup attempt." She pulled out a faded newspaper clipping from the white velvet bag and. It was encased in a protective plastic sleeve. She didn't need her glasses to read it. Dani knew what it said. She handed the document over to Sapphire, who gently held it in her hand.

"It's in Spanish," Sapphire said. "I don't remember my Spanish." She knew that Farrell didn't speak Spanish either. She looked at Sofia and Judith. They both lived in South Florida, where the Spanish language was prevalent. "Can either of you read Spanish?" Both shook their heads sheepishly.

"It doesn't matter," Dani said. "It's all lies anyway."

"So, their death was not related to a political coup?" Sapphire asked. *Explosion during a failed political coup* were the words Sapphire had emblazoned in her brain. That's what she was told and that's what she believed her entire life. "How can you be sure?"

"I have a gut feeling that an insidious government official learned of the formula. Perhaps a corrupt inspector who came to the farm and saw their make-shift lab. Somehow, word had gotten out." Dani let out a sigh of frustration. "I can't unravel what truly happened, but I do believe it was related to the formula and not a coup attempt, as the newspaper reported." Dani wished she knew more. She only had her suspicions. Instead of speculating and confusing Sapphire further, Dani simply said, "I'm sorry, Sapphire. I wish I knew more." She had lost her good friends that fateful Tuesday forty-six years ago. The same fateful Tuesday fifteen-year-old Sapphire had become an orphan.

Chapter 38
Butterfly and Hummingbirds

The group sat in silence as they absorbed the awful story of Jane and Andre's deaths. A lone butterfly fluttered through the garden. Hearing about her parents' deaths brought back a flood of emotions that Sapphire couldn't identify. Thirty-seven was too young to die. They'd taught her so much about life and navigating her role in the world, but they never had the opportunity to teach her about grieving. Sapphire hadn't grieved the loss of her parents. She didn't know how. Plus, it was easier to pretend that they were still alive, far away.

Now, raw grief washed through her. It felt bottomless. Sapphire tried to take a deep breath, but her chest was tight. She recognized the feeling from when Fisher died. The same heaviness in her chest. The difficulty in taking a deep breath. This was grief. And though the pain palpated, Sapphire was relieved to finally grieve the loss of her parents all those years ago.

The butterfly landed on her shoulder. Its pale violet-blue wings shone like silver in the sunlight. The colors blended in with Sapphire's sundress. Hummingbirds sipped sweet nectar from the feeders hanging on the trees. Observing the fluttering wings, helped Sapphire feel connected to the earth. She breathed a little deeper.

Judith took Dani's hand. "That must've been so painful for you. And so lonely."

Dani's eyes brimmed with tears. "I honored Jane and Andre's wishes. They were determined to keep you safe, Sapphire. There were so many times over the years I almost contacted you. I didn't because it would be selfish of me and disrespectful to your parents." She hoped Sapphire would understand. "I inherited the responsibility of ensuring your safety. Your Aunt Star and I talked about it and decided it was best for you to avoid any connection to the secret formula. That meant no connection to Aromaticus and no connection to me."

Sapphire heard Dani's words but couldn't process the message. The butterfly floated off her shoulder and circled a red flower. Her thoughts floated too, back to being fifteen and suddenly parentless. "I was away at boarding school when my parents were killed," Sapphire said. Dani understood Sapphire's need to replay the moment.

"Yes, Sapphire," Dani said. "Your Aunt Star looked after you. She made sure that you visited her on Sanibel often and kept you separated from anything to do with the secret formula."

More hummingbirds gathered, mesmerizing the group. They fluttered in place inches from the feeder. Sapphire's brain moved slowly as it tried to form her questions. Sofia, Judith, and Farrell quietly followed the exchange between Sapphire and Dani. Sofia knew that it was important for Sapphire to process the information at her own pace, and they were all willing to patiently wait.

Sapphire finally spoke up. "What was Aunt Star's involvement with the formula after my parents died?"

"Before they were killed, your parents gave the written details of the secret formula to Aunt Star," Dani said. "They worried about their safety and wanted to ensure the formula's legacy. Aunt Star developed an intricate code to keep it secure." Dani wasn't prepared to reveal where the code was kept. Not yet.

"Did you continue to research more about the formula after my parents died?" Sapphire asked. "The labs were destroyed, right?"

Dani nodded. "Yes, the contents of the labs at Aromaticus and your parent's farm were both destroyed, and the research on the formula ceased.

But over the years Aromaticus continued to research other rare and exotic plants. The medicinal value of microbes in the soil rivals the importance of the plant leaves they nurture. Soil temperature is the current focus," she said. Farrell, Judith, and Sofia listened with interest. "Tropical climates promote rich nutrients in the soil. Cold climates inhibit growth. That's why we maintain a factory and laboratory here on Kauai and in Asheville. It was part of Aromaticus' mission statement. And Jane's vision of the significance of microbial organisms was spot on."

"Wow!" said Sapphire. "My mother was ahead of her time." She always admired her mother, but her admiration of her mother as a scientist had swelled over this past week. "My mother would be so impressed that you're following her interest in soil composition."

Dani's phone vibrated. She read the text from Kai. *Still on for the Coffee Plantation tour?* She had forgotten about it. Maybe the timing wasn't right. Unable to gauge the mood, she decided to simply ask. Judith noticed Dani's indecision and asked, "Is everything alright?"

"Oh, yes," said Dani. "It's just that I'd forgotten I planned a tour of the Kauai Coffee Company. Are you still interested now? We can sample the variety of coffee flavors." The others held back waiting to hear what Sapphire wanted.

"Sounds great," Sapphire said. She looked at Judith, Farrell, and Sofia. "That's if you're all interested in going now." All three responded with a resounding YES."

Dani texted back to Kai. *We'll meet you in front in five minutes.* She heard the familiar car engine and the gravel under the tires as Kai pulled up the drive. How much longer would Kai be available to help her when she came to Kauai? H would be busy studying. Dani knew he was special. Kai had a promising future. It was inevitable that he would pursue higher dreams than being her occasional driver and assistant. It warmed her heart that Farrell would mentor him. A benefit to Farrell as well as Kai.

Sapphire stretched her limbs as she rose. They all filled their thermoses with mint water and gathered their hats. The butterfly and hummingbirds flew away, never knowing how much their performance was appreciated.

Chapter 39
Kauai Coffee

Kai was all smiles as the group piled into the car. "Hello Miss Lake. How are you today?" He felt especially lucky to be a tour guide to Dani's guests. Now Farrell wanted to mentor him. It was such an honor. Farrell's confidence in him helped Kai believe in himself more than ever. At age twenty-six, Kai wasn't ready to take on the world, but at least he could manage Farrell's new properties in Princeville. He couldn't wait to get started!

"Hello, Kai," said Dani. The others greeted him warmly. He tipped his hat to each one of them and began his tour guide role as they drove away.

"Kauai Coffee Company has over four million coffee trees growing over thirty-one hundred acres. It's the largest coffee grower in the US."

Sofia added *coffee growing* to the list of industries that would suffer if the nutrition formula was substituted for food. Struggling poor nations relied on their coffee crop to sustain their economic stability. With such fragile economies, how would these nations survive? Dani had said Andre noticed Jane not drinking her morning coffee, his first clue that something was different. Drinking coffee was a ritual enjoyed by people all over the world. No Starbucks? No baristas? Would that ever be possible?

"Kauai Coffee Company not only grows their own beans, but they also roast and package them," Kai continued. "McBryde Sugar Company was the forerunner of Kauai Coffee in the early eighteen hundreds. In 1987, they transformed into Kauai Coffee and prospered until Hurricane Iniki damaged the crops. Four years later, Kauai Coffee made a resounding comeback and …

Sofia was interested in the history but couldn't concentrate. Intrusive thoughts about the nutrition formula stole her focus. Were the others also thinking about the formula and how it would affect so many aspects of daily life?

Soon they arrived. Kai parked the SUV, and everyone exited. "The aroma of coffee is luscious," Sapphire said. The single-story A-frame structure was the size of a small home. It was painted in colorful pastel colors. "Oh, how quaint."

The scent grew stronger as they approached the entrance. Sofia's mouth watered. She could almost taste the coffee. "Can't wait to try their different varieties." They walked through the door to the visitor center with a small gift shop displaying coffee and souvenir trinkets. Beyond the gift shop was the tasting lounge with a video describing the history of Kauai Coffee. The group continued outside through the back door to their tour.

Kai joined the group as they walked the self-guided tour, exploring the process of roasting coffee beans. Farrell said, "I always wondered how coffee was produced. This is fascinating." They continued on, captivated with each station along the way.

After their tour, the group gathered in the lounge for a coffee tasting. They were enthralled with the variety of flavored coffees. "Scrumptious," said Sofia.

Ding. Farrell received a text. He glanced at it and smiled. "I've bought a winter home here on Kauai!" Never one to mince words, his news was right to the point. "Just learned my offer was accepted." Sapphire beamed.

Judith's eyes widened. Sofia's jaw dropped.

"How wonderful," said Dani. She had suspected something was up with all his drives to Princeville but assumed it was a business interest. "I've noticed how comfortable you feel here on Kauai." Would Sapphire join him? "All of you seem to feel comfortable here," Dani continued. "Kauai is like that for many people."

"Sapphire's going to design the renovations and decorate the home," Farrell said. "She even gave it a name." He turned to Sapphire.

"Celestial," Sapphire said. "You'll love it. It's right on the beach up in the northern part of the island. There's room for all of us."

"I hope you'll join us," Farrell said to Judith and Sofia. "And you can be *my* guest, Dani." Farrell proudly described the features of the home.

Sofia heard *chef's kitchen*. Who would need a state-of-the-art kitchen if people no longer ate? *Baking cookies with Star.* Like Jane, Sofia added more and more to her list.

"Kai will oversee the renovations," Farrell said. Kai grinned. "Kai will also manage a vacation rental I plan on purchasing."

"We can go swimming in the ocean when we're here," Sapphire said to Sofia. "Like we did this week." It was so relaxing and so much fun. Sapphire hoped Sofia would stay for the entire winter.

Sofia wasn't sure what she wanted to do. She had just moved to Sedona a year ago. Her home in Ft. Lauderdale was now on the market. She couldn't live in two places. How did people do it? Yet, she missed the ocean. Their week on Kauai reminded her of that. "Yes, I'd love to visit," Sofia said. "Thank you, Farrell, for your gracious offer."

Judith felt warm inside. Visiting Farrell's home on the island would mean more time with Dani. But how often did Dani come to Kauai? Aromaticus had a factory and lab here, but Judith didn't see Dani going to work once. "Where's Princeville?" she asked.

"The northern part of the island," Kai said. "About an hour's drive. The drive could take twice as much time during rush hour traffic. There's only one road going up there."

An hour's drive? Judith didn't like that. How often could she see Dani being so far away from Mango? Oh, they'd figure out the distance. An hour wasn't that far, after all.

"I'd love to visit," said Judith. "Thank you, Farrell. It'd be lovely to spend more time on Kauai."

"We have one more day here," said Sapphire. "We fly home Saturday." She was ready to return to Sedona. Her head swirled with more questions for Dani. But for now, Sapphire needed a break to assimilate all that she learned this week. Sapphire turned to Kai, "What do you suggest we see before we leave?"

"The Napoli Coast," he said. "You can't drive there, however. Miss Dani, I can arrange a boat or helicopter tour." Kai had cousins who were tour guides for both. He looked at the group. "Or maybe you'd like both a helicopter tour and a boat tour."

"Can we save the Napoli Coast for our next visit?" asked Judith. "I'd love to go swimming in the ocean for our last day." She glanced at Sapphire and Sofia. "Would you both go with me?" Judith wasn't sure of her stamina and stability but having her women friends next to her would be comforting. "You've been swimming all week and it sounds glorious. I can't leave Kauai without taking a dip in the ocean."

Sapphire and Sofia smiled at each other. "Sure, Judith," said Sapphire. "We'd love to take you swimming."

Sofia felt tense over her list of what she would miss if food was no longer needed. Floating in the ocean would relax her. "I'd love to go swimming one last time before leaving Kauai. It'll be many months before staying here at Farrell's when we'll have the opportunity to swim in the ocean again."

"Farrell," said Dani. "Tomorrow morning, I'd like to show you a business proposal I've been working on. That is if you don't mind." A final review from fresh eyes was needed. And she trusted Farrell. He clearly had a great business acumen. Plus, he was a lifelong close friend of Sapphire, so he was family.

"My pleasure, Dani," said Farrell. "I'm honored to assist you." Whew. He wouldn't have to go swimming even though Sapphire had insisted he bring his bathing suit. Perfect excuse! He would much rather see Dani's business proposal. Maybe she'll also tell him how she abstained from alcohol.

"Okay," said Kai. "I'll schedule your Napoli Coast tours next visit." He was glad to have the morning off so he could get a head start on his reading. The book list for the master's degree program was intimidating. He'd take it one step at a time. "Miss Lake," he said. "I've arranged the dinner reservations you requested for tomorrow night."

"For our final night together, I thought you all might enjoy dining at Beach House," Dani said. "Makani's looking forward to seeing all of you again." Dani looked forward to seeing Makani. After coming to Kauai for so many years, he'd become a good friend.

"Okay, great idea," said Farrell.

"I loved Beach House," said Sapphire.

"I'm really glad to go back there," said Sofia. She added *going to restaurants* to her growing list of things people would miss. Plus, the restaurant industry would suffer horribly. Makani, the maître di would lose his job. It was his passion.

"Let's go back to Mango and rest before dinner," said Dani. "And tomorrow afternoon I'll give you a tour of the Aromaticus factory." Dani already missed Sapphire and her friends. She still had the evening and one more day to share the rest of the story.

Chapter 40
Sapphire's Plan

While everyone rested in their rooms, Sapphire pondered her parents' untimely deaths. Who would've wanted them dead? She showered, put on a fresh tee shirt and jeans, and decided to talk to Farrell about it. Without much thought, she knocked on Farrell's door. "Come in," he said. "Oh, Hi Sapphire," He was seated at the window bench with his laptop open. "Just doing some work."

Sapphire sat on the bench next to him and crossed her legs. "I was thinking," she began. "If Dani didn't believe the reports about my parents' deaths, why didn't she investigate further?"

Farrell looked up from his work. "Hang on a moment." He saved his document and closed his laptop. "What kind of investigation could Dani have done? Times were different forty-six years ago and it was a foreign country."

"Yes, but they were American citizens," said Sapphire. "Wouldn't our government have been concerned? Two young American farmers get killed in a suspicious explosion and no reaction from their country?"

"There was a lot of drug trafficking going on, with a major cartel in Columbia," said Farrell. "It was very dangerous times."

"What about now?" asked Sapphire. "Do you think the government would open an investigation into the deaths of my parents? There's no statute of limitations or anything, is there?" She would not be satisfied until she got answers. "I need more information than Dani is sharing." She brushed the hair away from her face. "I'm determined to demand justice for my parents. They didn't deserve to die."

Farrell took Sapphire's hands. "Sapphire, if you're sure that you want to investigate further, I know who we can contact."

"Thanks, Farrell," said Sapphire. "I was hoping you would understand."

"Do you remember Devon Newton, Jared Silver's young FBI partner? Maybe he'd be a good person to contact," said Farrell. "He's based out of Miami, near Judith."

"Of course, I remember him," said Sapphire. "We all worked together to investigate Fisher's death. Newton cracked the case with his clues." She felt hopeful. "When we get back home, I'll reach out to him. I could meet him in person and stay with Judith."

"There's not much to go on, Sapphire," said Farrell. "And I'm not even sure the FBI does this sort of thing. It's a long shot." Sapphire slumped, looking deflated. "Newton can direct us to the right agency," Farrell quickly added to give her more hope. "If it's not the FBI's jurisdiction." He stifled a yawn.

"Okay, thanks Farrell," said Sapphire. "Glad we're having dinner here at Mango tonight. I'm tired too." She gave him a quick hug. "We'll contact Newton when we get home."

Chapter 41
Aunt Star

That evening, the group gathered for dinner in the dining room. Sofia and Pearl had cooked a second large platter of eggplant parmesan when they prepared the first. "I'll heat the eggplant and make a salad," Sofia said. "The second day is always better since the sauce gets to marinate." Sofia appreciated being in the kitchen even more now than before. The formula could make that pleasure extinct if people stopped eating. "Is there a local market to pick up fresh Italian bread?"

"I'll go out and get it," said Farrell. He felt comfortable driving around the island after learning directions from Kai over the week. Farrell wanted to go grocery shopping to experience the feeling of being a resident, not a visitor. "I know where the market is."

An hour later, Sofia carried out the large platter of eggplant from the kitchen. "Dinner is served," she said. She had set the table with fresh bread, herbed dipping oil, grated cheese, and salad. Although the others offered to help, Sofia insisted she wanted to serve. Would the ritual of serving food be over if the formula replaced the need for eating? She filled the plates and passed them around. "Bon appetite."

"This is even better the second night," said Dani. "You're right Sofia. Thank you for making two platters." Was the mood right to talk about Aunt Star tonight? Dani hoped so. She needed to tell Sapphire about the decision she and Aunt Star grappled with. Sapphire seemed unusually quiet. Sh had wait and see how the evening went.

After dinner, Sofia brought the dishes to the kitchen. The others offered to help but she waived them off. The kitchen was her sanctuary. A place she could escape to for time alone.

The group retreated to the outdoor garden and sipped coffee from Kauai Coffee. The moon had risen, bathing the patio with a warm glow. When Sofia rejoined them, Sapphire began asking Dani questions. "Did you and Aunt Star remain in close contact after my parents died?"

"We did at first," said Dani. It'd been a shock to them both, and they needed each other for consolation. "I was worried about your aunt's safety, so we were careful. We didn't know who else was after the formula. So, we couldn't appear close. Any suspicion of Aunt Star secreting the formula could put her in danger." She took a sip of coffee. "I was the only person who knew that your parents entrusted Aunt Star with the formula."

Farrell poured himself another cup of coffee. Was Dani still in danger? He gazed at Sapphire protectively. Could she be in danger as well?

"But what was she supposed to do with it?" asked Sapphire. "Aunt Star wasn't a scientist." Her aunt had been very wise and certainly creative. "She kept it a secret all these years?"

"She did," Dani said. "Your aunt was an amazing woman." Dani had admired Aunt Star for her calm demeanor. "I visited her a few times the first year after your parents died. We talked about the right thing to do with the formula. Should we give the formula to a medical organization? If so which one? Or perhaps a non-profit for third-world countries? Or keep it hidden? The decision was overwhelming, but we wanted to honor your parent's wishes and —"

"But what *were* their wishes?" Sapphire interrupted. Her frustration had an edge she hadn't intended to show. "I mean, what was my mother planning to do with the formula had she lived?"

"Your parents and I spent hours discussing that," said Dani. "Your mother wanted to first understand all the medical effects and the formula's stability under different temperatures. She also wanted to find a means to produce it without destroying the ecosystem. We discussed the ethics. Should we provide it to the world? Was it moral to withhold a life-saving discovery? We had heated debates before we couldn't have contact anymore. We examined it from different perspectives, often playing devil's advocate." The words *world hunger* haunted Dani. She could still hear Jane's voice and feel her torment.

"The world wasn't ready for a life-altering formula," Dani said, "No matter how beneficial it could be. We didn't know who to trust. If Big Pharma got their greedy hands on the formula, they'd focus on making a profit as their bottom line. Or worse, the government would control the distribution and the formula would get caught up in endless regulations. Your mother's wish was for Aunt Star to keep the formula safe until the world was ready for it."

Dani shook her head. "Alas, the world is no more ready now than it was when your parents were alive." She hoped the next generation would change that. "Government and pharmaceutical companies still haven't devised a safe means to supply prescription drugs at reasonable costs to all. Instead, it has just gotten worse over the years. And the current environmental damage to the Amazon Rainforest is disastrous."

"Were shady representatives from those organizations after Aunt Star?" Sapphire asked. "Why did you believe she was unsafe?" Sapphire recalled the words from her dream. *Keep the formula safe until the world is ready for it.*

"I suspected I was being followed the few times I visited Aunt Star," Dani said. "Once, early on, there was a break-in at Aunt Star's home. It was very suspicious because nothing was missing. But Aunt Star's Aromaticus essential oil bottles had all been drained. It frightened us." Sapphire's eyes widened. "This happened soon after your parents died."

"What about Aunt Star's home on Sanibel now?" Sapphire asked. "Are you worried that it's being watched, after all these years?"

"Someone out there believes there's a great money-making opportunity," said Dani. "Maybe it's someone from years ago. Maybe it's the urban legend that rises in the scientific community every several years." Was she sounding paranoid? "Aunt Star's collection of Aromaticus essential oils was missing when I arrived at her home after she died. All the empty bottles were gone as well."

"I could go to Sanibel Island," Judith said. "I've vacationed there before. It's a four-hour drive from my home in Miami." Sleuthing around had been part of her previous career. Judith missed the challenge. "I'll pose as a prospective buyer. Who would suspect an eighty-one-year-old woman of spying? I could speak to the neighbors, bring in inspectors and take notice if anyone is watching. I have a friend who's a retired FBI agent. I could ask him to come with me." Was Agent Silver in town or traveling the world with his great-nephew?

"That could be very helpful," said Dani.

"I received an email from Aunt Star's neighbor Betsy," said Sapphire. "She saw a realtor, the man you sent over to the house, Dani. Agent Silver could easily pose as a realtor."

Dani blanched as white as the shining moon. "I didn't authorize any realtors to enter the home," she said. "Vultures. How did that realtor get in?" The hair on the back of her neck stood up. Maybe she hadn't been paranoid after all.

"That would be a big help," said Dani. "Your friend also needs to be your bodyguard, Judith. I wouldn't want anything to happen to you."

Judith gave Dani a knowing smile.

Dani continued. "Your friend could also sweep the house for cameras and bugs. When I went there, I wondered if cameras were watching me take things out of the house. That's why I only took the shawl and ring for you, Sapphire." The two most important things. Dani hadn't had the heart to return.

"Thank you for sending me those treasures, Dani," said Sapphire. "Those heirlooms are all I need to remember Aunt Star." She had left both heirlooms at home in Sedona for safekeeping. "And now I have the photos of my parents too."

"And you also have the formula," said Dani. "To keep safe until the world is ready for it."

Sapphire gulped. *Have?* No one had given her the formula. Had Dani meant she *would* have the formula? Was it hidden in one of the white Aromaticus bags? Sapphire was full of questions again. But she spotted Dani stifling a yawn. This wasn't the time. Sapphire would have to wait.

Chapter 42
Who is After the Formula?

Sapphire pulled Judith aside as they all went to bed. She needed to talk to her in private. No need to worry the others. "Will you have a cup of tea with me in the kitchen?"

"Yes, good idea," said Judith. "Perhaps some chamomile tea to help us sleep."

Once the tea was brewed, they sat at the kitchen table "I need to ask you something," said Sapphire. "Weren't you working for The Witness Protection Program when my mother discovered the formula?"

"Yes, Sapphire," Judith said. "I was. Why do you ask?"

"I was wondering the extent of danger my family was truly in," said Sapphire. "What kind of criminals were you protecting witnesses from?"

"Very powerful criminals," said Judith. "They were ruthless. Terrorists, racketeers, kidnappers." She sipped her tea. "There were attempted murders of some of our protectees." She shook her head. "Greed and power were always the motivation."

"Could it have been criminals like that who were after the formula?" asked Sapphire.

Judith nodded. "Certainly."

Sapphire's eyes grew wide. "I remember the only time Aunt Star got cross with me," said Sapphire. I was seventeen. Aunt Star forbade me to go out at night with some new friends. I snuck out anyway and met my friends at a beach bonfire. When I returned home, Aunt Star screamed at me." Sapphire swallowed hard. "I'd never seen her like that. *Ever.* It frightened me. I cried. She cried. We hugged and I promised never to sneak out again. I didn't understand why she was so protective. Looking back, I think she might've been afraid. For my safety. From those kinds of criminals."

"Dani said that there was more than one time when her essential oils were stolen," said Judith. "Maybe she had a reason to be fearful."

"Do you think there could still be danger after all these years?" asked Sapphire. "Who would still be after the formula?"

"Dani was spooked when she went to Aunt Star's house," said Judith. "And the essential oil bottles had been drained again. There may still be someone out there who knows of the formula's existence."

"Do you think I could be in danger?" asked Sapphire. "Should I be worried?"

"I don't know, my dear," said Judith. She looked at Sapphire with distress. "I honestly don't know."

Chapter 43
The Business Venture

Judith awoke early the next morning eager for her swim. *Uh Oh.* She didn't have a bathing suit. When she originally packed to spend the week in Sedona, she had no idea she would end up near an ocean. Would Dani loan her one? Judith padded down the stairs in her robe and slippers and found Dani and Farrell in the garden already ensconced in their business meeting. "Sorry to interrupt. Do you have a bathing suit I can borrow, Dani?" Luckily, they were the same size or at least appeared to be.

"Of course, Judith," said Dani. She dashed to her room and returned with a bathing suit. "Keep this, I've never worn it. It still has the tags." Dani hadn't swum in the ocean for a very long time. She preferred to walk along the shore and collect shells. Several unused swimsuits sat in her drawer. She was delighted to give Judith a personal gift. Especially something as intimate as a bathing suit.

Whew! The right size. "Thank you," said Judith. She could tell she had interrupted a serious discussion and didn't want to linger. "Off I go." She hurried back upstairs to get ready for her swim.

Dani and Farrell were both on their second cup of coffee. The papers Farrell had just reviewed sat on the table between them. He turned to Dani. "I see this proposal has been evolving for more than a year. That's important. A decision as big as this deserves a lot of thought and consideration over a long time."

"Oh yes," said Dani. "I've contemplated this for several years. I've waited until I could be sure. Then I waited until I continued to feel sure for another year." Dani let out a breath. "I'm ready to do this." Sh had owned Aromaticus for thirty years, buying it with her savings when the previous owners retired. They were happy to sell it to Dani. She had already been promoted to president after having risen through the ranks. What did Farrell think about her plan?

"Okay," said Farrell. "Your attorney weighed in on the legal ramifications." He made a note to vet the attorney. "Your accountant listed the financial considerations and tax implications." Dani was a formidable woman and clearly knew how to run a successful company. "There's one thing missing," said Farrell. He recognized the problem since Sedona was experiencing the same issue. "Affordable housing."

"I'm glad I showed this to you," Dani said. "I needed a fresh perspective from someone who's not close to the situation." Still, Dani felt stung. She had missed something crucial. "If I transfer Asheville employees to Kauai, they couldn't afford to live here, especially those with families." Many of them had been to Kauai and stayed at Mango, all raving about their experience. A free vacation, however, is different than paying rent or purchasing a house. Most of the local Aromaticus employees lived with extended family in homes they've owned for generations. Dani reached in her purse for lip balm and applied it to her lips.

"It's still a good plan, Dani," said Farrell. "I have an idea to resolve the problem." He hadn't yet put in an offer for the short-term vacation rental he was considering. His beach house contract diverted his attention. He sat up straighter in his chair. "I'll partner with Aromaticus to purchase affordable housing for the relocated employees who choose to move here." Farrell had seen a vacant lot for sale that would be perfect for building a small housing community. "We'll offer a variety of homes with either rental or purchase options, including financing." Farrell quickly calculated the cost of building and the timeline. "Construction will take about eighteen months to complete. That is if there are no zoning or permit delays." He shook his head. Of course, there always were these sorts of delays.

"Hmm, it's an interesting proposal," said Dani. "If we offered affordable housing to employees, we'd lure a good number of transfers." She hoped. "I've wanted to close the Asheville factory and merge it with the Kauai site for some time now. You'll see this afternoon that Aromaticus owns a second building. We have room to expand. It just needs some renovations to scale our operation."

Out of the corner of her eye, Dani saw Sapphire and Sofia peek out onto the patio and quickly retreat to the kitchen. She had set up coffee, fruit, and scones indoors for them. Farrell didn't notice as he scrutinized the second part of the proposal Dani had handed to him.

"Wow," said Farrell. "This is big." It shouldn't have taken him by surprise. After all, Dani was far past retirement age and had no heirs. "Selling a company to employees is not a new concept," he said. "But *giving* it away is a magnanimous gesture." He scanned a chart listing the number of shares based on the number of years employed. Dani had proposed to give away her entire company to Aromaticus' loyal employees. "Are you absolutely sure you want to do this, Dani?"

"Yes," said Dani, without skipping a beat. Her voice exuded confidence and she loudly proclaimed, "YES, I AM."

"Everything okay out here?" Sapphire asked as she ran into the garden. Dani didn't realize how loudly shd spoken.

"Yes," said Dani. "I'm sorry I worried you." She smiled at Sapphire, feeling moved to see her concern. "We're good here."

Farrell and Sapphire exchanged a glance before Farrell gave the slightest nod to Sapphire. She disappeared swiftly back inside. He sipped his coffee.

Farrell studied the chart further. The proposal contained additional bonus shares awarded to groups of family members. The more years with the company, the more shares an employee would receive. Plus, families would receive bonus shares. "So, if a husband and wife both work for Aromaticus, they get an additional share as a couple?"

Dani nodded. "I'm rewarding loyalty and recognizing family commitments." Dani admired the family values of the Hawaiian culture. She had thought about this additional bonus for a long time. "Consider Kai, for example." Dani raised her hand and held up each finger as she listed his family members. "Kai, his mother, his father, and his grandfather all work for Aromaticus." Four fingers were raised, with only her pinky curled into her palm. Dani respected their work ethic and valued their dedication. Her proposal would honor Kai's family and others who'd worked for Aromaticus for many years. "They deserve to own a part Aromaticus."

Farrell turned the pages. Legal, tax and financial implications were all documented. He took another sip of coffee. Who would inherit *his* company? He had no heirs and no employees. Sapphire was his age and didn't need money. He'd explore options for charitable giving. He wanted to keep finding ways to help others. It had already helped him have more sobriety. He grabbed a scone from the table and took a bite. Should he ask Dani about her struggles with drinking? Farrell couldn't find the words. He opened his mouth to speak, then closed it.

"Farrell?" said Dani. He hadn't meant to drift off. "Is there something else that's worrisome in this proposal?" Was he holding back his opinion to spare her feelings?

"No, Dani," said Farrell. "Not at all. Merging the two factories and giving your company to the employees is truly elegant."

"But there's something on your mind," Dani said. "Just come out with it." Did he have any further reservations from a business perspective that she had overlooked?

Farrell pursed his lips. In barely a whisper, he finally uttered, "I, um, wanted to hear more about how you stopped drinking. If, um, you don't mind talking about it." Dani put her hand on his shoulder and nodded her head slowly. Her small hand was warm and radiated love.

Dani placed her papers back in their folder and stood up slowly. "Let's go for a walk. Get your hat and thermos. It's going to be a long walk."

Chapter 44
Sobriety

Farrell and Dani walked side by side along the beach. They stepped carefully to avoid the foamy waves washing up that threatened to creep up their ankles. Deep turquoise hues saturated the cloudless sky.

They strolled silently along for a long time before Farrell spoke. "I've struggled with a drinking problem for most of my life. Admitting it aloud is a big step for me." He sighed deeply. "I've tried to control it by limiting the amount I drink, but that hasn't worked."

"Controlled drinking didn't work for me," Dani said. "I wanted to have an occasional glass of wine or a celebratory sip of champagne." She tried more than once, only to find herself drinking more each time. "It does work for some people," Dani said. "Unfortunately, not for me." She adjusted her hat and sunglasses. "Or maybe it was fortunate. I had no choice but to abstain completely."

"I wondered about that," said Farrell. "I've gone for a month at a time without drinking. I was miserable. I constantly had alcohol on my mind. Might as well have been drinking."

"You know Farrell," Dani said. "It's not about what you drink. Or how often. Or how much." She picked up a shell. After examining it, Dani threw it back into the ocean. "It's the purpose it serves. For me, it quelled my loneliness. Except that when I drank, I had self-loathing on top of loneliness, making me feel ten times worse. I didn't have any other way to cope with my life and couldn't bear to face my grief. Those were dark days." Dani frowned. "In rehab, I began feeling connected again to others, and that gave me hope." The rehab facility had also given her a break from the pressure of her day-to-day routines. The staff encouraged her to develop healthier and more balanced routines, and she had.

"Glad rehab worked for you," Farrell said. "It's not for me." He had no interest in telling strangers about the things that tormented him. "I'm finding pleasure in new ways, helping others." Farrell took a long swallow from his thermos. The water quenched his thirst. "Conquering this is important to me. I can do it on my own, like I've done everything else in my life."

"There are lots of paths to sobriety. If you want someone to talk to, I'm here," said Dani. "And Makani would be honored to listen as well." Dani knew firsthand that Makani was a great listener. "You don't have to do this alone, Farrell. Support from others really helps." She turned to face him. "Perhaps you will join Makani and me at an AA meeting some time. Let me know when you are ready."

"Makani struggled with a drinking problem?" asked Farrell. "He seems so happy-go-lucky and comfortable with himself. Is that how the two of you became friends?" Farrell had noticed the comfortable rapport between them.

Dani said, "Yes, I sat at the bar at Beach House for dinner one evening. It was my first year here after Jane and Andre died. I drank mango iced tea and Makani offered to buy me another." Dani had appreciated the maître di coming over to talk with her. "He sat down next to me, and we hit it off right away. We learned that we had something important in common. We were both newly recovering alcoholics."

Squeals of delight pierced the ocean breeze as Sofia, Sapphire, and Judith giggled. The three ladies held hands as they emerged from the waves, stumbling to the sandy shore. They glistened in the sunlight with beads of salty water from head to toe. Farrell suddenly felt tempted to run into the ocean beside them. Instead, he gave each lady a wide hug, getting wet. Dani smiled seeing Judith in the bathing suit she gave her. "This was the best idea," Judith said, looking radiant. "I'm so glad I went into the ocean. Thank you, Sapphire. Thank you, Sofia. You both inspired me."

Sofia, Sapphire, and Judith wrapped themselves in beach towels. The five friends plodded in the sand, making their way back to Mango. They were still laughing as they brushed off the sand from their feet and shook out their beach towels. "Let's meet downstairs for a light lunch in an hour," said Dani. "Then we'll tour Aromaticus."

Chapter 45
Aromaticus Factory Tour

After devouring sandwiches and salad, Kai welcomed Sapphire, Sofia, Dani, Judith, and Farrell into the SUV. They all sported a healthy tan, despite applying sunscreen and wearing hats all week.

"How's the application for the business program coming along?" Farrell asked Kai after he climbed into the front passenger seat.

Kai adjusted the mirrors—Farrell had been the last driver of the SUV. "Submitted it already," he said proudly. "The curriculum looks awesome. I read some of the required text this morning."

They left the driveway and headed down the main road. Farrell gave Kai a pat on his shoulder. "Shows real dedication. Keep me posted."

"The factory is just up ahead," Kai announced to the group. "We'll all need to wear PPE to go through the labs." He looked in the rearview mirror at confused faces. "Personal protective equipment. Contamination of the slightest amount would lead to disposing of the expensive essential oils. Dani gave Kai a trusting nod.

"Okay," Sofia said. "We understand, of course." The others nodded. "Do you give tours of Aromaticus often?"

"I won't be your tour guide today," Kai said. "My mother is very excited to show you around."

"Pearl is conducting the tour?" asked Sofia. "I was hoping to see her again. I can't wait to learn how essential oils are produced. I have no clue about the process of extracting oils from plant leaves." This was going to be fascinating.

They pulled up to the factory and parked. "Look at that bright white finish on the outside of the building," said Sapphire, squinting for a better view. "Looks like sparkling diamonds." Square and rectangle structures were adjoined in a unique formation. "A very interesting looking factory."

Kai pointed to the lot next door. "That abandoned factory will be retrofitted when Aromaticus expands our operations."

The group walked along the white stoned path. Chirping birds weaved their way through the flowers and trees that lined the entire walkway. Judith breathed in the sights and sounds. "Nice welcoming committee," she said. "What a treat."

The front door was stunning with carved mahogany reaching up in a tall archway. "One of the employees is a wood carver," Kai said. "Employees are encouraged to express their creativity here. You'll all see why everyone on the island wants to work at Aromaticus. Miss Lake truly cares for her employees and shows it in every part of the workplace." Dani smiled, allowing Kai to shine.

Kai led them through the door and to the host on duty. "Hello, welcome to Aromaticus," said the middle-aged-looking man. He smiled warmly. "I'll let Pearl know that you're here."

"Each week a different employee is the front entry host or hostess," said Kai. "They greet all employees and visitors with a warm smile."

"I want Aromaticus' employees as well as visitors to feel appreciated the moment they walk through the front door," said Dani.

The group gazed around the tall lobby in awe. Huge paintings portrayed ocean waves and mountains high in the blue sky. "They're so colorful and striking against the white walls," said Sapphire. "Kauai landscape, right?"

"Yes," said Kai. "We have some very talented artists employed here at Aromaticus."

Sapphire, Judith, Farrell, and Sofia stood motionless. "It's like being in a museum," Sofia said. If the lobby was an art museum, what was the rest of the factory like? Farrell walked over to a framed certificate on the wall. "What's this about?"

"It's our membership in the National Association for Holistic Aromatherapy and their code of ethics," said Dani. "Aromaticus proudly surpasses industry standards."

Pearl emerged exuberantly to greet her guests. She wore a brightly flowered shirt, lightweight khaki-colored pants, and white tennis shoes. "Oh, this is our Aromaticus uniform," Pearl said as she pointed to the tiny silver script logo on her shoulder. Sofia wanted to work there just so she could wear the uniform. She embraced Pearl in a giant hug. The others greeted her warmly. A relaxed vibe hung in the air. Pearl motioned them to follow her through the next doorway.

"Here is our first stop, the Hydration Station," she said. Today's water flavors are Mango-Lime and Strawberry-Vanilla. "Please help yourselves". Pearl filled a glass for herself. The others followed suit. Everyone placed their emptied glasses in the bin before moving on.

"Next is our cafeteria," Pearl said. "We call it our Nutrition Station. Employees who enjoy cooking take turns to staff the kitchen." Pearl pointed to the stack of to-go containers piled on the counter. "Employees have the option of taking a meal home for themselves and their families."

The group followed Pearl through a long hallway to the next room. The sign in front of the floor-to-ceiling glass window read *Kids Station: Children are our Most Valuable Asset.* "We have daycare for our employees' children," Pearl said. Soft classical music played in the background. Children's artwork covered the walls.

"Amazing," said Sofia. "What a great perk for the employees."

Children's laughter filled the hallway as the group moved on. "I can't wait to see the next station," said Sofia. "We haven't reached the part of the factory where the essential oils are produced."

Pearl directed the group to a bin with the PPE. After everyone suited up, Pearl led them through a set of double doors into the first factory workroom.

"Large blow-up photos of colorful butterflies covered the high walls. In each photo, the butterflies perched on different plant leaves. "Those photos were originally taken many years ago by your father, Sapphire." Warmth filled Sapphire's heart. She stared at the photographs taking in every detail. The butterflies, the flowers and the plant leaves seemed to be giving her a message. Did the others see it? Was this a message from her parents? *Keep the formula safe* sang the butterflies. No one else seemed to hear it.

"Essential oil is a concentrated liquid containing chemical compounds from plants," said

Pearl. "In this room we distill the oils from the plants using a cold press system." The group observed the employees feeding plant leaves through the equipment at their stations. Huge piles of the leaves could be seen in bins next to each one.

Pearl led them to the bottling room next. "Here the employees monitor the machinery that fills the glass bottles with our oils."

"They look so pretty," Judith said. They strode to the next room.

"Lastly, the labeling room," said Pearl. "The group observed more employees maneuvering machinery as each bottle received an Aromaticus label.

Next, they passed a lab with a viewing window. "We can't go in there, but you see we have our master chemist developing new formulas," said Pearl.

Sapphire peered through the glass. Would the master chemist develop a world changing formula like the one her mother did? Was there a new secret lab at Aromaticus where chemists were researching life-saving formulas? Surely, her mother couldn't have been the only chemist with a passion and a dream.

"Our final stop is going to be the garden," said Pearl. "You can remove your protective wear now." Pearl motioned to a bin for them to place their coverings as she removed hers.

When they all stepped outside, Pearl pointed to plants neatly lined up in rows like school children. "I see mint and lavender," said Sapphire. "Several different varieties." Hmm. Dani told us that a certain variety of mint enhanced the endangered plant used in the secret formula. Could it be one of these? *Keep the formula safe, until the world is ready for it* continued to echo in her brain.

"Our garden grows the common varieties of plants used to produce our essential oils," said Pearl. "We have plant and herb farms in other parts of the island as well." She looked at Dani. "Conservation and respect for the land are paramount."

"Let's get these folks back to Mango," Kai said as he appeared, approaching the group. He kissed his mother on the cheek in an uninhibited display of affection. "They've got dinner reservations in an hour."

"Here's a parting gift from Aromaticus," said Pearl. She handed a mini white velvet drawstring bag to each of them. "A token of appreciation for your interest."

Judith peeked inside her bag. She squinted at the tiny label on the bottle but couldn't read it. She took a whiff of the unopened bottle and immediately recognized the scent. "Lavender, Mmm. It smells heavenly. Dani must have told Pearl this was Judith's signature scent.

"Ooh, I wonder what scent mine is," said Sapphire. She opened her bag and removed the tiny glass bottle. "Spearmint. I love it. What did you get Sofia?"

"Mine is ylang-ylang," Sofia said. "Pearl, isn't this your scent? I recognize it."

"Yes, Sofia," Pearl smiled demurely. "You mentioned you liked it that day we worked together in the kitchen."

"Yes, I love it," said Sofia. "Thank you for remembering."

"Okay Farrell," Sapphire teased. "Give it up. What'd you get?"

"Oh, let me see," said Farrell. He made a grand dramatic gesture of opening his bag and unscrewing the bottle. Then he held it up to his nose without examining the label. "Hmm, I think it's peppermint. Very strong. Smells like one of those red and white swirled hard candies." Farrell took another whiff. "I like it."

"Miss Lake told me you like those candies," said Pearl. "That's why I chose that scent for you."

Sofia hugged Pearl as they all said goodbye and piled back into the SUV. As Kai exited the parking lot, he pointed to a small patch of white flowers unlike any of the others they'd seen on the island. "Miss Lake planted those." He looked over at Dani who nodded slightly.

Kai slowed down to a stop as the group peered out the windows. A small plant stake stood in the ground with the label Jandre. "Those flowers are a unique variety found here on the factory grounds. Miss Lake named them."

"In honor of your parents," Dani said. In a whisper, she murmured *Jane* and *Andre*. "They're very rare and endangered." A purple butterfly sailed through the air and landed on one of the plants. Judith snapped a photo with her cellphone.

A sense of familiarity reached out to Sapphire from the exotic white flowers dancing in the breeze. She closed her eyes, put her hands together at her heart, and bowed ever so slightly.

Chapter 46
Champagne Toast

The group arrived home and prepared for dinner at Beach House. Farrell thought about what Dani said. *Controlled drinking.* It hadn't worked for her. She tried it several times. It worked for some. Would it work for him? Farrell wanted to order a bottle of champagne at dinner tonight to celebrate his new home. Yet, he wasn't interested in the alcohol content as much as the tradition. He could hear the cork popping and see the bubbles rising. Stemmed champagne flutes clinked in his ears. His mouth watered from the tingling taste on his tongue. Farrell would have to find another traditional custom to celebrate tonight. He'd ask Makani for advice.

Sapphire towel-dried her long hair before tackling the blow drier. What a relief to let her hair dry naturally all week. No time for that tonight. She pulled out a flowing dress for the occasion and slipped on strappy flat sandals. Sapphire had already packed her suitcase, except for a few final items and clothes. It'd be way too full to include the collection of white Aromaticus bags. Maybe Dani had an extra suitcase to loan her.

Sofia inhaled the scent of her ylang-ylang essential oil. She applied some to her wrists and pulse points on her neck, the way her mother taught her. It made her feel good. Maybe it would become *her* signature scent. The past week on Kauai was a dream. She looked forward to going home to Sedona. And to return to Kauai in the winter.

Judith selected her favorite scarf as she prepared for dinner. The turquoise silk draped down her simple black tank dress. She would miss Dani. Their friendship had revived her. How nice to spend time with a contemporary. She planned to invite Dani to visit her in Miami.

Dani selected a pale blue blouse that matched her eyes, as she contemplated the past week. Tonight would be about celebrating friendship and new beginnings. Sapphire's last night here. She had waited to share her story for so long. Had she left anything out? She already gave Sapphire a coded copy of the active ingredient in the secret formula. Sapphire just didn't know it yet.

Kai was quiet as he drove the group to Beach House. He'd miss each one of them. Especially Farrell. Virtual communication was so unsatisfying. He was glad Farrell would be spending time on Kauai so they could each other in person. Another glorious sunset greeted them as they arrived at Beach House. Kai dropped them off and drove away.

Makani's voice was full of excitement as he greeted his old and new friends again. "Welcome to Beach House." The same dramatic flair and tuxedo adorned him. Farrell strode up ahead of the group and talked quietly to Makani. Makani's eyebrows rose in response. "I've got you covered, my friend." The two men shook hands and Makani seated the group. He handed menus to each. They sat at the same round table they dined at a week ago. The sunset was different but equally breathtaking.

Judith's cellphone dinged. "Sorry, I brought my phone with me because I'm waiting to hear back from Jared Silver." She looked at the text and announced, "Oh, good, he is back home in Miami and will go to Sanibel Island with me next week."

"The retired FBI agent?" Dani asked. "I feel better about you having someone with you, especially someone with experience at spotting bugging devices." Her brow creased. "Maybe I'm overreacting. I'm just worried someone might be watching and listening, hoping to secure the formula."

"If there're bugging devices in the home, Jared will find them," said Judith. "And he will be discreet. Where on the island is Star's home?"

"Near the lighthouse," said Sapphire. She'
had been there often enough to know her way.
"Directly on the beach off Periwinkle Way. The
bedroom I stayed in is the first one on the left."

"Thank you, Judith," Dani said. "It's a big
relief for me. A very big relief. I'll give you the keys
when we get back tonight. And the alarm code."
Dani had been able to talk Star into getting a house
alarm, but she wouldn't agree to have a company
manage it. "It's not connected to a monitoring
company, but it screeches loudly."

Dani opened her menu. She always ordered
the same thing. Would her guests want something
different?

"Dani, would you order the same courses we
had last time?" asked Sapphire. "I loved everything."

"Yes, please," said Sofia. "It was all wonderful."
Fresh seafood in Sedona is hard to come by. That
was one thing she missed from Florida. And her
best friend Lena. Sofia closed her menu.

"I'll have the same thing too," said Judith. "I
hate struggling to decide what to order." Her mouth
watered at the thought of having the macadamia-
nut-crusted snapper again.

"Me too," said Farrell. "Everything we had
before will be perfect. Maybe this time, I'll have
room for dessert. Tiramisu, mmm." There would be

one thing different. Farrell spotted Makani approaching, as promised.

Makani carried over a silver wine bucket on a stand and placed it in front of Farrell. Inside was a bottle surrounded with ice. The bottle had a white linen napkin wrapped around it. A waiter placed champagne flute goblets in front of each guest. "Sparkling white grape juice," Farrell said. Dani smiled. Makani unscrewed the cap. The liquid bubbled up and spilled over the top. He poured a tiny amount into Farrell's glass and waited for him to taste it. Farrell put the flute to his lips and took a sip. "Superb!" It did taste good. Better than champagne. "Thank you, Makani."

Makani poured each of their flutes with sparkling white grape juice. "There's not a trace of alcohol in this, Miss Lake." Non-alcoholic wine and champagne had tiny amounts of residual alcohol, left over from the removing process. He knew even a trace amount of alcohol could trigger cravings in some alcoholics.

"I'd like to propose a toast," said Farrell as he held up his glass. "Makani, would you join us, please."

The maître di poured a glass for himself. He'd had the waiter bring extras since patrons often spilled or dropped the delicate flutes. "I'd be honored," he said. They all raised their glasses and waited to hear Farrell's toast.

"I want to honor our host, Miss Dani Lake." All eyes turned to Dani, who blushed. Judith placed her hand on Dani's hand. "The consummate hostess," Farrell continued. "Over the past week, I've gotten to know Dani as a woman of integrity." He hadn't rehearsed his toast and hoped it would come out right. "You trusted me, you trusted all of us as Sapphire's friends. You opened your arms, your home, and your heart." Farrell swallowed hard. "Dani, you introduced me to the beautiful island of Kauai and my new friend, Kai. I'm excited to buy a home here. Meeting you has changed my life."

"Here, here," said Makani, with tears in his eyes.

"To Dani," said Sapphire.

"To Dani," Judith echoed.

"Thank you, Dani," said Sofia. "Beautiful toast, Farrell."

Dani let out a breath. "To Jane and Andre."

"Yes," said Sapphire. "To my parents."

With smiles all around, everyone sipped their sparkling white grape juice.

The group sat quietly for several moments until the waiter arrived. He took their order and removed the menus from the table.

Chapter 47
Encore

"Dani," said Sapphire. "What Farrell said is true. You've created an amazing memory for us all. You honored my parents' lives and ensured their legacy." The others nodded in agreement. "My mother's flower garden and my father's butterfly photographs brought their presence to Aromaticus. Plus, the entire work culture is a tribute to them." Her father's photographs continued to intrigue Sapphire. Why had she heard the words from her dream when she viewed them?

Dani let a single tear slip from her eye. Judith handed her a tissue. The Jandre flowers always touched her. She had made sure to plant them in a far-off corner of the gardens, where they wouldn't draw attention.

Dani dabbed her eyes and stood. Sapphire stood too. They shared a deep embrace.

"I just have one favor to ask of you, Dani," Sapphire said.

Uh-oh. Dani held her breath and waited.

"Do you have an extra suitcase I can borrow?" Sapphire asked. "I can't fit all the Aromaticus bags of memorabilia in mine."

Dani let out her breath. *Whew*! "Kai is at Costco now," she said. "He's picking up some supplies for me. I'll contact him. He can get you one there." She retrieved her cellphone from her purse and sent Kai a text.

"There's a Costco on Kauai?" asked Sofia. She loved shopping at Costco. If the formula replaced food, their entire food department would be eliminated. Another item to add to her list of things that would change in the world.

"Yes," said Dani. "It's near the airport in Lihue."

"Thank you, Dani," said Sapphire, feeling sad to be leaving in the morning. It was a bittersweet feeling since Sapphire also looked forward to being back home in Sedona.

Their dinner arrived. Sapphire, Sofia, Judith, Farrell, and Dani ate in silence. They ordered the tiramisu for dessert and spooned up every bit. For an encore, the sun went down in a spectacular burst of color.

As they left the restaurant, Makani kissed Dani on the cheek. She embraced him in a warm hug. He gave the other ladies a big hug as well. "I look forward to seeing you all again."

"Thank you for helping to make this a

memorable evening," said Farrell. When Makani reached out his hand for a handshake, Farrell put his arms around him in a bear hug. Sapphire put her hand to her heart. She loved seeing Farrell show his emotions.

Kai was waiting out front to drive the group back to Mango. He bounced out of the driver's seat and popped open the trunk. They all peeked inside and saw a small-sized suitcase with wheels. "I hope this is okay, Sapphire."

"Thank you, Kai," Sapphire said. "It's perfect." She would miss him. They piled into the car and Kai drove away. Five minutes later, they arrived at Mango.

"I'll see you in the morning." Kai was taking them to the airport very early. The others said good night. Sapphire, Farrell, and Sofia climbed the stairs to their rooms.

Judith stayed back. Would Dani invite her for tea? Their last night together.

"Tea?" Dani said to Judith as if reading her mind.

"That would be lovely," Judith said. "Let me help you prepare it." She followed Dani into the kitchen. Judith put the kettle on the stove while Dani set up delicate cups and saucers. Dani poured once the water boiled. They sat at the kitchen table and sipped their tea. "I want to show you photos of Miami and my home," said Judith. "Perhaps you'll visit me there sometime." Judith fished her cellphone out of her purse and browsed through her photos.

Dani scanned the photos as Judith scrolled to find the ones of her home. "Wait," said Dani. Her heart skipped a beat. "Are those pictures of the shawl? Star's shawl that I sent to Sapphire?" She hoped her voice sounded casual and didn't reveal concern. Why would Judith have photos of the shawl on her phone?

"Why yes," said Judith. She had taken the snapshots back in Sedona. "The weaving was unique. I'd never seen that pattern before." Was Dani concerned? Did Judith overstep? "Sapphire said it was okay me to take snapshots."

"Oh, yes!" said Dani. "The stitchery is very beautiful." Her voice was an octave higher. "I knew the weaver on Sanibel who created it." Dani relaxed her voice back to normal. "Unfortunately, she's no longer alive."

"That's why I've never seen it before," said Judith. "It's one of a kind."

"Yes, it is," said Dani. "It certainly is." The look she gave to Judith said that she would say no more about it. Judith didn't ask. Dani sipped her tea. Unanswered questions hung in the air. Why was Dani upset and secretive about the shawl? Did it have something to do with the formula? Aunt Star? Judith felt more determined than ever to research the stitching pattern.

Dani sat pensive and silent. Judith assumed that she was tired. The ladies finished their tea and said good night. A final good night for their last night together on Kauai.

Sapphire waited until she heard Judith come upstairs and return to her room. Dani would still be awake, but not for long. Quickly, she padded down the stairs and knocked on Dani's door.

"Come in," said Dani. *Why was Judith back so soon? Did she suspect I was holding back information about the shawl?*

Chapter 48
The Formula

The door opened. Sapphire walked in and immediately started speaking. "If you trust me, why haven't you given me the formula?" Her words spilled out as an accusation. "You've waited a long time to meet me and tell me about my parents. You've honored my parents' wishes by keeping the formula secret and protecting me all these years. Now, that I am here and you've told me about it, why haven't you shared it?"

Dani felt taken aback by Sapphire's boldness. "You're so much like your mother, Sapphire. You look like her and now you sound like her." Sapphire stared at her.

"There's a chemistry to developing a formula," said Dani. "Formulations are a multistep process where the active ingredient is mixed with other components. Natural substances, including the active essential oils, are combined to produce the final product." Sapphire stood erect and tilted her head. Was Dani going to give her a chemistry lesson? Sapphire continued to stare at Dani.

"I understand that the formula is complicated and is important to you," said Sapphire. "You either trust me or you don't."

"What will you do with the formula?" asked Dani. "Do you think that the world is ready for it now?"

"Is that why you're holding back?" asked Sapphire. "You want assurances that I'll make the right decision? I haven't decided what I will do with it. I only just learned about the formula, and I always take time to consider important decisions." Sapphire gazed out the window. The moon cast an eerie glow on trees silhouetted against the sky. "My strong sense of intuition has served me well. Perhaps my parents were always with me. I've felt their presence guiding me throughout my life. My connection to them has now grown stronger, thanks to you. You've given me that gift. Jane and Andre will continue to enlighten me towards the right decision. My heart remains open to their guidance."

Dani continued to be struck at how much Sapphire looked and sounded like Jane. Her eyes watered at the bittersweet memory. "Aunt Star directed you to the active ingredient," she said. "It'll all be clear very soon. The safety of the formula is dependent on concealing it in coded format. A code that Aunt Star developed. For you. Your mother entrusted Aunt Star with her daughter and her formula. I'm helping Aunt Star and your parents by honoring their wishes." Dani dabbed her eyes with a tissue. "She made me promise to make sure you received the shawl and ring."

Sapphire's agitation grew. Aunt Star's shawl and ring? What did they have to do with the formula? She remembered the ring's curious initials. "Who is JJM?" asked Sapphire. "They're inscribed in the ring."

Dani looked away. "Perhaps it's part of your legacy."

Sapphire stared at Dani again. My *legacy*? Why did this have to be so cryptic with clues and secrets?

Watching *The Wizard of OZ* every year with Aunt Star popped into Sapphire's mind. Aunt Star always made sure Sapphire learned from Dorothy and her friends. Answers come from within. Every visit to Sanibel, Aunt Star encouraged Sapphire to tune into clues in search of true meaning. Her aunt had trained her to find her intuition. Was she training Sapphire for finding the formula all that time? But why?

Dani stood silent; her lips tight. Was she holding back from saying more? Or was Dani just tense from their talk. Either way, Sapphire knew she wouldn't get any more tonight. She said good night to Dani and traipsed up the stairs. She would have to wait until she was back home to unravel the clues and cryptic messages. She tiptoed down the hallway, collapsed into bed, and fell into a deep sleep. *Keep the formula safe* whispered in her head as she opened her eyes the next morning.

Chapter 49
The Trip Home

Kai arrived before sunrise to drive the group to the airport. Farrell carried all their suitcases down the stairs and helped Kai load them into the SUV.

Dani hugged each of them goodbye at Mango. She preferred to say goodbye from there. Plus, there was no room left for her in the SUV. She handed Judith a keychain of a palm tree with a set of keys. Then she handed her an envelope containing a single piece of paper with the code for the alarm system at Star's home on Sanibel Island.

The sunrise displayed vibrant colors offering a final Kauai farewell. As Kai drove off, Dani waved from the doorway of Mango. She let out a sigh of relief. The visit had been a success. Dani had shared everything she planned to and more. A big weight was lifted from her shoulders, and an abundance of love replaced it.

When they reached the airport, Farrell helped Kai unload the suitcases. The group checked them at the outside baggage station. Farrell held on to Sapphire's smaller suitcase. It contained the white velvet bags and their precious contents. Too precious to check as baggage. It would go in the plane's overhead compartments. They all said their goodbyes to Kai. "I'll see you soon," Kai said. "Mahalo." He got back in his vehicle and drove off. The SUV was empty, but Kai's appreciation and hope filled the space.

The group made their way through check-in and security. Judith directed them to the lounge where they enjoyed coffee and muffins while they waited for their flight. Judith's cellphone dinged. Her brow furrowed. "Jared says there's a hurricane approaching Florida next week. Appears to be heading directly to the southwest coast of the state. If I want him to go with me to Star's home on Sanibel Island, we should get started as soon as possible." Judith was always a quick thinker and learned to be flexible with travel plans. "Sapphire, I should fly back to Miami when we arrive in Phoenix. I'll check with the desk concierge here for flights."

Sapphire nodded. "I understand. Thanks so much for coming to Sedona on a moment's notice to be there for me." She smoothed her hair away from her face. "And then to Kauai for another week."

Judith approached the front desk concierge in the lounge and returned to her friends five minutes later. "Okay," she said. "I'm booked on a flight home to Miami this evening. I have a two-hour layover in Phoenix. She calculated the time change but was confused between Hawaii's time zone, Arizona's, and Florida's. "I'll eat dinner or whatever meal it is at that time."

Sapphire's brow creased. Several devastating hurricanes had hit Florida over the years. Aunt Star's home withstood the hurricane-force winds, although her neighbors' homes suffered significant damage. "Be careful, Judith. I don't want you to go over there if it's dangerous weather." Sapphire hesitated before continuing. "And we still don't know what threats could be waiting at Aunt Star's home."

"That's why I'm going back to Miami tonight. Jared said he'll take me over to Sanibel this weekend. The hurricane's not scheduled to hit for several days later." Although, hurricane forecasts can be off. Jared would exercise caution. He was not one to charge into hazardous situations.

As on the incoming flight, Farrell sat next to Sapphire. Sofia sat next to Judith across the aisle. Sapphire wanted to sleep but so many thoughts ran through her mind. "I wonder if I'm the right person to have the responsibility of safeguarding the formula," she said in a hushed tone.

Farrell took her hand. "The formula couldn't be in better hands," he whispered.

"Farrell," she said. "I don't know if Dani gave me the formula." She kept her voice very quiet. "Remember, she said *you have the formula* not *you will have the formula*." Sapphire sighed. "Could it be in one of the white velvet bags in my suitcase? Or maybe it's at Aunt Star's house?"

"I doubt it," said Farrell. He repositioned his seatbelt as the plane took off. "Dani didn't want to go back there to collect anything. She only wanted to know if there were cameras and bugging devices."

"I'll look through everything in the bags when I empty them out at home. There's probably something tucked into one of them," said Sapphire.

"You learned so much about your parents." That's more important than the elusive formula." He was practical. "What good is it anyway, if you can't produce it."

"But Farrell," Sapphire said. "The formula would change the world." How could he not think it was a big deal? "It's bigger than the internet." She began to raise her voice, then looked around to see if anyone was listening. The passengers nearby were sleeping.

Farrell rubbed his chin. "The internet has its pros and cons too." Was Sapphire thinking of providing the nutrition formula to an organization for further research? "Can you imagine the environmental impact on the rainforest?" Fisher had shared his passion for protecting the environment. "Our ecosystem is fragile." Farrell was on a roll. He spoke in an emphatic whisper, "Your parents didn't release the formula because they cared about not damaging the environment. They wanted to protect the Amazon Rainforest, not have industries trampling on the lands, exploiting it."

"Okay, Farrell, I get it." Sapphire felt stung. "I care about the environment too. You know, Dani said that my parents had heated debates about this. I see both sides. I understand why they wanted to preserve the formula for a future time when the world would be ready. I'm going to get some sleep now." Sapphire was too keyed up to sleep but she needed a break from debating with Farrell.

"Sorry, Sapphire," Farrell said. "I didn't mean to accuse you of being insensitive to the environment." It was complicated for Farrell. Fisher had devoted his life to protecting the environment. They'd talked about these things all the time. He missed Fisher. Spending time with Kai reminded him of how much he missed Fisher. The two men were nothing alike, but Farrell hadn't spent time with male friends since Fisher's death. His male professional acquaintances only talked about business. Kai and Farrell talked about life. And although Kai was almost young enough to be his grandson, Farrell learned a lot from him. He didn't yet have the words to explain that to Sapphire. "I guess I'll try to get some sleep too."

Across the aisle, Judith and Sofia also discussed the formula. "Would you try it if you had the opportunity?" Sofia whispered Judith. She felt so conflicted. On one hand, she loved the life-saving possibilities. On the other, she felt a deep loss when she envisioned a world without food. "I'm not sure we were meant to artificially extend life."

"I have misgivings too," said Judith, also whispering. "But the plants used to create essential oils aren't artificial. What's more natural than plant leaves? Especially if organically grown."

"I guess you're right," said Sofia. "But if people live longer, it'll disrupt the natural order of souls moving through lives, as they learn lessons through their spiritual journeys."

Judith smiled as she teased Sofia. "Spoken like a true Sedona resident. And you've only lived there a year."

"Metaphysical, new age, spiritual, divine, sacred, ecclesiastical," said Sofia. "I hear these terms and it's all semantics." She put her hand on her heart. "I know there's something that holds us all together. It doesn't matter what you call it."

"You're right my dear." She placed her hand on Sofia's arm. "It's called love," said Judith. "We felt the love vibrating in the air during our time on Kauai. It wasn't a change in atmospheric pressure or elevation."

"You had a special connection with Dani from the start," said Sofia. It was so sweet to observe. "It's as if the two of you'd known each other your entire lives." Sofia missed her best friend, Lena. They had that connection. Time, nor distance, diluted their bond.

Judith smiled. "I felt comfortable with her right away. I was quite surprised. I'm going to miss her. A lot. I invited her to visit me in Miami." Judith hoped she would come.

Sofia yawned. "I'm going to take a nap." She usually couldn't fall asleep on planes, but maybe this time would be different.

"Me too," said Judith.

The two ladies fell fast asleep. Sapphire too. Farrell closed his eyes, feeling blessed to be surrounded by an abundance of love. He reached far back in his heart and told his younger self, *see, it turned out okay after all.*

Chapter 50
The Butterfly Photographs

Two days later, Sapphire, Sofia, Judith, and Farrell had returned to their normal routines. It was business as usual for Farrell, and he was busier than ever. Sofia prepared eggplant parmesan using Pearl's recipe. Her friends gave rave reviews. She also wore her new signature scent, ylang-ylang.

Judith was on her way to Sanibel Island with Jared Silver. He was going to sweep Aunt Star's house for listening devices and cameras. Judith would pretend to be a prospective buyer with Jared as her realtor. The two would talk with neighbors and inquire if anyone had been in the home.

Hi Judith, Sapphire had texted that morning. *Say hello to Jared and tell him I hope he visits Sedona again soon. Have a safe trip.* She was glad they would be there and back before the hurricane hit the coast. Would Jared notice if there was anything pointing to Aunt Star's suspicious death?

With Aunt Star's shawl around her shoulders, Sapphire happily planned the interior design for

Celestial, the home on Kauai. She would follow Fisher's custom and hire local artisans to imbue Celestial with Kauai's traditional culture. Sapphire methodically unpacked her treasured Aromatics bags with photos, news clippings, awards, and lists from her parents. She poured through each one leisurely. Where would she place each treasure? The photo of her father proposing to her mother will grace her home in Sedona.

Next sapphire studied the butterfly photos taken by her father. She felt so grateful Dani had given them to her. They were as spectacular as the blow-up versions hanging on the factory walls in Aromaticus. She decided she would hang her father's photographs in Celestial.

Sapphire brought the photographs to Joe at Sedona Framing. She had trusted him with many beautiful pieces of artwork over the years. "Could you please help me select the best mounting, matt borders, and frames for my father's photos?" she asked Joe. "They were taken over 40 years ago."

Joe peered closely at each one. "These are magnificent. The flowers and leaves in the background give the butterflies dimension and character. Your father managed to keep both the butterflies in the foreground and the leaves in the background in sharp focus. He was a skilled photographer."

Sapphire smiled.

"Settings on cameras were manual at that time," Joe continued. "No automatic focus. No camera phones." He took out his magnifying glass and pointed to a small caption in the corner of one photograph. *He pua laha 'ole.* "Do you know what that means?"

Sapphire shook her head. "I have no idea."

"Sounds Hawaiian," said Joe. "You don't want me to crop that out, do you?" He handed the magnifying glass to Sapphire.

One by one, Sapphire studied each photograph. They all held the same inscription. "Oh," said Sapphire. "That's my mother's script." Her heart leaped. "Please make sure to leave it showing." She snapped a photo of the inscription with her iPhone and wrote down the words on a piece of scrap paper. "I'll look up that phrase when I get home."

Sapphire stuffed the paper in her purse and hurried off to other errands. All the while, her mind kept returning to Judith and Jared. They'd be at Aunt Star's home on Sanibel Island later today. What would they find?

By the time Sapphire got home, she forgot about the inscription.

Chapter 51
Brewing Storm

Jared picked Judith up at six AM for the three-hour drive to Sanibel Island. The route over Alligator Alley through the Everglades was serene. "Doesn't look like a storm is brewing," she said. It felt like the old days at WITSEC, going on adventurous work assignments.

Jared was retired from the FBI for a year. He put off retirement when he became widowed and could no longer fulfill his dream of traveling with his beloved wife, Bonnie. Judith encouraged him to embrace his retirement. Jared's spunky great-nephew, Taylor became his traveling partner.

"How was New Zealand?" Judith asked Jared.

"Incredible," he said. "Taylor planned everything. Did you know that New Zealand is two islands?"

"No, I didn't," said Judith. She wanted to hear more, but the bridge in the far distance caught her eye. "Sanibel Causeway is ahead." As they drove over the bridge, she sat up straighter and craned her neck to catch a first glimpse of the Sanibel Lighthouse. She couldn't wait to get to Star's home.

"There's the lighthouse," Jared pointed to the left off in the distant horizon. "Is Kauai anything like Sanibel?"

"Kauai is like Kauai," Judith said. The lush tropical island was unique. "Imagine Sanibel, more beautiful, with less humidity, fewer mosquitoes, and less no-see-ums." Judith found the keys in her purse, along with the alarm code. She handed both to Jared when they reached the other side of the bridge. "You're my realtor so you should have these." Judith was getting into her role. Many tourists dreamed of owning a beach refuge. It was an easy role to play. "Turn left over here. Periwinkle Way."

"Slow down," she said. "The house is coming up on the right." Judith scanned the house numbers until she found the dolphin-themed mailbox. "Sapphire painted that design one year during her annual visits to Aunt Star."

Jared pulled into the empty driveway. As they exited the car, he scanned the roofline for hidden cameras. All he spotted was an outdated security camera obscured by a tree limb. "Are you sure that Aunt Star never had security cameras installed?"

"Dani said Aunt Star refused to," said Judith.

Jared tucked his briefcase under his arm. He carried a clipboard in one hand and the dolphin keychain in the other. "Stay here," he told Judith. "I want to check it out first." He punched the alarm code on the keypad. Telltale scratches were noticeable on the cover plate. Had someone tampered with the alarm system? *Beep beep beep* chirped softly as it disarmed. Jared disappeared into the house.

After a full five minutes passed, Judith was worried. What was Jared doing? Did he find cameras?

Finally, Jared emerged, all smiles. "You're going to love this home, Judith. It's a perfect beach getaway. Just what you're looking for." Under his breath, without losing the winning smile, Jared whispered to Judith. "Your friend was right, there are cameras and bugging devices inside. They appear to be motion activated. Keep up your role. I believe we're being seen and heard."

"If it has the wide unobstructed beach view that you promised," said Judith, "I will love it." She put on her scrutinizing buyer face and followed Jared inside. Judith could tell right away that Sapphire had a hand in decorating the home. Familiar beach décor adorned the white walls, with turquoise and aqua hues throughout. "Simply elegant," said Judith. "So far, I like the energy."

Judith went from room to room, being careful to not touch anything. She could tell which room Sapphire slept in. It had a faint aroma of mint. There was a small bookshelf in one corner with books lined up neatly in size order.

Jared ushered Judith toward the windows in the living room. "And here is your beach view," said Jared continuing to use a raised voice. As promised, it was spectacular.

"Wow!" Exclaimed Judith in high-pitched tones for the benefit of the listening devices Jared had noticed. She took out her iPhone and snapped a photo of the ocean. "I'm sending this to my daughter right now." Since she was pretending, she might as well give herself a pretend daughter. Judith texted the photo to her pretend daughter and added the message *I want to take a book from the bookshelf in the front bedroom.* The text went to Jared.

After he glanced at the text, Jared turned to Judith. "So, if you want to make an offer. I suggest we do so right away."

"Yes," said Judith. "I'd love to."

"Let's go in here and get to work." Jared guided Judith to Sapphire's bedroom. He scribbled some figures on a piece of paper and handed it to Judith. "Here's the amount I think the seller will accept."

Judith read Jared's note. *Get your book quickly. I'll block the camera hidden in the light switch.* "I can swing that amount," she said, continuing her buyer role.

Jared positioned his body in front of the light switch to block the hidden camera. He stretched his arms and pulled his shoulders back. "That car ride really cramped my back," he said for the sake of anyone watching.

He gave Judith an imperceptible nod. She kneeled at the bookshelf and swiftly scanned the book titles. Her eye fell on a particular book. That was the one. She slipped the chosen book inside her large purse. Judith didn't need to act when she groaned upon standing. Her creaky bones and stiff joints were real.

They left the home as they found it, minus one book. Their mission was accomplished. Back in the car, Jared played the weather station which tracked the storm. *Category four* and *headed toward the southwest coast of Florida* blared with a loud warning.

"What did you see in the house?" Judith asked. "Were there really cameras like Dani suspected? And bugging devices too?"

"Yes," Jared said. "Old fashioned and outdated but they appeared to be hooked up and recording.

My buddies with the FBI will track down who installed them and find out if anyone is monitoring them."

"Please let me know right away, as soon as you get answers." said Judith. "I want to let the others know."

"The FBI will figure it out," said Jared. "And I'll let you know as soon as they give approval to release the information."

"You played a convincing realtor, Jared. I wonder who set up the cameras," said Judith. "And how long they were there."

"We'll get to the bottom of this." Jared turned up the radio as another storm report warned of hurricane-force winds getting closer. "We got there and out just in time," he said. "They're evacuating the island."

Chapter 52
Demolished

Two days later, as predicted, a category four hurricane touched down on the southwest coast of Florida, destroying most of the homes on Sanibel Island. The Sanibel Causeway bridge collapsed like tinker toys at three places into San Carlos Bay. Sapphire phoned Judith as soon as she heard the news. "Aunt Star's house was leveled," Judith reported to Sapphire. "Sorry I couldn't retrieve anymore items for you before the hurricane hit." Judith hadn't yet told Sapphire about the book she filched on her trip.

"I have everything I want from the house," said Sapphire. "Aunt Star's shawl, her ring, and my memories. I'm just relieved that Aunt Star wasn't alive to see her beloved island destroyed."

"I'd like to fly out to Sedona," Judith said. "I have something to show you. As soon as air traffic is up and running on a regular schedule." Thousands were stranded in local airports waiting to get home while airlines scrambled to reschedule flights.

"It'd be lovely to see you, Judith," said Sapphire.

"Great," said Judith. "I'll see you in about a week, I hope." Everything would make more sense when she gave Sapphire the book, especially when she read the inscription.

Chapter 53
The Reveal

Judith arrived at Sapphire's home two weeks later. Sofia and Farrell had gathered at Sapphire's for their little reunion. "I think Judith has something important to tell me," Sapphire had told them. "Maybe it's about the formula."

Judith hugged each of them enjoying a familiar aroma drifting from the kitchen. The table was set with a large salad and crusty Italian bread. "Sofia, did you cook our favorite meal? And is that mango iced tea?"

"Yes," said Sofia. "We're recreating the meal we had at Mango. I tried a tiramisu recipe. Hopefully, it'll taste better than it looks."

"Well, what are we waiting for?" said Judith. "Let's eat." Farrell carried her suitcase to her usual guest room while Judith washed her hands. They all gathered at the table and dug in. Most of the dinner conversation was about Farrell's new home on Kauai. The sales contract was moving along smoothly, and closing was in two weeks.

Farrell's plate was empty first. He wiped up the last bit of sauce with a piece of Italian bread.

Soon they all enjoyed generous goblets of tiramisu. "Makani wants to see a group photo of us," said Sapphire.

Farrell set up a tripod that as they each posed with a forkful of messy tiramisu halfway to their smiling mouths. "Perfect," said Farrell. "I'll send it to Makani."

"After dessert, I want to show you the photos I had framed to hang at Celestial," said Sapphire. "I'm so pleased with the way they turned out."

Judith said, "I'll be right back." She quickly retrieved the book from the guest bedroom and slipped it inside an Aromaticus bag Sapphire had given her.

Farrell and Sapphire leaned the framed photos against the living room walls. "They're stunning," Judith said. "Those frames really make the colors pop." She noticed an inscription at the bottom of each framed photo. She put her reading glasses on and peered closer. "What does that say?"

"It's my mother's handwriting," Sapphire said. "I had to look it up. It's a Hawaiian expression. *He pua laha 'ole.* It means *the flower not common.*"

Judith's eyes widened. "Those flowers behind the butterflies. We've seen those before." She scrolled through her snapshots of Kauai from her cellphone.

"Here it is." She held up her phone for Sapphire, Farrell, and Sofia to see.

They all gathered close to the phone. Judith's hand shook. "May I?" Sapphire gently took the phone in her hands. What was Judith so nervous about?

"Enlarge my snapshot with the edit feature," Judith said. "And hold it up next to one of the butterfly pictures." Sapphire did as instructed. "That picture is from Kauai Coffee," said Judith. "Remember? Dani planted those flowers. They were a rare variety and your mother's favorite. She named them Jandre."

"A rare variety?" said Sofia "And *flower not common* is on each of your father's butterfly photographs in your mother's script?" Sofia remembered something else. "Dani told us that she and your parents observed the butterflies in the garden." She pointed to one of the framed photographs. "They watched them for hours."

"Right," said Sapphire. "My parents and Dani took note of which plants the butterflies were drawn to." She squinted at the leaves on the unusual white flowers. "The leaves in your cellphone photo look identical to the leaves in my father's butterfly photographs." Sapphire's heart beat faster.

"The leaves are quite unusual," said Sofia. "Maybe Andre was photographing the leaves."

"Sapphire, please bring Aunt Star's shawl here," Judith said. Sapphire spied the white velvet bag by Judith's side as she hurried to get Aunt Star's shawl.

Farrell placed his face inches from one of the framed photographs. He was as close to the leaves as the butterflies were. "I wonder if these flowers grow in the Amazon?"

"Here's the shawl," Sapphire said, gently handing it to Judith.

"Please put it on, Sapphire," Judith said. "And stand next to the framed photographs."

Wrapped in Aunt Star's shawl, Sapphire stood next to one of her father's framed photographs. Farrell's jaw dropped. "I see it," he said.

"See what?" said Sapphire. "What do you see? Tell me!"

"Please allow me to put it on," said Sofia. "You stand back and look." Sapphire gently handed Aunt Star's shawl to Sofia. "Now stand back, farther," Sofia said.

Sapphire sat on the couch. She peered at her aunt's shawl, then her father's framed photograph, then back at the shawl. "Is that a leaf pattern woven in the shawl? Oh my! The design woven in Aunt

Star's shawl is the same as the leaves in the photographs."

"And the leaves are the same as the ones in my snapshot of your mother's favorite flowers," said Judith.

The room remained silent as everyone stared at the photographs. The butterflies now took backstage to the leaves. The green hues vibrated as the leaves appeared to be blowing in the wind.

Chapter 54
Hidden in Plain Sight

Sapphire, Farrell, Sofia, and Judith stared at the leaves with new eyes. "What does this all mean?" Sapphire asked. No one had an answer. She eyed the Aromaticus bag in Judith's lap. "What's in the bag?"

"Oh," said Judith. "I took a book from your room in Aunt Star's house the day Jared and I visited Sanibel Island." It still felt unreal to her that the island was now devastated, and Aunt Star's house demolished. Judith removed the treasured tome from the bag. It was large and heavy. The title on the spine had drawn Judith to it. "This was required reading when I began my training program for the Witness Protection Program sixty years ago. I still own a copy, with underlines, highlights, and notes scribbled in the margins." She cradled the book lovingly, then offered it to Sapphire.

Sapphire glanced at the book as she returned to her seat. "That's not *my* book," she said. "I've never seen it before."

"It is now," said Judith. "Read the inscription." Judith had read it several times.

Sapphire read it to herself, then read it aloud. "Happy Birthday, Sapphire. May the strength and determination of generations of women before you provide loving warmth and be your guiding star."

She sighed. "Aunt Star must have planned on giving me the book for my birthday. But COVID kept me from traveling." Sapphire silently repeated the words from the inscription: *strength, determination, warmth,* and *guiding star.* She glanced at Sofia with the shawl wrapped around her shoulders. Did *warmth* refer to the shawl? Did *generations of women* refer to her mother and Aunt Star? She peered at her ring. Was the star-sapphire gem her *guiding star*? Sapphire felt her heart beat through her chest.

"What's the title of the book?" asked Sofia.

Judith recited, "Hidden in Plain Sight: The History of Women in Steganography."

"Isn't that the old-fashioned shorthand that secretaries used to use?" asked Farrell.

"No, that's *STEN* ography," said Judith. She slowly pronounced each syllable. "*STEG AN O GRA PHY* is the practice of hiding information in plain sight."

"You mean like a secret code?" asked Farrell. "Like the secret codes you used to communicate with Fisher when he was relocated?"

Judith nodded. "Words or symbols can be incorporated into weaving. It's known as name drafting." Judith stared at the shawl wrapped around Sofia. Sapphire and Farrell stared at it too. Sofia looked down at the edge of the shawl. The unusually shaped green leaves stared back at her.

Sapphire leafed through the pages and selected a passage to read aloud. "Steganography was used as a tool for communication between women. The fiber revolution and the information revolution defined women's roles in the history of cryptography." She read more keywords that jumped out at her. "Tantalizing, Leveraged for Secrecy, Networking, Security."

A sheath of paper fell from the pages and sailed to the floor. Sapphire lifted it into her hands. A faint scent of mint escaped. "The letterhead reads *The Sanibel Island Weavers*," Sapphire announced. "It's dated June 18, 1971. I would have been twelve at that time, three years before my parents died." She continued reading aloud.

> *Dear Star, Thank you very much for your generous donation of a floor loom. I'm sorry that the hobby didn't work out for you. Your one creation was stunning. Eye strain and joint pain in*

the fingers are common struggles for weavers. Our group auctioned your loom off to the highest bidder at our annual fundraising event. At your request, a portion of the funds was donated to the J. N. Ding Darling National Wildlife Refuge.

The Sanibel Island Weavers

"I've gone kayaking in Ding Darling on Sanibel," said Sofia. "It's the largest undeveloped mangrove ecosystem in the United States." She' had always loved seeing the birds and exotic plants.

"Your one creation was stunning," murmured Sapphire. "Did Aunt Star weave this shawl? I don't remember any looms at her home."

"Dani told me that she knew the weaver who created the shawl," said Judith. "I was showing her photos from my iPhone. She noticed the picture I'd snapped of the weaving. I thought the pattern was interesting. When Dani spotted the picture, her voice changed. She had a strange look on her face too."

"Did she say anything else?" Sapphire asked.

Judith thought back. "Dani said that the weaver was no longer alive."

"The shawl looks like it was skillfully woven by an experienced artisan, not an amateur," said

Sofia. "If Aunt Star taught herself to weave, that would be pretty amazing."

"Aunt Star was an amazing woman," said Sapphire. "My mother was the one who shone since she was a scientist, but Aunt Star had impressive skills. I really admired her. She taught herself to cook, bake, garden, draw, and paint. And so much more."

"Could she have taught herself to weave?" Sofia asked. "Wouldn't that have been hard to do?"

"Aunt Star taught herself anything she wanted to learn," Sapphire said. "I guess you could call her a Renaissance woman."

"I wonder what type of leaf that is," said Farrell. "Fisher downloaded an app for me that identifies plants. I still have it." He found the app on his phone and took a photo of the plant leaves on the shawl. "Unable to Identify," he read aloud. "Let me try the leaves on the butterfly photographs." He held the camera close to the leaves and snapped the photo. The app again displayed *Unable to Identify.*

"Try this one," Judith said. She found her snapshot of the white flowers that Dani had planted by the exit of Kauai Coffee. "I'm going to forward it to you." Taylor, Jared's great-nephew had showed her how to share photos from her iPhone. The satisfying sound of *swish* sent it soaring through the internet.

"Got it," said Farrell. "Let me upload it to the app." Sapphire held her breath. Judith crossed her fingers. "It's displaying the thinking logo," Farrell reported as he stared at the screen.

Finally, the app displayed a response. "Third time's a charm," said Farrell. He read the caption aloud. "Unnamed rare exotic plant, indigenous to the Amazon Rain Forest. ENDANGERED."

"Dani named that flower Jandre," said Judith. Her eyebrows raised. "Remember?"

"In honor of my parents," Sapphire said as she shot out of her seat. "Didn't Kai tell us that McBryde Gardens originally owned the land now occupied by Kauai Coffee?"

"Yes," said Farrell. "And McBryde Gardens was one of the gardens at the National Tropical Botanical Gardens." The room had grown dark. He stood up to turn on the lights.

"Where your parents had their first lab," said Sofia. "Maybe Jandre is the leaf they used to produce the main ingredient in the nutrition formula." She spoke faster than usual. "It's rare and exotic, grows in the Amazon, and is endangered."

"But didn't Dani also say that a common mint leaf enhanced the properties?" asked Judith.

Sapphire quickly removed the ring from her finger. "I didn't know what the inscription meant. Could *JJM* stand for Jandre Jandre Mint?"

Everyone focused on Aunt Star's shawl again. Sapphire and Judith spoke at the same time. "Mint leaves interspersed with the Jandre leaves." The room buzzed with excitement.

Sofia sprang up and opened the flashlight function on her smartphone for closer examination. "Those initials could've been inscribed at any time," she said. "Maybe Aunt Star had them engraved on the ring."

Farrell pulled Sapphire closer to the shawl. "The pattern is two Jandre leaves, then one mint leaf, and then it repeats," he said. He pointed to a leaf. "Sapphire, is that a mint leaf?"

"Yes," Sapphire said. "Spearmint."

"So, two Jandre leaves for every spearmint leaf," Farrell said. "That could be the formula. Two to one ratio!"

"Remember the book's inscription?" Sapphire asked. Her words spilled out quickly. "*Generations of women*: my mother, Aunt Star, and Dani. *Warmth*: the shawl. *Guiding star*: the ring." Sapphire took a quick breath. "The shawl has the pattern of Jandre, Jandre, and mint. The ring has the initials JJM. The butterfly photographs show the Jandre leaves." Her voice reached a fevered pitch. "Dani planted my mother's favorite flower where my mother discovered the formula. She named the flowers Jandre." Sapphire grinned at her friends with satisfaction.

"The active ingredients for the formula," said Farrell.

"Yes," said Judith. "But where's the full formulation?"

"The book!" cried Sofia.

Sapphire quickly flipped the pages. She couldn't take the time to turn them gingerly. Even so it was taking too long. She held the book up on its side and frantically shimmied the pages. A single paper sailed to the floor. She snatched it up. Her eyes raced back and forth on the paper.

"It's full of chemistry symbols," exclaimed Sapphire. "In my mother's script. The formula!" She bounced out of her seat and showed the paper to the others. "Look, *JJM*," she said, pointing to the one symbol she knew.

Everyone sighed with relief. They'd found the formula.

"What now?" asked Sofia.

Sapphire clutched the paper close to her heart. *Keep the formula safe* vibrated in her mind.

Keep the formula safe until the world is ready for it. A shared secret hung in the air. *Keep the formula safe.*

Chapter 55
The F.B.I.

Jared could think of nothing else in the past two days since visiting Star's home with Judith. It had taken him only five seconds to recognize the ancient recording devices and cameras. While Judith was waiting for him, he'd called his old FBI partner Devon Newton. The conversation played over in his mind.

"Hey boss," said Newton. "Great to hear from you, old buddy. What's going on?"

"Hi Newton," said Jared, relieved he got ahold of him right away. "I'm fine. Listen, I've got a favor to ask you."

"Yeah, of course, boss," said Newton." Anything you need, you know I'm here for you. Hit me up."

"I'm here at this house on Sanibel Island with Judith Saltan," said Jared. "She's waiting outside right now so I need to be quick." Judith would become suspicious soon. "Sapphire's Aunt Star lived here until she died a month ago."

"I remember Judith and Sapphire very well," said Newton. "We all worked so well together last year to investigate Fisher's death."

"Judith's friend came here to clean it out and thought the house might have cameras and listening devices," said Jared. "She was spooked. I told Judith I'd sweep the house for bugs."

"Sure, boss," said Newton. "What do you need?"

"Well, it's kind of weird," Jared said. "There are these ancient cameras here and recording devices that are government issue. I can't believe it. They look like they're from fifty years ago. I'm texting you the serial numbers now and the address of the home."

"I'll search the database to see who they were issued to," said Newton. "Got it. Hold on," he said. "I'm on it now."

"Thanks, buddy," said Jared. "Please hurry, Judith won't wait much longer, and I don't want her to know that there's FBI equipment here. Too confidential and who knows where it'll lead." She would come charging in very soon.

"Whoa," said Newton. "Those devices were stolen." He scanned the report quickly. "You're right. Fifty years ago. They were never found, but the agency had a suspect." Jared heard Newton tell his new partner to get moving. "I'm on my way out to the house now," he told Jared.

"Thanks, buddy," Jared said. "I'm texting you the alarm code and leaving the key under the back porch. I gotta go." He put on his best realtor smile and swung into action with Judith.

The hurricane touched down two days after Jared's visit to Star's home, demolishing most of the homes on Sanibel Island.

The ringing of his smartphone brought Jared back to the present. He answered right away.

"Hi partner," said Newton. "We retrieved the devices. Dusted for fingerprints and it led us to the culprit."

Whew. Jared had hoped Newton would be able to retrieve the ancient equipment and track down the person who planted it. If Jared wasn't retired, he'd have investigated himself.

"We were able to close an old case," said Newton. "Over fifty years ago a scientist named Duke Earnst approached the FBI. He claimed to have information about a secret nutrition formula. Duke expected a reward and called it a referral fee. Said it was his patriotic duty to offer the formula to the United States before other countries. Duke had no proof and was written off."

Jared continued to listen intently.

"After several years of unsuccessful attempts to garner interest from the agency, Duke applied for a technician job with the FBI. He was somehow able to pass the screening process and began the training program. But he washed out before the end of his first week. Deemed psychologically unstable and a risk to the agency. There was suspicions Duke was responsible for the theft of equipment. Nothing in the report about the FBI investigating that. The serial numbers of the bugging devices matched the serial numbers you sent me."

"Incredible," said Jared. "Good work!"

Newton continued. "Ten years later, a CIA operative working undercover to combat drug trafficking ran into Duke in South America. Our operative reported that Duke had tried to sell a secret nutrition formula to the Columbian government, claiming to know where the formula was hidden. Duke was ignored initially, but finally met with a team of corrupt government inspectors. They took an interest but demanded proof. Duke promised to direct them to the formula for a fee. The operative lost his trail when our government abruptly pulled him off the drug trafficking task force for security measures. Violence in Columbia had escalated and was out of control. No further reports of Duke had surfaced. Until now." Newton stopped to take a breath before continuing.

"We picked up Duke Earnst at his home in Fort Meyers Beach, Florida. In addition to theft of FBI equipment, he's now a suspect in several murders. He's in custody with the FBI, pending charges."

"Great detective work, partner," said Jared. "Let me know when I can notify Sapphire and her friends." He knew the routine. The complete investigation would take time.

"One more thing," Newton added. "I found an FBI old timer who remembered this guy. He said no one in the agency took him seriously, even when he threatened to sell the formula to other countries. They called him Duke the Kook."

"Glad you could tie up an old case," said Newton. "Sounds like you've got more work ahead of you. Thanks for letting me know."

"Anytime, boss," said Newton. "So, where are you and Taylor traveling next?"

"Taylor's taking a course in high school about the environment. He's studying the effects of the internet on climate change and the world's response to the global crisis," said Jared. "We've booked a trip to the Amazon. Taylor wants to see the Rain Forest before it disappears."

Chapter 56
Reversal of Fortune

Duke squinted his eyes. The feed from his ancient video camera showed activity! He hadn't turned it on in days. When he switched it on, he saw a recording from the day before. Coffee splattered from his mouth as he sputtered aloud. "Who's in the house?" Staticky voices broadcasted from the hidden audio microphones. A woman's voice. *This house is simply elegant. So far, I like the energy here.* Next Duke heard a man's voice. *And HERE is your beach view.*

Duke scratched his unkempt beard. Huh, a realtor was showing the home to a perspective buyer? Phew! At least the family was not back to remove all the contents.

"There's still time to find the formula," he exclaimed out loud. "It must be there." He'd better get back there before the house is sold. He still hadn't completed sifting through every item in Star's house. Surely the formula was hidden somewhere in her belongings.

Duke poured himself another cup of coffee. He drank it down in one long swallow. A nosy neighbor had confronted him last time he was there to search the house. He squelched her suspicions by acting like a realtor.

After he downed another cup of coffee, he left to take a walk on the pier. When he returned, he prepared for bed with a plan for the next day. He would go back to Star's home and resume his search. His old locksmith tools worked like a charm the first time. It was easy to filch a spare key from Star's drawer and copy the alarm code he found hidden in her jewelry box.

The next morning, Duke woke up in a frenzy. His reflection in the mirror was disheveled with hair flying in all directions. His beady eyes never saw the secret bugging devices Newton planted behind the mirror. He never suspected the FBI entered his house while he walked on the pier the night before.

Duke ranted out loud to his reflection. "It's got to be in that house. I won't stop until I find it!" He paced his small bathroom. Forty-six years ago, he'd been so close to wrapping his hands on the secret formula. "Stupid Columbians!" He'd told them about the formula. He was set to make millions. Then the Columbians spotted the secret lab on Jane and Andre's farm. They double crossed Duke. Tried to cut him out of the deal. "But I showed them. Blew up that inspector's office. Who knew Jane and Andre would be there?"

At least he wasn't caught. Gullible government officials believed his anonymous tip. Jane and Andre Dover were tied to an underground subversive group. It all wrapped up neatly. Duke returned to his reflection. "I'm brilliant. Always have been and always will. Soon the world will see!"

Duke's coffee cup was empty. He plodded to the kitchen to brew more. He never noticed the spy device hidden in one of the stove dials. When the coffee was ready, Duke gulped large swallows of bitter black coffee. Then he continued his rant. "Yes, I'm brilliant. Wasn't caught for killing Jane and Andre. And wasn't caught stealing the spy equipment from the FBI. I was so clever to enter their training program just to steal the devices."

Duke started to pace back and forth in his kitchen. "Never got caught spying on Star's home either. She had no idea who took her Aromaticus bottles. Too bad the secret formula wasn't in any of them. And it wasn't in the ones I took after I killed her. Stupid lady! I had to poison her."

If only Star had told him where the formula was, he would've left her alone. He gave her a chance. She refused. How else could he sift through everything in the house? She drank her favorite tea daily, unaware of the tasteless poison he'd sprayed on her dried mint leaves. Being a brilliant chemist had its advantages. No one would ever suspect him. No autopsy. As far as everyone knew, an old lady died peacefully in her sleep.

Duke maneuvered through his living room, now pacing around the couch. He turned on the television and found the news channel. Duke didn't see the bugging device hidden in the knob on the coffee table. He was on his sixth cup of coffee.

"I know it's hidden somewhere in that house! I'll remove every floorboard. I'll smash every stick of furniture. I'll rip out all the electrical wiring. I'll pull out the drywall. I'll open every plumbing pipe. I'll tear down the ceiling. I'll knock over every beam. I'll —

"Wait." What was that he heard on TV? A hurricane was coming? Scheduled to land right here? In Ft. Meyers? Evacuation orders in place? Not me! I'll ride this one out. "Nothing can kill me. I'm cleverer than nature. I'm more powerful than any hurricane. I'm brilliant and immortal. Once I get my hands on the formula, everyone will be in awe and revere me. I'll have the respect and admiration I deserve. I'll be awarded the Nobel Prize. The world will know that I am a genius.

Finally!" His screechy laugh reached a frenzied pitch.

"Duke's cackling sounds like the wicked witch of the north," said Newton. The other two agents chuckled. Their black van was only one block away. "We've got enough," said Newton. "Let's go pick him up."

Chapter 57
Sedona and Kauai

A month later, Silver finally broke the news to Sapphire about the murders of her parents and Aunt. Sapphire felt stunned. Then saddened. Although she felt disturbed by the news, it provided Sapphire answers to her lingering questions. The clarity helped her make an important decision: what to do with the formula.

Sapphire was filled with questions and concerns about the formula's fate. If she released it, would it remain in reputable hands? How could she prevent big pharma and government agencies from controlling it? If she held on to it for now, and later entrusted it to someone to *keep safe for the future*, who would be the right person? This sacred mission required someone who cherished the environment. It also had to be a person younger than her by several generations. Could this person help her with the beginning steps of releasing it? Then the person could follow through, monitor, and protect it for future generations.

Sapphire realized she needed help to sort all this out. She generously applied her Aromaticus spearmint essential oil to her temples and wrist pulse points. Aunt Star's shawl rested on her shoulders. The star-sapphire ring encircled her finger. The photo of her father proposing to her mother at Spouting Horn hung on the wall facing her. Sapphire sat in meditation, focusing on Sedona's red rocks through her open window. As always, they could lead her to answers.

When she arrived on Kauai the following week, Farrell and Sapphire inspected the completed renovations at his beach home in Princeville. "The new wooden staircase to the ocean shore looks sturdy," said Farrell. "And that was a great idea to add a small shower at the base of the path to wash off the sand before we enter the house."

Sapphire admired the octogen skylight. "It's just like I envisioned. Look at how the sunlight shines through the stained glass and paints beautiful colors on the floor." She had decorated the home in white, aqua, and deep ocean turquoise hues.

For the final touch, Sapphire created an intricate sign. Dani arrived just as Kai proudly pounded the stake into the ground in front of the home. Then they all stood back and admired the intricate letters. *CELESTIAL.*

To celebrate the posting of the sign, Farrell, Sapphire, Dani, and Kai rested outside on the new beach lounges, sipping mint water. Kai handed Farrell the building permits. "I thought you'd like to see these for yourself," said Kai.

"Granted in record time," Farrell said, after studying them. "Never seen that before."

"Governmental officials were thrilled to support housing for Aromaticus employees," said Kai. "The property had already been zoned for residential homes. The construction timeline is ahead of schedule. It'll be completed in about a year."

At sunset, Farrell told Sapphire his story as they walked on the beach. "I was only fifteen and have no memory of what happened," said Farrell. He explained how he was accused of forcing himself on his girlfriend. How his father sent Farrell away to save his political career. "I was drunk that night, but to this day, I can't believe I'd ever force myself on anyone." He sighed. The last ray of sun dropped below the horizon. "I tried to talk to her, but our parents forbade us to have any contact."

Sapphire hugged Farrell and said, "I'm honored that you finally told me."

"It really is a relief," said Farrell. He had more to tell Sapphire. "I finally swallowed my pride and accompanied Makani to my first AA meeting."

Sapphire smiled. "Will you continue attending?"

"We'll see, maybe," said Farrell. "*One day at a time* is the mantra I learned at AA. I phone Makani from time to time. He's a good listener, and a good friend."

The next morning Dani welcomed Judith and Sofia for a visit. Within hours of their arrival, Farrell, Sapphire, Sofia, and Judith marveled at the caves, waterfalls, and magnificent mountain formations of the Napoli Coast. "Breathtaking," said Sofia. "This helicopter tour is amazing as you promised, Kai."

That evening, Judith and Dani sipped their tea and discussed their upcoming transatlantic cruise. "A great way to celebrate your retirement," said Judith.

Dani nodded. "It will be wonderful to travel for pleasure instead of business."

Makani and Farrell attended an AA meeting the following afternoon. On the way out, Makani asked Farrell, "Will you be my guest for dinner tonight at Beach House? And please bring Sapphire, Sofia, Dani, and Judith." He paused for a moment. "Invite Kai and his parents too."

"Will you recite the *Pono Pledge*?" Farrell asked.

"Of course," Makani said. "Only this time, I want you all to join me."

"It would be my honor," said Farrell. "My great honor, indeed."

Epilogue
Six Months Later

For three nights in a row, Sapphire heard her mother's voice. *The time is coming soon to release the formula. The world is almost ready.*

The first night Sapphire thought it sprung from a place of hope in her heart. When the same message whispered in the air the next night, Sapphire wondered if it was her imagination. The third night, Sapphire believed her mother was speaking to her.

The message reverberated throughout her home. *Soon. Release the formula soon.* Every room whispered the same message.

After Sapphire received a special phone call, she finally knew what she needed to do. She was ready to begin the long process.

A week later, the entire team gathered in Sapphire's living room. The team included a new member. She would need a lot of help. Dani and Judith sat side by side. Next to Judith was Jared Silver and his great-nephew Taylor. Sofia and Farrell sat next to Dani. "I've asked Taylor to join us today," Sapphire began. "He represents hope for our next generation. I want you all to hear his story firsthand." She motioned for Taylor to speak.

"Uncle Jared and I explored the Rainforest last month," said Taylor. "It was so cool to learn about endangered plants and medicinal practices. During one of the ecotours, I cut my arm on a razor-sharp palm frond. A native woman applied a sweet-smelling oil. It was derived from a rare plant native to the Amazon. It healed the cut within hours and no scar remained." He rolled up his sleeve and held out his arm for them to see. "Plants are magic medicine."

Jared observed proudly as Taylor continued. The others listened with rapt attention. "The native woman who applied the ointment introduced me to her grandmother. She was one of the tribal elders, in her nineties. Uncle Jared and I stayed after the tour was over and talked to her. The woman told us about a beautiful American scientist she met almost fifty years ago. She referred to her as Miss Jane."

Dani gasped. "Sapphire, your mother!"

Sofia turned to Sapphire wide-eyed.

Sapphire nodded with a smile. She had heard the story from Jared last week, the morning after her third dream. That's when she knew the time had come.

"The tribal elder ignited my passion to share medicinal treatments from the Amazon," said Taylor. "I've applied to several universities to study botany with a concentration in environmental science."

"And that's not all," said Jared. "Tell them about your plans for your last year in high school."

"I won an international contest. The prize is an internship at a high school in Brazil. I'll be an exchange student for a semester to study endangered plants in the Amazon Rainforest."

Farrell grinned, his heart full of hope.

"Sapphire, you were right," said Dani. "Your parents guided you. She placed her hand on her heart.

Sapphire wrapped her shawl a little tighter around her. She twisted her star-sapphire ring encircling her finger and gazed at the photo on her wall. Andre was bent down on one knee looking up at Jane, with love in his eyes. Jane's eyes returned his love. They were so young and innocent. Spouting Horn gushed its geyser high into the sky, spreading their love to the world.

Acknowledgements

Writing fiction requires the ability to let one's imagination flow while observing the exciting process. Learning to accept feedback from my writer's group was a humbling experience. Our humor helped me enjoy the writing. I am grateful to my editor, writing coach and book designer, Naomi Rose. She encouraged me to polish my words, providing better clarity to the reader. It was a pleasure to work with someone who shared my passion for the story.

I am grateful to my family members for demonstrating their interest and encouragement in my writing as well as all aspects of my existence. My devoted husband Ron, my wondrous children Jesse, Joshua and Sara, my remarkable parents Dotty and Eddie, and my loyal sister Lori. My best friend, Dana, has been my rock for over fifty years.

Establishing new friends later in life has been an unexpected bonus. I appreciate the support and encouragement of old and new friends who read my first book and have waited patiently for this next one in the series. I deeply appreciate each one of you including the new friends I have yet to meet.

Lastly, I wish to acknowledge the thousands of individuals and families who have entrusted me to guide them throughout the course of my career. I have had the privilege to witness the resiliency and strength of families as they demonstrate grace, dignity, perseverance, creativity, and a sense of humor amid the most difficult struggles. My admiration of thousands of individuals and families overcoming obstacles with limited support fuels my life passions and provides hope for our future.

Authors Note

Aromaticus Kauai is entirely fiction. Any character resemblance to actual individuals is purely coincidental.

Aromaticus is a fictional essential oil company. I have no knowledge of a secret formula. Description of this formula is a fantasy of my imagination. I hold only a rudimentary knowledge of chemistry, and the life-changing formula described has always been a fascination of mine.

I fell in love with the stunning island of Kauai and enjoyed visiting the locations depicted in *Aromaticus Kauai.* Tree Tunnel, Spouting Horn, The National Tropical Botanical Gardens, Waimea Canyon, Kauai Coffee, and The Napoli Coast are breathtaking sites the reader is encouraged to tour when visiting Kauai. The lovely restaurant, Beach House exists, however the maître di Makani is fictional. Poipu, Lihue, Princeville and Hanalei Bay are real towns on Kauai.

Sanibel Island in Florida did suffer a hurricane in real life, as described in the novel. The homes on Sanibel Island, and in Poipu and Princeville were designed in my imagination.

In *Aromaticus Kauai*, your friends from *Quitclaim Sedona* are back, and you can join forces with them in their exciting journey. If you enjoyed reading about the characters described in *Quitclaim Sedona* and *Aromaticus Kauai*, please look for further novels from Renae Lapin delving deeper into the individuals described in this story.

I wish to thank you, my readers for sharing your time and interest. Please let me know if you enjoyed reading *Aromaticus Kauai*. I welcome emails from my readers.

With much appreciation,
Renae Lapin
Renae Lapin Mysteries
RenaeLapinMysteries@gmail.com

About the Author

Renae Lapin has been blessed with immeasurable gratification and success in her career as a Family Therapist over the past 45 years. Thousands of individuals and families have honored her with their trust, supporting them to identify and achieve their goals by unlocking their own wisdom and strength.

Taking her experience out of the therapy room and into her writing, Renae Lapin's first mystery novel *Quitclaim Sedona* depicts rich character and relationship development. Great passion for her profession is reflected in the authenticity of her beloved characters, bringing them to life as everyone's best friends. In her second mystery novel *Aromaticus Kauai*, the characters are welcomed back as the reader's enduring friends.

Dr. Renae Lapin, Psy.D. maintains her professional license as an LMFT, Licensed Marriage and Family Therapist in Arizona. In her semi-retirement, Renae Lapin provides Critical Incidence Stress Management, supporting businesses by addressing the immediate impact of crises in the workplace.

Renae Lapin is a proud resident of Sedona where she enjoys creating stained glass and hiking the Red Rock trails while humbly accepting the solemn responsibility of stewardship of the land. *Quitclaim Sedona* is her love letter to Sedona.

Two trips fifteen years apart to the island of Kauai inspired the author to enchant her readers with its beauty. Enjoy visiting Kauai, and become enthralled with its natives and their culture through the eyes of the characters in this second mystery novel. *Aromaticus Kauai* is Renae Lapin's love letter to Kauai.